MW00906624

The Labyrinth
of the
Capricious Priest

MERLAINE HEMSTRAAT

To Vince,
Thanks for your
support!
Merlaine Hemstraat!

Copyright © 2017 Merlaine Hemstraat

All rights reserved. No part of this book may be reproduced without written consent of the author.

This book is a work of literary fiction and should not be construed as real. The names, places, characters and events are a product of the author's imagination. Any similarities to persons (living or dead), actual events, locations and organizations are entirely coincidental.

Full Moon Publishing, LLC

Glade Spring, VA

Website http://www.fullmoonpublishingllc.com

Cover Design by Lee Helton

ISBN: 1946232459
ISBN-13: 978-1946232458

DEDICATION

To all dramatis personae...every story is a legend...

CONTENTS

CHAPTER ONE

Life is a capricious mistress…bestowing upon her ardent flames the whims of her pleasure…yet upset that temptress and she casts her stormy brow, unfurling her wrath…unpredictably…fancifully and erratically…

***

Wiping sweat from his brow, Aaron Emerson slunk down a hallway towards his office for the last time. Clutched in his hand, was his notice of termination of employment from his workplace.

"How the hell will I break *that* news to my wife?" Aaron muttered under his breath.

Aaron pondered that question and many more while he collected his personal things from his former office. Shoving the items haphazardly into a box, he wanted to put as much distance between himself and the office, with all the prying eyes, burning a hole into his back.

Clearing his throat from the doorway stood one of his colleagues.

"Aaron, I just heard. Man, what a blow! What reason did they give for your lay-off?" asked his colleague Donald Fenway, with concern creasing his freckled face.

Don's reddish brown hair shone under the fluorescent lighting.

Glancing towards Donald, Aaron shrugged as he went through the drawers in his desk. *News sure travels fast at the office.*

"Ah shit, does it really matter now? What's done is done. I just don't know what I'm going to say to Maiya. She'll be devastated."

"Doesn't Maiya still work?" inquired Donald as he moved towards Aaron ready to help him with his box.

Without looking up, Aaron nodded as he continued to empty his desk contents.

"Yeah, but only part-time; if you can believe it, she does love her job at the funeral home. She's still a receptionist you know."

"I didn't know, but hey someone has to do it right? Okay, so you'll have some money coming in until you can get back on your feet," stated Donald, while placing his hand on the rim of Aaron's box.

Shaking his head, Aaron straightened up as he began to move his box to his chair seat.

"Maiya doesn't pull in much with her part-time work." Sighing, he continued lamenting. "This is *really* going to upset her. We'd been making plans for a much-needed vacation. I guess this news dashes our dreams of a trip now."

Donald Fenway moved towards his friend and stood looking

up at Aaron's tall frame. His short brown hair was tousled and Aaron's sea-blue eyes appeared flashing and dramatic.

"Listen; if you need anything… let me know. I mean that. Things might get tight so let me know and I'll see what I can do."

Smiling briefly, Aaron nodded. "Thanks Don, I really appreciate that but we have some savings so things aren't as grim as all of that just yet however, it does mean that we can't go on vacation as we'd planned. Oh well, something is bound to turn up somewhere else. You know what they say, when a door closes, a window opens somewhere else."

"That's right Aaron, I have heard that many times before and it's true. Look, I had better get back to my office or I'll be next. Keep in touch and tell Maiya that we'll be having you over for a barbeque very soon. I'll ask my wife to plan something for a week or two from now," Donald stated as he turned towards the hallway leaving Aaron with his stormy thoughts.

***

As Aaron pulled up at a stoplight, he reflected on all that his life had become.

"Twenty-three years at the same job, with the same employer is quite an accolade these days. Most people are lucky to keep their jobs for more than a few years. What the hell is wrong with corporate Canada anyway?" Aaron lamented aloud.

"Although I've worked for the same firm for over two decades and they've become an integral part of my life, woven into the very fabric of my existence, it is time for a drastic change. I'll be damned it I seek similar employment…no, I'll start out with something ground-breaking," Aaron resolved, as he pressed the accelerator in his car.

The trouble was Aaron didn't have a clue as to what that ground-breaking new employment would be.

***

Maiya Emerson stood near the doorway of the funeral home where she worked four days a week as a receptionist. Dressed in navy blue, Maiya looked sombre yet approachable. Her French heritage gave her a slight accent and provided her with an aristocratic countenance, that she prided herself on. Maiya turned heads wherever she went and the funeral home was no exception.

Maiya's long raven tresses offset her almond-toned flawless skin punctuated by her cardamom colored eyes. Her skill with make-up artistry was exceptional as Maiya's frosted bronze colored lips completed her stunning palette.

***

The afternoon had been quiet at *Lytton's Funeral Home* in Toronto.

Maiya shifted some flowers from the back room where the florists delivered arrangements for the families of the deceased, entrusted to the funeral home.

Bringing the flowers into one of the rooms that a man occupied, Maiya arranged the floral creation near the casket. Stopping briefly, she glanced in at the deceased person and mentally remarked that the older man appeared quite distinguished even in death.

"This is Mr. Galbraith resting in this room, "Maiya remarked quietly, under her breath.

Hearing the light tread of footsteps nearby, she ceased all conversation.

Turning around, Maiya noticed Thomas Fieldstone, the managing funeral director standing at the doorway.

Walking quickly towards him, she closed the French doors behind her and stood next to Thomas Fieldstone.

"Everything is ready for this evening Tom," Maiya remarked, as she began to move slightly back from her position next to her employer.

Nodding his head, he smiled at her. "Thanks Maiya. It should be fairly quiet as we only have Mr. Galbraith resting here tonight. Some members of his family will be along to speak with me soon. When they arrive, please get me from my office upstairs or ring me in the prep room if I don't answer my extension.

"I'm expecting another person to arrive from one of the hospital morgues sometime soon so they will keep me busy."

"Certainly Tom," replied Maiya as she began to move towards the front doors of the funeral home.

***

While standing by the front doors, Maiya's mind wandered to her husband, Aaron. Smiling to herself briefly, she basked in thoughts of him. After a few moments, she began to experience an unsettling feeling while she stared out towards the street. *What was the cause of that feeling?*

***

Aaron Emerson poured himself another drink as he glanced at the clock near the sideboard in the dining room of their spacious apartment house. *2:25 pm. It was far too early to get drunk.*

Registering a mental note to make that drink his last for the afternoon, he settled on the couch in the living room while he stared outside their large window.

Absently stirring his drink with his index finger, Aaron conjured up ways to put off telling his wife the truth of him being permanently laid off from work.

"I could pretend to go into work each day for a while but what good would that do when the money stopped coming in?" Aaron asked himself aloud while holding his drink.

Aaron had been given a 'package' from his employer that consisted of three months' salary plus fifteen thousand dollars. His employer would keep him on the payroll for the next three months with full benefits.

While he sipped his drink, Aaron decided it wasn't a bad package for twenty-three years of continuous service however, it could have been better.

"If I had been given fifteen thousand dollars plus six months' salary it would have been a much softer blow," Aaron lamented sadly.

Sighing, Aaron took another drink.

***

After another ten minutes, Aaron got up to refill his drink.

"Didn't I say this would be my last drink for the afternoon?" His hand reached out for the ice bucket and he waited. "To hell with promises; some things were meant to be broken," Aaron declared aloud.

"Shit, I don't want to encounter Maiya so early in the day and half cut, no less. I better get out of here and continue my binge in some bar," Aaron still spoke aloud.

***

Deciding to drive and park his car until later, he pulled into at a local mall. Without a definite destination, Aaron wandered along until his feet brought him to a local bar about three blocks away.

***

Grabbing the door to *Spanky's Bar and Grill*, Aaron figured it was a decent place to spend the next few hours.

Once inside Aaron passed by the usual 'bar flies' lined up along the polished wooden bar top.

A few heads turned his direction more so out of curiosity than acquaintance.

A waitress approached as Aaron was studying the menu.

"Hi there, I'm Melissa and I'll be taking care of you today. What'll you have?"

Aaron looked her up and down and smiled. "Thanks Melissa maybe I'll have some fries with gravy and a tall beer; whatever's on tap will do."

"You got it!"

Watching her walk away, Aaron grinned. Immediately thinking of his wife, he frowned, as he knew he shouldn't even be looking at the young chicks. Maiya was an exotic beauty as well as an elegant and classy lady. Chiding himself, he began to look around the bar.

The interior was decorated in a south-western theme that suited him. By mid-afternoon, there weren't a lot of patrons but those that were there were likely regulars.

Melissa arrived with his beer and set it before him. "There you are. Your fries with gravy will be out in a few moments."

Smiling, Aaron nodded at her. "Thanks dear."

Turning his way, Melissa smiled. "You bet."

Aaron reached for his tall glass of beer and began washing his sorrows down his throat.

Over the top of his glass, he noticed a man who appeared to be a priest; complete with clerical collar. Raising his eyebrows, Aaron set his glass down as he watched in fascination while the man appearing to be a priest sat down at the bar. It seemed that the clergyman was going to have a drink.

A couple of the other patrons glanced in surprise at the priest but went back to their own affairs.

Aaron couldn't help himself; he was intrigued. Never expecting to see a priest in a bar in the middle of the afternoon, he thought he'd seen everything.

Deciding to get up and bring his drink over to the bar, he sat down next to the priest.

Presently Melissa came by with his fries. "So you've moved to the bar? No worries. Here you go, now if you need anything else, just holler."

Aaron chuckled at Melissa's choice of words. "Sure, you bet."

Seeing the priest, Melissa walked around and handed him a menu. "Hi there, I'm Melissa and I'll be taking care of you today. Can I bring you something?"

The priest who appeared to be in his mid-forties answered in a surprising way. "Melissa I could use some taking care of. Okay, give me a steak with all the trimmings done rare and a tall glass of beer; on tap is okay."

"You got it," Melissa said as she took his menu away.

Aaron wondered if her lines were a script.

Glancing back to the priest, he watched the clergyman with great interest. Catching his eye, he attempted a smile.

The priest smiled back then turned towards Aaron. "Do I know you? You wouldn't happen to go to *St. Simeon's Church?*"

Aaron fingered his beer glass as he studied the priest's face. "No, no I don't usually go to church although I suppose I should. My wife, she's French, she likes to go but I don't think she goes to *St. Simeon's.* I think maybe she goes to one of the churches downtown."

"Fair enough. Hey, don't think just because you're seated next to a priest that you have to explain why you don't go to *St. Simeon's* or any other church for that matter." Sighing loudly, the priest continued speaking. "I should introduce myself. I'm Father or Reverend Kubelik, Frank or Franco Kubelik."

Extending his hand, Aaron replied, "I'm Aaron Emerson and I'm pleased to meet you Father Kubelik. Which do you prefer? Reverend or Father? Do you prefer Frank or Franco?"

Chuckling lightly, Father Kubelik spoke. "I prefer Reverend Frank Kubelik but any of the above will do. My real name is Francesco Kubelik but because I'm ordained, I can use either title. Somehow 'Father' doesn't seem to fit with a guy like me."

A few minutes passed as the two men sat together.

Taking a long drink of his beer, Aaron set his glass down. "Oh? Why is that? What kind of a church is *St. Simeon's*; Catholic? I mean priests are allowed to take the odd drink aren't they?"

Rev. Kubelik grinned. "Oh they can do a lot more than that depending on their denomination or character I should add."

Chuckling lightly Aaron nodded in agreement. "Yes I suppose so although we tend to stereo-type priests or anyone in the clergy don't we? I wonder why we do that. Anyway, it's none of my business either way."

Rev. Kubelik's food and drink arrived as he turned back towards Aaron. "*St. Simeon's* is Anglican actually which means it's kind of a cross between Catholic and Protestant but much closer to Catholic. High Anglican churches are the closest to true Catholic churches however *St. Simeon's* is not a High Anglican church per say. No, it's more so my character that doesn't fit in with being referred to as 'Father' or using the title."

Aaron watched Rev. Kubelik bless his food then begin to eat.

Looking at his own untouched food, he started to consume his fries with gravy, which were still quite warm. Discovering he was captivated by the young priest, he couldn't take his eyes from him.

After the two men finished eating, both leaned back and continued swigging their beer.

Turning towards Aaron, Rev. Kubelik searched his face. "Well you know my occupation, how about you? What fun things do you do to pass the time of day?"

Laughing slightly, Aaron liked how he asked him what he did for a living.

"If this had been yesterday I would have told you I was happily and gainfully employed at my job of the past twenty-three years, but today I got the boot, so to speak. My profession was professional paper shuffler."

Rev. Kubelik wore a serious expression as he considered what Aaron had told him. "I'm very sorry to hear that Aaron and I'm sure that you'll find something else soon. I will pray for you. May I ask what your background is? You said you worked at the same job for twenty-three years but in which sector?"

Draining his glass, Aaron gave his attention to the priest. "The company I used to be employed by for the last twenty-three years specialised in medical supplies. My position was an administrative assistant to the Vice President. I know that sounds weird because it's usually a woman in that role but the VP was a golf buddy of mine. Therefore, twenty-three years ago he gave me the job because he felt I could easily do it and they needed someone they could trust.

"To make a hell of a long story short, things worked great for years until my buddy, the VP passed away a few months ago. Now the joker they hired doesn't like me and wanted to hire some chickie for the job. You get my drift."

Draining his beer-glass, Rev. Kubelik shook his head in disgust. "That sure sucks if you don't mind me saying so. Wow, what a blow. Your good friend passes away and everything goes to hell in a hand basket if you'll pardon my saying so."

Laughing loudly, Aaron decided he really liked Rev. Kubelik. "I don't mind you saying so at all and in fact I was just thinking what an interesting man you are and what an especially unusual priest you are."

Melissa arrived to collect their glasses and take their orders for more beer.

"Does your wife work? Rev. Kubelik asked as he waited for his second beer.

"Yeah, thank God she does but only part-time. Still, it's better than a kick in the pants so at least we won't starve. I did get a good 'package' as they held the door for me on my way out if you know what I mean and we do have some savings but otherwise, I'm screwed because who is going to want to hire a guy like me at my stage in life?

"I keep thinking that I don't want the same kind of work and to try something new, although what that is now I can't imagine."

Melissa arrived and set the new beer glasses down in front of the two men.

Taking his second beer glass in his hands Rev. Kubelik nodded. "You sure sound like a guy with his head screwed on so I can't see how you'll have any problems finding something else, but something new, I guess that depends on what it is."

"Now take myself; I've been a priest for my entire adult life and I really love what I'm doing and I wouldn't give up serving God for anything. Lately I've been feeling something similar to you like as if I'm making the motions and maybe my talents could be used elsewhere, but definitely still serving God."

Raising his eyebrows, Aaron considered the priest's story. It appeared they had more in common, than he had originally thought.

"What do you think you could do and still serve God?"

Fingering his beer glass, Rev. Kubelik considered Aaron's question. He wasn't sure how much he should divulge of his real feelings and his true situation on the matter.

"Oh there's quite a lot of missionary work and opportunities with social agencies and the like. I do have lots of options here and overseas for that matter but I guess I'm having a bit of a mid-life crisis."

Laughing slightly, Aaron was indeed surprised. "Do you mean career-wise or otherwise?"

"Otherwise."

"Wow, that's different. I apologise because I know that sounds very stereotypical which is what I was just saying a few minutes ago. So can you not marry?" Aaron asked as he took a drink of his beer.

Rev. Kubelik hesitated, as he once again wondered how much he should divulge about himself, his life and his current situation.

"Let's just say that absolutely, in the Anglican denomination, priests can marry and we have female priests too. No, it's more so a matter of my suitability to marriage although I'll always serve God no matter what happens.

"The part I'm having problems with is mixing the two. I want to and I will serve God forever. However, I also have these quirky sides to my nature. I feel as if maybe I should go on a long sabbatical and travel the world and see many cultures and then come home and apply what I've learned and that might include me sowing some wild oats along the way."

Studying the priest, Aaron realised he could be quite a lady killer if he wanted to be. Although Aaron would have never figured him for that kind of guy, perhaps he really did have a problem in those areas. It would be quite a conflict indeed.

While Aaron studied Rev. Kubelik, he noticed that he was quite good looking with his sultry jet-black hair and deep dark chocolate eyes. His features looked Mediterranean and he showed no signs of aging.

"Well I wish I had some insight for you Rev. Kubelik but I don't. I suppose you could retire temporarily then travel and do what you need to do then return to the priesthood. It is an interesting and strange conundrum you find yourself in."

Nodding slowly, Rev. Kubelik agreed with him. "It is that, isn't it? I know, that is my difficulty; part of me wants and needs to be a priest serving God and then there is this other side of me which hankers for the wild side of things if you get my meaning."

Shaking his head, Aaron understood, but continued to find it hard to think of a priest in that predicament.

"May I ask your parentage or background?"

"Sure, I don't mind telling you my background. My surname is Czech but I'm adopted so I doubt if I have one drop of Czech blood in me. From my physical appearance, I would say I'm a Spaniard or at least with some Spanish roots but I could be Portuguese, Brazilian or French."

"Those are exactly the regions of the world I thought you were from. Wow, that's interesting. Have you been to Spain, Portugal, Brazil or France before?"

Laughing lightly, Rev. Kubelik shook his head. "No, not yet but I'm afraid if I go to Spain, Portugal, Brazil or France and see those beautiful and stunning looking women, I doubt if I could contain or control myself. I know I could marry one of them but personally, I want to marry all of them. You see my problem; I love women and I love intimacy and I really am having a very hard time separating my two natures.

"From a religious point of view one would say I am afflicted with the evil spirit of lust. I would agree that that is my problem but then again is it just. Maybe in my case it goes much deeper than that. It's a real debate either way and I guess one could almost describe it as a paradox."

Whistling lightly, Aaron couldn't believe what he was hearing; a wayward hankering priest. How difficult was that? Yet was this because society seemed to think priests weren't supposed to have *those* kinds of feelings? At least Rev. Kubelik knew he had some challenges but really *how* difficult were they? Who was *he* to judge the priest; Aaron decided judgement shouldn't be left to anyone human to be sure.

"Well I'm out of my element here and I really can't judge anyone so I guess Rev. Kubelik the problem lies with society's perception of how a priest should be or conduct himself," admitted Aaron thoughtfully.

Nodding with satisfaction, Rev. Kubelik agreed with him. "You are so right and there lies my problem; like I said a strange kind of paradox. I'm in a sort of fish bowl and whatever I do; I am or will be judged by people. Now God on the other hand has the full right and authority of judgement and yet he is only too aware of my and all of our many faults.

"I've prayed about this but I still can't find any peace and that isn't because God hasn't tried to talk to me about it. It is my free choice and will to follow the path that I take. God never forces himself on anyone. He gave us full choice at creation."

Both men ordered a third beer then sat back and smiled at each other.

"Rev. Kubelik, I must say I am really enjoying our

philosophical and religious conversation. I know this may sound odd, but you make religion and going to church attractive. You are an incredibly interesting man and priest and I hope we can meet again after today. I know you said you are the priest at *St. Simeon's* so I know where to find you."

"Aaron, please don't think that your comment was odd; it was honest and I'm flattered. I've enjoyed this too and by all means, I do hope we can meet again as well. I'm not the only priest at *St. Simeon's*. Although I am the main incumbent or priest, there are two others who assist me as well. If you wish, you should bring your wife and come to one of my services sometime then we could grab a bite to eat together afterwards?"

"I might just take you up on that Rev. Kubelik," Aaron admitted honestly, as he studied the fascinating young priest.

Taking a long swig of his beer, Rev. Kubelik set down his glass as he spoke. "I do want to thank you for being so open-minded and non-judgmental with me. Many people would have either moved from this spot next to me or given me a verbal beating for what I'd shared with them. You have been a friend to me today and I needed that. I only hope I have helped you somehow by me talking about myself. Sometimes that helps us to hear about others then we have a fresh perspective about ourselves."

Smiling warmly at the priest, Aaron felt he could read him well. He had helped him with his own problems. Although Rev. Kubelik hadn't given him a lead to finding work, he had inadvertently talked about himself and taken Aaron's mind from his problems for a while.

Glancing at his watch, Aaron knew he needed to leave to be home before his wife arrived from work.

Leaving some money by his plate, Aaron turned towards the priest. "You know, I really hate to leave. I could easily sit here and talk to you for hours however my wife should be home soon so I guess I better get going."

Rising from his chair, Aaron stopped for a moment. "I really *will* come by and hear one of your sermons one day soon. I would really like that and I do hope we can become friends beyond today."

Grinning broadly, Rev. Kubelik stood for a moment to shake Aaron's hand. "My pleasure and absolutely we are already friends now so don't be a stranger Aaron. You do that, you come and see me anytime and we'll go from there. I'll be looking for you and your wife at one of my services."

"Thanks Rev. Kubelik, I will and you can count on seeing me again. We are friends now and we both have some things and some ways to help each other. Talk to you and see you soon!" Aaron said amicably as he let go of the priest's hand.

Turning towards the front door of *Spanky's*, he headed out into the early evening of a Monday night.

Rev. Kubelik held his beer glass turning it around and watching the remaining liquid sloshing about in the bottom. He liked Aaron Emerson and had enjoyed and benefitted from their conversation. Truly hoping that he would attend a service in the future, Rev. Kubelik drained his glass then set it down.

Reaching into his pocket, Rev. Kubelik left adequate money to cover his bill then he left *Spanky's* heading out into the evening. The night air was welcome to wake him up. Walking along, he pondered all that he had shared with Aaron Emerson and hoped it had not been too revealing. Dreading returning to an empty apartment, Rev. Kubelik pressed on towards what he presently called home.

CHAPTER TWO

Aaron Emerson wasn't at all sure if he wanted to tell his wife the 'good news'. *Just maybe I'll wait. Maiya won't know and what she doesn't know won't hurt her, at least until later.*

Seeing his wife's car in their driveway, Aaron prepared to act as if everything was the 'status quo'.

***

While doing the dishes, Maiya Emerson glanced over at her husband. "Did I tell you I'm off tomorrow? Yeah, the boss' assistant over-booked me and another receptionist so we drew lots to work and I lost. Anyway, it will give me an opportunity to clean up some things I need to do."

Aaron felt like yelling. *Damn it all, now what will I do all day? Maybe I should just tell her the truth?!* Sighing loudly, Aaron prepared for the worst.

***

An hour after their shouting match, Maiya Emerson finally calmed down.

"So Aaron, what will we do now? What are your plans? Have

you got any?"

Holding another drink in his hand, Aaron began to explain his position.

"Maiya, you must think I'm a fool. Of course, I've got a plan. Besides, I told you things aren't that bad. In fact, they will be just fine for some time. Eventually we could be screwed but not for a hell of a long time."

Taking a long swig, he set his drink down on the night stand by his side of the bed. "Maiya haven't I always kept things going and figured things out? Well give me some credit. Anyway, I've got a couple of ideas I want to float first then we'll see how things go."

"Like what? What are those ideas you want to float?" Maiya asked as she folded her long legs across her side of the bed.

Pausing, Aaron thought for a moment. "Well as a matter of fact I met a really interesting priest today and he might be able to help me get another job or find another career. Either way he's offered to help me."

Maiya was intrigued. Sitting up straighter, she spoke. "That doesn't sound like you. How did you meet this priest? I've never known you to go to church."

"Well I didn't meet him in a conventional church but sometimes church is where you make it."

"What? I don't get it," Maiya said with frustration in her voice.

Shaking his head, Aaron continued explaining. "Oh, don't

worry about the details Maiya, the point is I've made this terrific friend and he's *going* to help me. I'll probably see him tomorrow or the next day so we can go from there."

Getting up, Maiya Emerson walked over to the mirror. "Maybe I should try another line of work myself."

Feeling his blood begin to boil, Aaron got up quickly and held his wife's arm. "Don't you dare! You stick to the conservative and quiet funeral home and let me come up with a new line of work."

Running her hands over her sumptuously attractive body and surveying her exotically lovely face, Maiya laughed a little. "Oh really? Well we shall see. I might just do it anyway. For now I'll stay where I am but in the future, who knows?"

Quickly taking his wife into his arms, Aaron began kissing her erotically. "It would seem that you need a reminder about how great a lover I am…"

***

An hour later while Maiya soaked in the bath tub, Aaron went down stairs for another drink. Recalling the mind-blowing sex they experienced, Aaron felt energised and ready to tackle anything. Remembering his priest friend, Aaron could see how sex or the lack of it, could make a man half-crazy if they allowed it. Sex or the lack of it, could drive a person to madness if they over or under indulged in it. Aaron considered how sex was the one form of emotion and activity that provocatively altered a person.

"Maybe that was Rev. Kubelik's problem; maybe he needed to find the kind of woman who would tire him out and leave him so satisfied that he'd never hunger for another. He needed a nymphomaniac," Aaron speculated aloud.

Laughing slightly to himself, as he stirred his drink with his fingers, Aaron wished he knew such a woman for his friend.

Strangely, his mind went to his own wife Maiya. Feeling surprised that he considered her the kind of woman the priest needed Aaron marveled at his thoughts.

"What the hell am I suggesting; that I let my friend borrow my wife for the night?" he pondered incredulously.

Aaron sat down on the sofa downstairs as he heard the water running again in the bathtub. Picturing his wife's sexy naked body as she bathed, Aaron knew she would be perfect for his friend.

Giving his head a shake, he stopped. "I must be going out of mind! Why the hell would I even *think* such a thing? Where did *that* come from?"

Catching his breath as he got up, Aaron resolved to put *those* thoughts as far away as he could hide them in his mind.

***

After lunch the next day, Aaron Emerson decided to visit *St. Simeon's Church*. He truly hoped Rev. Kubelik would be in.

Opening the heavy wooden doors, Aaron quietly went inside the beautiful and hallowed church. Unsure of what to do, he crossed himself as he continued inside.

When he entered the sanctuary, Aaron noticed a couple of people praying or sitting in the pews. Not seeing a priest at present, Aaron went towards a pew and sat down.

The highly vaulted or arched ceilings were magnificent as were the stained glass windows and the central High Altar. Aaron could see the church had an enormous pipe organ, which he could imagine, sounded incredible. Closing his eyes for a moment, he drank in the reverent ambiance and sanctified surroundings.

From beyond, a door opened and a male who appeared to be a priest began walking through the church. As the person drew closer, Aaron could see it was not his friend.

Deciding to stop the priest, Aaron got up and began motioning to him. "Excuse me, but may I speak with you for a moment?"

The priest stopped and came towards him. "Certainly. Would you prefer to speak in private or here? I'm Father Andrecki."

"Hello Father Andrecki. No, here is fine. I just have a quick question. When will Rev. Kubelik be in?"

Starting for a moment, Father Andrecki stared at Aaron Emerson. "I beg your pardon but you did ask for Rev. Kubelik?"

Raising his eyebrows, Aaron nodded his head. "Yes I did. Is there something wrong?"

Glancing around them quickly, Father Andrecki lightly touched Aaron's arm as he led him away from the other parishioners.

Wondering at the priest's unusual behaviour Aaron waited.

Standing directly in front of Aaron, Father Andrecki formulated his answer. "I know this is going to be a shock but Rev. Kubelik passed away six months ago."

Aaron's mouth opened for a moment, as he stood transfixed,

unable to believe his ears. Frowning tensely, he spoke. "Father Andrecki, let's make sure we're talking about the same priest."

After Aaron Emerson described in detail Rev. Kubelik, the other priest looked grim.

"I know this comes as a real shock but I assure you it's true. I officiated at his funeral mass. God knows I had the hardest time doing so but it is something a priest must do. Do you have a few moments? If so, please come into my office and we can talk privately," Father Andrecki suggested hopefully.

"Yes of course I can come and speak with you and quite frankly, I have to because this makes absolutely *no* sense to me whatsoever because I had three beers and dinner with him last night at *Spanky's Bar and Grill*," Aaron explained with great passion in his voice.

At the mention of *Spanky's Bar and Grill*, Father Andrecki turned around and stopped. Then, thinking about it further, he continued onwards inside the inner rooms nearing his own office.

Aaron was shown inside and asked to sit down.

Father Andrecki closed the door and locked it from the inside. Once seated in front of Aaron he began to tell his story.

"For whatever reason you believe you met with a person who identified themselves as being Rev. Kubelik. As I said, he passed away six months ago. I have his death notice and the personal obituary from his funeral in a file in my desk."

Opening a drawer, he retrieved a brown folder and handed it to Aaron. "Here, see for yourself," Father Andrecki, offered while he monitored Aaron's response.

Aaron Emerson read the documentation that did appear to prove that Rev. Francesco Kubelik had passed away due to an accident, six months earlier on February 19, 2016.

Looking up at Father Andrecki Aaron shook his head. "I don't know what to say. I really am at a loss for words. Whom did I eat, drink and talk with, his ghost? I tell you this guy was as real as you or I and he was extremely convincing. Why should he pretend to be someone he isn't? Why is this fellow impersonating a priest and *that* priest specifically?"

Shrugging his shoulders Father Andrecki's expression was kind. "Mr. Emerson, I really am sorry about this and I do wish I could tell you who you ate dinner with, but are you certain they said they were Rev. Kubelik? I mean just maybe, their name might have been similar."

"Not a chance Father. If that were true, why did he direct me here? Have you ever had another priest with a name close to his and am I the first person or only person to come in here and say this?"

"Mr. Emerson you are the first person to mention this and I have no explanation for why this person directed you here. Nevertheless, I am glad they did, whoever they are. You are always welcome here and I hope you come back for this is the house of the Lord."

Unable to move or understand the situation, Aaron Emerson remained in his chair. His mind sprinted from one speculative thought to another.

"May I get you something? I know you may wish a few moments of private thought," offered Father Andrecki.

"Yes, thank you, I guess a little water would be nice," Aaron answered absently.

Rising, Father Andrecki excused himself as he went for Aaron's water.

***

Sighing loudly, Aaron ran his fingers through his hair as he struggled with the news.

"Exactly what is going on here? Why was this priest insisting Rev. Kubelik was dead? I know what I just read but I don't believe it. Ghosts don't drink beer, nor eat steaks with all the trimmings and they sure as my name is Aaron, don't talk about their hankerings for women!" Aaron muttered under his breath.

***

Father Andrecki returned with the water glass as he set it down for Aaron. Sitting opposite him again, he waited.

Taking a long drink, Aaron held the glass in his hands as he spoke. "Father Andrecki, I don't want to take up too much of your time. I appreciate everything you've told me and I guess I just need to process this before I accept it."

"I understand Mr. Emerson and please don't worry about taking up too much of my time. My time is for my parishioners and whomever God might send my way. For some reason unapparent to us now, the good Lord sent you to me and us here at this church so I feel I need to help you any way I can. If I can come up with something that will help to explain this, I'll get back to you if you'll leave me your number."

Nodding slowly Aaron agreed. "Okay, I'd appreciate that and please do share anything you think might help to explain this." Getting up, he extended his hand. "Thank you Father, I'll be on my way now. Here is my phone number."

***

Aaron's feet felt heavy and uncoordinated as he walked along towards his car. Unable to accept the news, something nagged within him that suggested there was a lot more going on than what Father Andrecki had stated.

Heading to a local library, Aaron Emerson sought information to collaborate Father Andrecki's statements. After using one of the computers and checking through various indexes, Aaron made some notes. The Diocesan website noted Rev. Francesco Kubelik's passing and a link was provided to a news story. When Aaron clicked on the link, he read the story that unfortunately didn't include a photo of him.

"No photo of the reverend…very strange…" Aaron muttered under his breath. "It was as though someone had purposely removed any identifying information."

Reading on, Aaron discovered that on February 19, 2016 Rev. Kubelik had been driving home from a meeting with a parishioner and a drunk driver had hit him and killed him almost instantly. Bad weather was also an attributing factor in the accident. The accused had been arrested; criminal charges had been laid as well as them losing their licence.

Staring at the computer screen, Aaron knew he needed to find a photo of Rev. Kubelik. Deciding to search through the website of *St. Simeon's Church*, he scrounged around for any photos of the priest. Strangely, there were none in any archival photos on their website.

Without knowing where the priest had pastored previously, Aaron couldn't follow that lead either. Moving to a seat near one of the windows, Aaron read through his notes as he thought.

Making a list of what he knew, Aaron stared out the window reflecting on the possibilities.

"Okay, so what do I have; there is proof that a priest named Rev. Francesco Kubelik had died in a car crash on February 19, 2016. We know he had been a pastor at *St. Simeon's Church* but whether he is the same man, whom I met last night at *Spanky's Bar and Grill* is another thing. If only I could find a way to secure a photo of the priest.

"If this man who impersonated a priest the night before at *Spanky's* wasn't a real priest or the real Rev. Kubelik then who was he and why was he going around pretending to be Rev. Kubelik?" he wondered aloud.

Aaron thought back to the night before at the bar. Melissa the waitress did not appear to know him so he likely was not a regular.

Glancing around him, he noticed he was alone. "What other businesses are in that same vicinity as the bar? Was there another church near there too? What else had the so-called priest said about himself? He had spoken of some of his vices and his presumed nationality. Were there any clues there? What kind of a joint was *Spanky's*? Was it a front for something else?"

Aaron's mind swam around furiously until he put his head in his hands for a rest.

Sighing, he got up to go home. He had to think and he had to run the surprising information by his wife.

CHAPTER THREE

Maiya Emerson had been shocked and a little incredulous of her husband's story.

Studying him sitting across from her, she struggled for a collaborative sounding comment. "Well, Aaron I must admit if anyone else had told me this story I would have asked if they were tight but since it's you who told me this story and when I remember what you said last night about Rev. Kubelik I'm inclined to believe you.

"The real problem as I see it; comprises of two points. The first point being why did this man pretend to be this particular priest complete with a really fantastic story about his vices and all of that stuff. I mean he didn't just say he was a priest, he said he was this *particular* priest. In other words, he called your attention to this particular Rev. Frank Kubelik and he wore his cleric's collar.

"The second point is because this man did call your attention to this particular priest what was his reason for doing so? I can't believe he was nuts so what is his actual reason for impersonating a priest? He gave you the name of a specific parish where he was the incumbent but why? It was as if he wanted to give you this particular identity as a sort of alibi and why did he go into such detail about himself? I also wonder if maybe he was leading you to that parish for a reason."

Aaron whistled at his wife. "Holy smokers you are one smart lady! I hadn't even got around to thinking those things yet but babe I think you have certainly nailed some of the crux of the issues. Yes, it is as though he was establishing a kind of alibi about himself only not so much his whereabouts but his identity. Why and why me? You also nailed it about his collar. That point alone suggests he wanted people to *know* or *assume* he was a priest. You could be right Maiya; maybe he was leading me to that church."

"Precisely and very well put my love; like I said before, all of these observations point to him wanting to establish his identity and not only *an* identity but a *particular* identity. We need to try to find a way to get a hold of a photo of this Rev. Kubelik."

Slapping her face, Maiya continued speaking as she shook her head in disbelief. "Of course, why didn't I think of this before? The funeral home! Which funeral home did Rev. Kubelik rest in? Who looked after his interment assuming he was buried? He might have been cremated but either way where did his remains go? You said Father Andrecki officiated over Rev. Kubelik's funeral. He would know the details of these questions and a lot more."

Aaron wore an excited expression on his face as he regarded his wife. "Okay baby, you look after the funeral home angle of this mystery and I'll look after some of the other points to this conundrum."

Maiya's face crinkled in puzzlement. "What other points? Who else can you speak to in order to get some inside information about this mystery? You don't know any police persons. I wish you did because that would be perfect."

"I don't know but something will turn up. All I know is this priest came into my life for a reason. I owe him this much to find out what happened to him."

"Well it's obvious a priest by the name of Rev. Francesco Kubelik died on February 19, 2016 but whether or not he was the man you ate and drank with yesterday afternoon is quite another matter," admitted Maiya as she got up to refill her drink glass. "Aaron I have to get some sleep soon because I'm up early tomorrow for work. Are you coming or do you want to stay up longer?"

Glancing up at his tall wife while she refilled her drink glass he nodded. "I think I'll stay up a bit longer. I'm not really tired and this thing has me so worked up I've just got to get to the truth."

Laughing lightly Maiya sat down next to her husband. "Well you won't solve it all tonight but I must admit it really is a brain bender."

All at once, Maiya had a thought. "Aaron, why don't I try going to *St. Simeon's*? Father Andrecki doesn't know me and neither does or did Rev. Kubelik. From your description of Rev. Kubelik, I know I'd recognise him but what about Father

Andrecki? What does he look like?"

Thinking for a moment, Aaron began to fill in his description. "Father Andrecki is about 6 feet tall, fairly well-built I should think and his hair is sandy colored with medium blue eyes. He speaks with a slight accent. I would think somewhere in Eastern Europe. I would put him in his early forties as well. Rev. Kubelik couldn't have been more than that age range either."

Nodding her head, Maiya mentally noted the priest's description. "Would you say Rev. Kubelik was about the same height and weight?"

Holding his drink in his hand Aaron paused. "Oh I see, you think that maybe Father Andrecki is Rev. Kubelik but with a sandy colored wig or hair piece on. Oh and his eyes would need some special tinted contact lens. Remember I said Rev. Kubelik had dark chocolaty colored eyes and jet black hair?"

"It's possible isn't it? So, were the two men about the same height and weight and build?" Maiya prompted, with interest.

Sighing loudly, Aaron reflected back to the two men's physical appearance. *It was plausible. The two priests may have been similar height, weight and stature but... that's incredible! Why the heck would one priest pose as two priests and yet why the hell not?* "I don't know Maiya, maybe? I can see what you're driving at and I like it but it seems a bit too far-fetched somehow and yet, it just might be the truth."

"This entire story is far-fetched so this component of it won't really make any difference. Well, it's food for thought. I have to get to bed. Come on up when you're ready."

Passing by him she stopped and came back to kiss him.

***

Aaron digested their conversation as he heard his wife upstairs getting ready for bed. She made a lot of sense and he liked her logic. Something nagged at him that Maiya had suggested; *the one priest posing as two.*

CHAPTER FOUR

Donald Fenway called the next day as Aaron sat at his dining room table making notes.

"Donald? How are you?" Aaron greeted him as he laid down his pen.

"I was wondering about you, old friend. I'm fine I guess although this place gets shittier by the day. You got out in time Aaron, you really did."

Sighing Aaron agreed. "It sounds like it. Are you working today or off?"

"Actually I work a half day today due to some extra personal days I have to use up before the end of the year. I wondered if you wanted to get together," Donald suggested hopefully.

"That would be fine Don and actually I'd really enjoy getting out and spending a little time with you. Sure... where and when?"

***

Aaron Emerson pulled into the parking lot of *Monk's Abbey Golf and Country Club*. Because he had been given a life membership from his old employer, the Vice President, E. B.

Vincents, he could come and go whenever he wished. It also gave him privileges few could afford. With Aaron's life membership, came extending invitations to guests to the country club.

Walking towards the ornate and heavy doors, he was greeted by Alexander Robinson, one of the country club's regular concierges.

"Good afternoon Mr. Emerson; great to see you again!" Alexander Robinson said enthusiastically as he held the door open for Aaron.

Smiling warmly at Alexander, Aaron stopped for a moment. "Oh Alex, I have a guest; Mr. Donald Fenway who should be arriving shortly. Please see that he finds me in *Friar's Lounge*."

"Absolutely! Have a great time Mr. Emerson and I'll be sure to see that your guest finds you in *Friar's Lounge*," Alexander Robinson promised.

***

Aaron always loved spending time at *Monk's Abbey Golf and Country Club* whether with his wife or some of his friends from work. The country club was part of a former Benedictine monastery. It had been built at the turn of the century however, over the years the building had been too costly to maintain.

Over the years, Aaron had heard that a wealthy Catholic patron had originally commissioned the monastery to be built. Unfortunately, when the patron passed away and due to a long estate court battle, the monastery ended up not receiving some of the endowments promised.

In the 1960's a private developer bought the aging monastery and had it made into a golf and country club retaining most of the original beauty and architectural features of the old monastery.

***

"Hello Mr. Emerson, welcome back! Would you like one of your usual refreshments?" Lydia, one of the bartenders asked him as she smiled graciously.

Smiling at Lydia Aaron agreed. "Sure, I think today I'd like to start with a *Fizzy Friar*. Oh and when my guest arrives please see that he finds me."

"My pleasure Mr. Emerson!" Lydia stated as she began to prepare one of Aaron's favourite drinks.

Aaron nodded and waved at several of the lounge patrons whom he knew personally.

***

Donald Fenway arrived at the *Monk's Abbey Golf and Country Club* about ten minutes after Aaron had seated himself in *Friar's Lounge*.

Getting up, Aaron shook hands with Donald Fenway. "Don thanks for coming!"

Glancing around appreciatively Donald took his seat. "Very elegant place!"

Immediately a waiter appeared by their table. "May I take your drink order sir?"

Donald Fenway nodded as he gave his order. "I'll have a tall beer on tap."

"Right away sir!"

Aaron sat back and surveyed his surroundings as well as his friend.

"This is one fabulous place isn't it? And it's the one benefit that no one could strip from me because E.B. Vincents had given it to me years ago and it is a life membership."

"Yeah E.B. was a really generous VP. I just wish he was still with us," admitted Donald Fenway with regret in his voice.

Donald's drink was delivered as the two men thought about E.B. Vincents.

"Let's toast old E.B.- To, E.B. Vincents; one of the great ones!" Aaron said sadly.

"Here, here!" agreed Donald Fenway.

Swigging his drink Aaron regarded his friend. "I know you're going to bring me up to date on the crap that's been going on around there. Geez in some ways I miss it and yet not in the least."

"Hey you said it! Sometimes I wish they'd sacked me alongside of you. Actually one of the reasons I wanted to talk to you was there was some man asking about you yesterday. Actually two men. I'm not sure who they really were but they said they were investors and they told us that you'd been helpful in brokering a deal for them in the past.

"Well naturally when we said you no longer worked there they just nodded and said okay and left. They didn't ask to speak with someone else in sales or administration. What do you make of that?" Donald Fenway asked as he regarded his friend across the small cocktail table.

Aaron shook his head as he took another drink. "Damned if I can figure *that* out! I've never brokered any deals for anyone in the past or at least any that I can remember and besides, I never worked in sales so who the hell are they kidding? Maybe they have me mixed up with someone else?"

Pursing his lips Donald shrugged. "Yeah I know that but obviously they didn't. I got the distinct impression they were some kind of investigators or something like that. They really had the 'cloak and dagger' look to them."

Hearing their description, Aaron became slightly alarmed. "Is that a fact? Who the hell is investigating *me*? I've done nothing and I pay my bills on time and I'm caught up with my taxes so there's nothing there. Besides, they don't send out cloak and dagger types and it sounds like something out of a movie."

"Well I just wanted you to know because there was something very unsettling about them. Just be aware Aaron. I don't want anything to happen to you," Donald stated seriously.

"Well thanks Don I can't tell you how I appreciate the warning. Say, what did they look like? I mean can you describe them in greater detail?"

Don put down his beer glass for a moment as he thought. "Let's see; the one man seemed like, no, they were both fairly tall about 6 foot or better and quite well built. They both wore black, and they had black hats with dark hair which I think was barely visible below the bottom or brim of their hats and of course they wore sunglasses."

"Geez friggin Louise! Like you said, real cloak and dagger stuff and right out of a movie. Obviously, they didn't want to be identified by any particular features. This is very disturbing and I'm quite concerned about this. This stinks of something nasty," Aaron admitted passionately.

"Have you somehow rattled some cages or maybe Maiya?" Donald asked with concern in his tone.

"I can't recall doing so and surely not Maiya. Who would she cross at the funeral home?" Aaron explained while his mind ran like an Olympic sprinter.

Sighing loudly Donald Fenway picked up his drink and drained his glass. He was growing increasingly concerned for his friend.

"I'm really sorry to have been the bearer of bad news. Maybe it's nothing but a practical joke."

"Some friggin joke," Aaron replied as his mind swam with disturbing thoughts.

After a second round of drinks had been ordered, something occurred to Aaron.

"You know Don; just maybe I can shed some light on this."

For the next half hour, the two men discussed the strange affair of Rev. Frank Kubelik.

"Boy if that isn't some story," Donald Fenway replied after hearing all the salient facts. "I'm inclined to agree with you that just maybe the two incidents or cases are related. Maybe by you asking about Rev. Kubelik at *St. Simeon's* you inadvertently rattled some cages. That has to be it Aaron. What the hell else could it be? After all, that priest knew where you used to work."

"Yes I did mention to Rev. Kubelik where I worked but that means then that he really is alive. It also probably means he is involved with something sinister. Shit! How did I get involved in this?!" Aaron lamented as he looked at the cocktail table in front of him.

"Wait a moment Aaron; it could just as easily have been that other priest, Father Andrecki. Did you mention where you used to work to him?"

"Not that I recall but who the hell knows at this point!" Aaron stated dejectedly.

"Well my money is on the other priest or maybe someone following you who saw you go into *St. Simeon's Church*. If someone were looking for Rev. Kubelik then they would be really interested in finding anyone who spoke to him or knew where he could be," reasoned Donald Fenway.

Running his hands through his short brown hair, Aaron Emerson began to calm down a little. "You might have something there, Don. Actually the more I think about this I'm inclined to agree with your theory about someone looking for Rev. Kubelik. Obviously they would be stationed near the church he used to pastor in.

"Okay, so maybe that is what this is all about and not about me personally. Okay; that I can handle. Shit, for a moment there I was really scared."

Nodding his head, Donald agreed. "That's the idea. Say Aaron, if you're up to it do you want to order some lunch?"

"I feel a lot more like eating now!" Aaron admitted as he caught the attention of the waiter.

Half an hour later, the two men dug into their excellent lunch. Aaron had ordered the grilled salmon with twice baked potatoes, vegetables and side salad. Donald had chosen the *Friar's Burger Plate* with all the trimmings.

"Boy the food here is great isn't it?" Aaron said between bites.

"You better believe it!" admitted Donald as he bit into his succulent burger.

While slicing a piece of salmon, Aaron had been thinking. "If Rev. Kubelik was wanted for something he must have either been a witness to something or maybe he was directly or indirectly involved with some event or crime or something. After all, don't priests listen to confession?"

Donald stopped bringing his beefsteak fries to his mouth as he considered Aaron's ideas.

"You might have something there Aaron. I didn't think of that but it's obvious! Of course, a priest has to listen to a penitent under the seal of the confessional. But do the Anglican priests offer private confession at the church or is that just Catholic priests?"

"I don't have a clue unfortunately but I or we can easily find that out," replied Aaron as he ate his twice-baked potato.

"Either way my guess is that just maybe Rev. Kubelik heard

something during confession or maybe while he was in the church or he witnessed something and now it's kind of like he's a marked man so to speak," Donald speculated.

"How are we going to prove something like that? If this event or act or words were heard under the seal of the confessional no one is going to tell us about it and for sure neither will Rev. Kubelik or Father Andrecki. But wait now, since we know that priests can't or aren't supposed to break the seal of the confessional why would anyone fear that Rev. Kubelik might divulge their secret?

"I mean if they said their piece in good faith to the priest why would they fear that he'd share it with someone and break the seal?" Aaron wondered.

"Maybe he didn't break the seal but they thought he did? Maybe it is a huge frame up and this Rev. Kubelik has gone into hiding. Maybe he staged his death so that those hunting him down would leave him alone?" Donald Fenway suggested as he finished his lunch.

Aaron put his fork into his broccoli and then stopped. "Just wait a minute Don. You might really have something there. That certainly could be what this is all about!"

Don smiled as he watched his friend. "Yes, but once again how do we prove it?"

"Well I admit I haven't got a clue but remember this: if we work on this theory or premise then we'll know which direction to go in and tailor our inquiries in those directions. I know we've bounced around a few theories today but damn it all they make a lot of sense," Aaron stated excitedly.

"Okay so where do we go from here?" Donald Fenway asked as he pushed his plate away from him.

Finishing up his lunch, Aaron Emerson wasn't sure where to go with their theories.

"I wish I knew. The problem is no one at *St. Simeon's* is going to tell us what really happened even if they knew and they might not know. On the other hand, if they know, they are going to be protecting Rev. Kubelik so they'll never give his real whereabouts away.

"If we could find a photo of Rev. Kubelik this might help. I've asked Maiya to check into the funeral home side of things in case she can uncover something helpful. I think that we should find out casually how often they offer confession at *St. Simeon's*. Maybe it's offered twice a year or some such thing. This might help to date when the good Father might have last heard from the penitent."

"That appears to be a sound plan Aaron. I think until some of these facts are filled in there isn't much else we can do. I will let you know if those hoods are seen hanging around or asking for you again," Donald offered seriously.

"Thanks Don, I really appreciate that! I just remembered that Maiya offered to go to *St. Simeon's* and see who she encounters."

"You know I've been wondering about that priest, the good Rev. Kubelik. It's what you said he told you about his certain vices he had. Now maybe this is a lot more common than we realise but doesn't that sound kind of weird or off colour, this priest admitting he had certain wayward thoughts and impulses. I mean does that sound realistic?" Don wondered as he sat back in his club chair.

"If you ask me, by him admitting to his problem with certain vices that is totally realistic. If he went around acting like he was so angelic I wouldn't be inclined to believe him. I mean maybe he might be legitimately pure but come on Don, what priest nowadays is so puritanical? Strangely that was the one feature which stood out that speaks to his credibility from my perspective."

"Okay, okay if you think it helps his case then that's fine with me. Time will tell but it just struck me as not sounding realistic but I might be behind in my views of clergy these days," admitted Don as he glanced for the waiter.

After ordering another round of drinks, the two men sat back and digested their theories as well as appreciating the country club's ambiance.

"Don I love this place and for obvious reasons but did you know about its history?" Aaron asked.

"No, I can't say I do."

After filling Don in on the history of the magnificent old monastery turned country club, Aaron had an interesting thought occur to him.

"This would be a great place to hide if someone was seeking shelter," Aaron suggested intuitively.

Immediately Don was fascinated. "What do you mean?"

"Well rumour has it that during the war old monasteries were often used to hide clergy or other people too. I guess I'm referring to the ancient wars of centuries ago but the idea is the same. These old cloistered halls used to have monk's cells or rooms where the monks occupied. Now maybe I'm getting that mixed up with rich estates hiding clergy but the point is old monasteries hid people in the past," Aaron explained as he folded his hands in his lap.

Donald Fenway considered his friend's newest theory and decided it had certain merits. "Actually you're right Aaron. The church hid Jewish people in monasteries, churches and even the Vatican during World War Two. These are well established facts not rumours so you are absolutely right.

"But back to your original point about this old monastery turned golf club retaining some of its old monk's cells; how do you know this?"

"Easy, my old boss E.B. Vincents told me some years ago. How he found out is beyond me. He may have had something to do with the original developer that restored, renovated and turned this fabulous old monastery into the golf and country club we find ourselves in today," Aaron explained.

"Now this is *really* interesting. Aaron my man, I think we might have finally latched onto something useful," stated Don Fenway with a smile. "How familiar are you with some of the club's more esteemed members?"

Aaron thought for a few moments.

"I admit I don't come here as often as I'd like to but I am quite well known just the same. I could make some discreet inquiries. I see what you're driving at and you know what… that might be how this all came about. If Rev. Kubelik has sought refuge in this old monastery turned golf club, he would have needed someone on the inside as a highly esteemed member to get him in so to speak, or possibly a staff member who is a trusted parishioner of *St. Simeon's*.

"On the other hand, we're assuming the good Father really is a priest. What if he isn't and he doesn't need anyone wealthy or connected to get him in here? He might be from a well-to-do family himself. Logistically, we aren't particularly close to *St. Simeon's* but what does that matter? It would be perfect for a secret place for the priest or anyone else to hide. Who would think of it?"

"We did," admitted Don Fenway reluctantly.

"Yes but that's because I'm a member here and because I know the history of this grand old place. Not everyone knows it or cares about it in quite the way I do. Don, I don't think this would come to many people's minds as a place for a priest to hide but if the good Father is actually a member here or he knows of a trusted member then they would realise this place had potential. For one thing, most people wouldn't even know or believe he's in hiding. Now we don't know it for certain either but I can't imagine what else it could be."

"Yes and we've been hashing theories around for hours and in your case for a couple of days. I think we're solid here so hopefully no one will catch on and those goons I told you about if they are following you they better not figure this out," admitted Don carefully.

"Naw, those kinds of hoods aren't smart enough to actually think of something like this," Aaron replied with a smile, "although who they work for might be. Okay, mums the word and let's keep our own counsel as we look into things as discreetly as possible. I'll keep you posted and you can do the same. Let's not say anything anywhere it might be heard."

"Agreed."

CHAPTER FIVE

.

Maiya Emerson sought out Thomas Fieldstone, the Managing Director of *Lytton's Funeral Home*.

Finding him in his office, she knocked on the open door. "Thomas, do you have a few minutes?"

Glancing up at her, he smiled. "I think I can spare that Maiya. Come on in. What's on your mind?"

After Maiya settled herself, she began speaking. "Thomas I was wondering how someone could find out what a deceased person looked like while they were resting at a particular funeral home. What I mean is supposing someone passed away and *Lytton's* took care of the service. If someone wanted a photo of someone who was resting at that funeral home how could they get it?"

"Well Maiya as you know we have several ways we provide photos of the deceased and as you also know they are always pre-death photos. Family generally provides them so we can include them around the home while the family and guests are visiting. Maiya you know all of this and it's part of your basic training.

What are you driving at?" Thomas Fieldstone wondered as he sat back in his office chair.

Feeling somewhat embarrassed she tried again. "Maybe it is my use of the English language which hinders me from explaining myself properly. Thomas let me try to tell you what I mean. If someone died say six months ago and their service was at some other funeral home in the city how would we or someone like me get a pre-death photo of them?"

"I could obtain this for you Maiya if I knew the funeral home but I'd need to know why," stated Thomas Fieldstone evenly, as he reached out to straighten some papers on his desk.

Watching Maiya's somewhat awkward countenance, he wondered about it.

Surveying her obvious beauty, he forced himself to bring his attention back to her queries.

Feeling she had no choice but to go into her lengthy account, she told her husband's story.

Ten minutes later, Thomas Fieldstone rubbed his eyes as he considered Maiya's account of the facts.

Sighing lightly, Thomas Fieldstone began his reply. "Maiya I can completely appreciate your husband's desire to try to help this priest but I'm not sure I could get involved in something like this without permission from a family member of Rev. Kubelik. Yes, I really doubt it and unless the reverend's photo was somewhere public like a website or social media, I couldn't secure it on these grounds.

"I honestly wish I could help you and your husband but that's the reality of it. If I think of something that could be helpful, I'll tell you. I know that sounds rather cold but this could be considered a prickly situation and we always have to be mindful not to get into those types of situations. Maiya, I do hope you understand me and our position here."

"Okay, yes and fair enough Thomas," Maiya said as she got up to leave his office.

***

Walking downstairs, Maiya Emerson wondered if there were another way to help her husband and his friend.

***

Thomas Fieldstone made some notes about their conversation then placed them in his wallet. He would literally do *anything* for Maiya but he had to be careful.

***

The two 'investigators' watched from their vantage point. They had observed Aaron Emerson's wife go into *Lytton's Funeral Home* hours ago.

Each cranking open a can of pop, they kept watching.

"Well it's obvious she works there. I wish we had not lost her hubby in traffic this morning," the smaller hood noted.

The larger man of the two hoods, nodded. "Yeah that was a bad break but we still have his wife and she's extremely easy on the eyes. I don't mind watching her one bit. Imagine her at a strip joint? Wow, she'd bring the house down!"

Laughing raucously the two men kept up their vigil.

**

Some hours later, Maiya Emerson left work and headed to the grocery store.

As she entered the parking lot, she noticed in her rear view mirror that a certain black vehicle appeared to be following her. She had noticed them not long after she left work. Feeling her blood begin to boil, she clenched her fists as she resolved to lose them pursuing her.

**

Casually entering the grocery store, Maiya watched from behind some bags of rice piled near the storefront that faced the parking lot near her car.

Within minutes, she saw the one man get out and come towards the store. The other man emerged and stood by the car, lighting a cigarette.

Maiya felt mysteriously excited as she wondered what she would do to get rid of the men. *Those fiends think I'll be scared of them well I'll turn the tables on them!*

Playing a cat and mouse game with them, Maiya led the one man around the store mysteriously and then she doubled back and stood behind him and called out loudly, "why the hell are you following me! Now beat it or I call the police!"

Turning around abruptly, Maiya had caught him off guard. "Look lady I don't know what you're talking about. I'm in here doing my shopping."

"Like hell you are! You've been following me since I left work at *Lytton's Funeral Home*," Maiya shouted as she began attracting a lot of attention, including that of the manager.

Walking quickly towards her, he kept his eyes on the man nearby. "Ma'am is this guy giving you some trouble! Hey Mister, get back here! John, call the police!" the store manager called out to his employee.

The suspect flew out of the grocery store and motioned for his friend to get going as fast as possible.

Maiya smiled triumphantly, as she wrote down their licence plate from her memory.

"Ma'am we've called the police so they should be here any moment. Can you tell me happened?" the store manager asked, as he led her to one side.

"Perhaps once the police come as I don't want to repeat my story three times. I want to thank you for helping me though. I really appreciate that!" Maiya stated with relief in her voice.

"My pleasure," the manager said as he kept studying her. "I must say you are very brave."

"Oh thank you! I got their licence number so the police should be interested in that," Maiya said as she held the slip of paper for him to see.

"I should say so!"

Hearing sirens outside, they both turned towards the front of the store.

"That *was* fast! I am glad though because those jerks could still be nearby. Those officers responding to the call must have been just down the street," Maiya noted with a smile on her elegantly beautiful face.

Presently two constables strode inside asking for the manager. Being directed their way, Maiya and the manager stood together.

The manager came forward. "Hi, I'm Jerry Waschinski and I'm the store manager. This brave lady here is the reason we called the police, that is to say on her behalf."

Glancing from Jerry Waschinski to Maiya the one constable began speaking. "Okay thanks Mr. Waschinski. Ma'am, please tell us your name and your story."

After Maiya had recounted her frightening experience and given them the licence number, she waited.

The other police constable took notes then said, "Ms. Emerson, you're certain that this same vehicle followed you from work?

"Yes I am and the reason I know this is because they were parked in the lot across from the funeral home and that's not allowed unless there is a funeral or visitation and today there wasn't one. There will be a visitation later tonight but not today during the day so immediately, I noticed this and kept this in my memory. Later I couldn't believe they were following me as I came here to do some shopping."

"Do you know why they might have been watching you while you were at work?" the other police officer asked as he held his pen poised to write.

"I can't imagine but now that you have their licence number it should tell us something about them and who they are," Maiya speculated wisely.

"Yes it will and I must say it was really level-headed of you to get their licence number despite the rest of this. You are a very brave woman indeed," the one policeman said as he surveyed Maiya with appreciation.

"Thank you! So, what will happen now?" Maiya asked as she glanced between the police constables.

"We've made our report and we're going to run this licence immediately and then we'll follow that up. If you encounter them again give us a call and here is the case number to quote," offered the larger of the two constables.

Turning towards the front of the store, they strode back to their police cruiser.

***

"Ms. Emerson would you like a cup of tea or coffee? I'd like to offer you a few moments to get over this," suggested Jerry Waschinski kindly.

Smiling at him broadly, she agreed. "That is very kind of you Mr. Waschinski. I'd appreciate a hot cup of tea."

"Please call me Jerry and it is my pleasure. If you'll follow me, you can sit in my office and have the tea. Just this way."

Maiya followed Jerry Waschinski into his small but neat office.

"Please have a seat and I'll bring you some tea," Jerry offered.

"Thank you Jerry, I really appreciate your kindness," Maiya responded as she looked around his office.

***

A few minutes later Jerry Waschinski returned with a steaming cup of tea for her. Setting it before her, he returned to his desk.

"That was quite an experience but you handled it so bravely. I am really pleased and proud of you," admitted Jerry as he studied Maiya's face and overall appearance.

"Why thank you and interestingly it kind of all started with a priest," Maiya stated mysteriously.

Raising his eyebrows, Jerry Waschinski could hardly wait to learn more of her story. "If you feel like telling me I'd love to hear about it."

Sipping her hot tea, Maiya smiled warmly. "Well I think that should be alright."

About ten minutes later, Jerry sat back in his chair as he digested everything Maiya Emerson had told him.

Leaning forward on his desk, he began speaking. "Ms. Emerson, I believe I know of or I've met Rev. Frank Kubelik."

Sitting up straighter Maiya was intrigued. "Do you really? Oh please tell me more about *that*!"

Smiling slightly, Jerry Waschinski shrugged. "Well there's not a huge amount to tell except that I do know of him and I've heard some of his sermons before at *St. Simeon's*. He's great! I love his unique style and the man himself, he's a real sweetheart. Oh yeah, great priest!

"But you say he's been killed? Wow, that's incredible and utterly horrible! I hadn't known because my wife and I moved so we go to another church closer to home now. Man, that's rotten! Rev. Kubelik; I can hardly believe it."

Maiya felt sure he was sincere and that he truly had not known the priest was allegedly deceased.

On impulse, Maiya had a thought. "Jerry, do you happen to have a photo of Rev. Kubelik? I mean maybe at home or know where I might find one of him?"

Thinking for a moment Jerry smiled. "Actually I think I do because a year ago he officiated at my niece's Baptism. Oh yeah, Rev. Kubelik is in a few photos. They're at home of course but if you come back here tomorrow I'll dig them out and show you them."

Maiya was proud of herself. "Yes I will happily come back tomorrow and have a look at those nice photos. When should I come?"

"Any time after we open at eight am. Gee, that's really sad Ms. Emerson. My wife will be quite bereft to learn of Rev. Kubelik's passing."

Drinking her tea Maiya agreed. "I know it is so very sad. I wish I had known him myself but my husband knew him instead."

***

The two police officers drove along with the details of the ownership of the car registered under the licence number Ms.

Emerson had provided them.

"Too damned bad the licence fizzled out. Of course, it is a stolen vehicle. I mean that would be too easy wouldn't it?" Constable Richardson stated as he drove along. "But we're on the lookout for it now and it's in the system so with any luck we'll catch those jerks."

Constable Rizzi nodded as he glanced around outside. Recalling Ms. Emerson, he smiled. "She was one cool lady. Imagine most people reacting as she did. She's a one in a million."

"She ought to be a cop," observed Constable Richardson. "I wouldn't mind having *her* on the police force wouldn't you?"

Grinning, Constable Rizzi agreed. "Oh yeah, now she would be a *real* asset to the force. But yeah, I think she'd make a great cop."

"One thing though; I keep wondering why the hell those goons were following her. What do you think?"

"Yeah that's been bugging me too. To all intents and purposes, she seems completely innocent and I'm sure she is and yet those thugs are following her, why?" Constable Rizzi remarked.

"Maybe they just like what they see and maybe she reminds them of someone. Who knows? But it sure is weird I have to admit. Well if they bug her again we'll have more to go by hopefully," Constable Richardson mused as they turned to drive down another street.

"Yeah there's no smoke without a fire so something made

them follow her. I wish we could really look into this but we haven't got enough to go on. I just hope she doesn't get hurt in any way. I just pray she stays brave and alive," Constable Rizzi said as he kept watching out the window.

"Well one thing's for certain; they knew we were called and they saw how brave she is. Those are huge points which might be enough of a deterrent for them," Constable Richardson stated as he focused on traffic.

CHAPTER SIX

Hearing the door unlock, Aaron Emerson glanced up. "Maiya, you're home a bit later than usual. Had to work late honey?"

Sighing loudly as she came in, Maiya plunked herself down on a chair as she threw her keys across the floor. "Just wait until I tell you *my* story!"

"Does this call for a drink?" Aaron asked as he waited for his wife to catch her breath.

"Yeah a big tall one!" Maiya stated as she began to spill her story for her husband.

Some minutes later, after Maiya finished recounting her adventures, Aaron refilled their glasses and sat down with a thump.

"What in the name of Mike is going on? This thing gets more sinister by the minute. Who *is* this Rev. Kubelik and where is he? Also what did he do in order to attract so much attention?"

Shrugging Maiya took another drink. "Who knows? But we know one thing; he's not deceased because if he was those goons wouldn't be following us."

Glancing over at his wife, he agreed. "You've put your finger on it baby. That is one irrefutable fact. There is no way a bunch of thugs follows people associated with the deceased and someone who apparently passed away six months ago, no less."

"We should go and talk to Father Andrecki only this time let him know we know what's going on," suggested Maiya as she put out her long legs in front of her.

"Sweetie let me tell you what Don Fenway and I figured out today. Well they are only theories but do they ever make sense!" Aaron said proudly.

After bringing his wife up to date on the gist of the theories formed earlier in the day he waited for her comments.

Shaking her head, Maiya was impressed. "Wow, you two really gave this some thought. I am impressed. Okay so how will you prove your theories?"

"Don Fenway and I have got some great leads to follow-up. For one, I need to find a way to take a look at the original plans from the 1960's developer and see what they kept or boarded or walled up. Secondly, I need to think of someone at the club that might have helped Rev. Kubelik hide at the country club assuming that he did.

"Thirdly, Don and I need to find out a lot more about confessions at *St. Simeon's* and how often they occur and when was the last confession for the good reverend. Fourth and maybe finally for now, we'd like to take another trip to speak to Father Andrecki. Don and I are convinced he knows what's going on. He has to."

"Okay those are great plans and I will get the photo from Jerry Waschinski," stated Maiya as she watched her husband. "But remember honey it's only a theory of yours that Rev. Kubelik hid at the golf and country club. We've not a shred of evidence to support this."

Frowning a little Aaron shrugged. "I know that but we have to start somewhere and don't forget my gut feelings are often right. This is a gut feeling and one that happens to make a hell of a lot of sense."

"Okay babe, I just wanted to remind you of that. I'll get a photo from Jerry Waschinski tomorrow."

"Yeah, that's awesome babe because that was another one of the points Don and I were toying with but now you've got that nailed down so we're good there," remarked Aaron as he lay back in his chair.

"Does E.B. Vincents have any other family who are still members of *Monk's Abbey Golf and Country Club*?

Aaron thought for a moment. "I have no idea Maiya but you might have something there. If there is someone related to him still holding membership they might be very useful to speak to."

"What can they tell us?"

Laughing slightly, Aaron began speaking, as he remained lying in his chair studying his gorgeous wife. "Honey, it was your idea, why did you bring it up in the first place?"

"I thought they might be the people or person who was the inside contact for Rev. Kubelik. Obviously E.B. Vincents knew of these monk's cells so maybe their relatives did too," Maiya said as she got up to get another drink.

"Yes sweetie that was my thoughts too. Since you brought them up I felt they might have been the inside connection," Aaron replied as he began to sit up straighter.

"Or they might have been the ones who called on the hoods," Maiya suggested as she dropped two pieces of ice in her drink.

Rising, Aaron joined his wife at their bar. "Now why the hell would they do that? If they called on the goons, wouldn't they just get on with it and capture the good priest? Why this cat and mouse game?"

Sighing lightly, Maiya Emerson stood next to her husband as he dropped ice in his drink. "Well that's just it, to make the poor priest sweat. Oh, they're brutes! Imagine picking on a poor priest. They should be ashamed of themselves!"

Aaron stood holding his drink as he considered his wife's ideas. Turning towards her, he smiled. "Baby, you might have something there. I'm really glad you said what you said a moment ago about E.B.'s relative or relatives.

"I might have gone in there, guns-a-blazing and made things fatally dangerous for the good reverend if he is hiding at the country club. I had really better be sure of who I speak to about this. I had really better be very careful and not tip my hand."

***

Dropping into the grocery store on her way to work the next day, Maiya waited for Jerry Waschinski to meet with her.

Five minutes later, Jerry Waschinski came towards Maiya but he wasn't smiling. "Ms. Emerson, hello and thanks for coming by. The thing is this; last night our home was broken into and ransacked."

"What!" Maiya called out loudly as she stared at Jerry Waschinski.

Glancing around him, he guided Maiya into an alcove near the back of the store. "Ms. Emerson, my wife and I went out to a show last night and for dinner and when we returned we had to call the police! The place was turned upside down and it would appear that the one thing they were looking for they found."

Already fearing she knew the answer she asked the question anyway. "And what was that?"

"The photos of the priest; Rev. Kubelik at my niece's Baptism. That was all that was stolen. Now can you believe that? I lay money on it being those hoods that were bothering you yesterday," Jerry Waschinski speculated.

"What do the police say?"

"Well they don't know of course but they didn't disregard my theory either. They're keeping an open mind and it's gone down in the report," Jerry explained.

Maiya Emerson thanked Jerry Waschinski and left the store heading towards her work at the funeral home. Her mind spun with discombobulated thoughts and theories.

Pulling into the staff parking area around the side of the funeral home, Maiya had a plan. Glancing at her watch, she saw she still had seven minutes until she had to report inside the funeral home.

***

Taking out her cell phone, she quickly called her husband. "Aaron, listen, I have to go inside to work in a moment but I am going to drop by *St. Simeon's* after work today. I should be finished around six pm. If you want to wait for me, you can either go with me or let me try going in alone to see what happens."

Aaron reached for his bagel in the toaster as he answered, "Yes baby, I want to be outside waiting for you just in case. You can go in alone to see who's there and what happens but I'm definitely waiting outside for you."

"Okay love, well I better go. See you over at *St. Simeon's* tonight," Maiya agreed as she ended the call while heading towards the side entrance of *Lytton's Funeral Home*.

***

Aaron hung up the phone as he grabbed his warm bagel and began spreading some peanut butter and honey on it. *Maiya hadn't mentioned the photos Jerry Waschinski promised to show her today. Had something gone wrong or maybe he hadn't come in yet?*

"Oh well, maybe she'll show me them later today or we'll drop in and see Jerry and his photos of the good reverend a bit later," Aaron mused out loud to himself.

While he ate his breakfast and made himself some coffee, Aaron wondered what else he could do to help his friend, the good

Reverend Frank Kubelik. Pouring the hot coffee into his mug Aaron pondered the question of whether the good reverend actually wanted help. Just what if he, his wife and his friend Don Fenway were knocking themselves out for nothing?

Sipping the hot liquid, he couldn't believe that. No, their meeting wasn't by chance. Just maybe Rev. Kubelik had purposely come to *Spanky's Bar and Grill* that afternoon of their meeting. While Aaron considered those lines of thought, he wondered what apartments were in the vicinity of *Spanky's*. Thinking back to the street scene, he recalled there were some apartments nearby within walking distance to the bar.

Glancing at the wall clock, he saw that it was nearing 10:30 in the morning. Leaving his coffee on the table, he rushed upstairs and got dressed.

Transferring his coffee into a travel mug, he grabbed his wallet and keys and headed back to the area of *Spanky's Bar and Grill*. He'd park and wander over to the apartment buildings in the area and take a look or ask around for anyone who might have known the good reverend. Just maybe he'd get lucky and find some old codger who knew him and knew where he was as well as what he looked like. If Aaron was really lucky, he might even find someone with a photo of him.

***

Entering the lobby of the first apartment building closest to *Spanky's* Aaron searched the names and initials on the resident list above the mailboxes. Faint smells of cooking mixed with industrial cleaner wafted towards his nose.

The elevator door opened and a woman with a load of laundry turned towards the opposite direction. On an impulse, Aaron decided to stop her.

"Excuse me ma'am? Could I ask you a question?" Aaron said with a friendly expression.

Eyeing him closely, the middle-aged woman looked a little wary. "Well I don't know. Do you live here?"

Keeping his distance, Aaron stood back as he continued to smile at the lady. "Well no I don't but I have a question that I hope you can help me with."

Still unsure, the lady shifted her load to her other arm. "Well what is it then?"

"Thank you very much. I was wondering if you knew of a Reverend Frank Kubelik and if he lived in this building," Aaron asked hopefully.

Shaking her head, she laughed slightly. "A priest, in here?! Not much chance of that. If you knew the kinds of tenants, they got in here now you'd need a priest to exorcise them! Yeah what a bunch some of em' are."

Nodding, he smiled at the woman again. "Okay, thanks for your help. I won't detain you any longer. I appreciate it."

Turning towards the door, he stopped as the woman had begun speaking again.

"Excuse me ma'am, what was it you just said?"

Remaining where she had stood previously, she repeated her

words. "I said, you should ask old Jensen who lives next door. He knows everybody! He's lived in that same house for going on fifty years if I'm not mistaken. Yep, he'll know if a priest lived or lives around here. Old Jensen hasn't anything else to do but watch from his porch and memorise the comings and goings of everyone in the neighbourhood."

Aaron's pulse quickened as he took in the information the lady had given him. "Ma'am, thank you *very* much!"

Nodding at him, she disappeared around the corner carrying her load of laundry.

***

Aaron quickly made his way across the front lawn to the sidewalk and stood surveying the old house next door, which did have a large porch and indeed sat an old weathered looking man with a blanket over his knees. Pausing for a moment, he wondered if he could just walk up to the old man's porch and speak to him.

Slowly he began to approach the old man's property. "Hello sir, may I speak with you for a moment?"

The old man watched Aaron approach his house then he put up his hand and waved him forward.

Seeing his gesture, Aaron strode closer and smiled at the old man. "Thank you sir. I just have a question. I was wondering if you knew of a priest named Reverend Frank Kubelik or you knew if he lived around here."

The old man motioned for Aaron to join him on his porch. "Come on up and have a seat. I don't bite. Yeah, I know the fella you're talking about but he don't live here anymore. He used to though. I saw him and I saw you a few days ago going into and coming out of that bar across the way.

"Yep, he was here a few days ago but then you knew that because you were in the same bar as him that afternoon. Yep, I saw him come out of there and walk towards his home then he never came back out again."

Aaron's mouth hung open slightly as he listened to the old man. "Sir, you're sure that you saw Reverend Frank Kubelik go into his home three days ago and you never saw him leave. May I ask where he lived?"

The old man studied Aaron as he sat near to him. "Why do you want to find him? Are you one of his parishioners?"

"No sir, we were very good friends. You're right; I did share lunch with him that afternoon three days ago at the bar across the street. It was the last time I saw him. I really want to find him so that I can make sure he's okay," Aaron explained honestly.

The old man looked out across the busy road as he considered Aaron's answer. "This place used to be such a nice area when I moved in here fifty years ago. Ah well, times change don't they."

Taking his thin arm and hand, the old man pointed across the road in a diagonal direction. Turning towards Aaron, he spoke. "Do you see that garage over there?"

Aaron's eyes followed the direction of the old man's arm and hand pointing. "Yes, I believe I see an auto-body garage over there."

Still watching Aaron, the old man kept pointing. "Well that's where Reverend Kubelik *used* to live."

Frowning slightly, Aaron spoke the one question, which burned, in his mind. "Why are you so sure Reverend Kubelik doesn't live there any longer?"

Laughing slightly, the old man put down his thin arm and hand. "That's easy; I saw them taking him away in a covered stretcher didn't I?"

Aaron gasped slightly as he came to terms with the full impact of what the old man had told him. "Sir, I'm a little confused. Are you telling me some ambulance crew removed the body of Reverend Kubelik on a covered stretcher a few days ago?"

Narrowing his eyes, the old man stared into Aaron's eyes intently. "I didn't say it was some people from the ambulance service. I said I saw *them* taking him away in a covered stretcher. Now who those persons were, I can't tell you but it was one of those cars that the funeral homes use. That's all I can tell you and I assume it was the Reverend Kubelik because I haven't seen him since and he always used to come and speak to me when he passed by.

"Not only that, but his cat has been looking for him too cause she's over here now with me. Her name is Giselle."

As if on cue, a calico cat got up from under a chair and came forward to see Aaron. Purring, as she looked up at him, all at once the feline jumped up on Aaron's knees and sat looking at him and purring.

Laughing slightly, as he began petting the friendly cat, Aaron couldn't believe what he'd learned. "Oh you're a friendly kitty aren't you? So, you're looking for the good reverend are you Giselle? Well so am I?"

Giselle meowed and then settled herself down on Aaron's lap as he continued to pet and stroke the lovely animal's fur.

"She likes you," the old man said with a toothy smile. "By the way, my name's Jensen. Just call me Jensen and not Mr. Jensen, okay?"

"You got it Jensen!" Aaron laughed as he continued to stroke Giselle's soft fur. "Yeah she's a lovely cat and so friendly. Well the good reverend would have a beautiful animal like her wouldn't he? But I keep thinking about what you told me. I mean, I just wonder who those people were who came to retrieve Reverend Kubelik's body?"

"Don't know and I couldn't see the name on the funeral car they came in. All I know is they took him away and loaded him into the back of their wagon so who they were, I haven't a clue. I just recognised that they were from some funeral home. I've seen enough of those kinds of funeral cars before in my day," Jensen admitted ruefully.

"I daresay you probably have and I've seen my share of them too for that matter. Well this sure does beat all, this strange conundrum. I mean I can't make head or tails of it all. It's the damnedest puzzle I've ever heard of and I'm in the thick of it," Aaron remarked as he studied old Jensen sitting watching him.

Giselle had fallen asleep curled up on Aaron's lap. Not wanting to disturb her, he let her be.

"Well if you ask me it was that woman who did it to him," Jensen remarked suddenly.

Affecting a double take, Aaron hardly knew if he had heard him correctly. "I say, could you repeat that? Something about a woman doing him in?"

Laughing slightly, old Jensen snorted as he repeated himself. "Yeah, you heard me right the first time. I said it was that woman who did it to him. She was always coming around in her fancy car and dressed to the nines she was. She was the kind you'd see at a country club."

Aaron started at the mention of the term country club. "Was she indeed. So she had that pampered look about her. Would you be able to describe her Jensen?"

Staring across the road at the garage, Jensen considered Aaron's request. He knew who she was, but should he tell him? "What did you say your name was?"

"Oh, I beg your pardon, but I didn't introduce myself. I'm Aaron Emerson."

Nodding slowly, Jensen understood at last. "Well let me think about it a little okay? Her description is kind of hazy in my memory just now. It must be my meds kicking in. Maybe if you come back another day soon I'll be able to remember more about her and that day when Reverend Kubelik left his home with those people."

Aaron wondered about the old man's sudden reluctance to tell him anything further. It might be that Jensen was having a temporary mind fog but on the other hand, it seemed that as soon as he told him his name the old man had clammed up.

Sighing, Aaron agreed. "Sure, I'd be happy to come back and see you another day soon. I should let you rest now as you may be growing a little weary.

"Thank you so much for helping me and speaking to me today. You've been a tremendous help."

Jensen smiled his toothy smile then nodded. "Okay, that'd be nice. You come back soon and come see Giselle too. She's gonna miss you."

Carefully, Aaron moved the cat and set her down on the chair where he had been sitting. "I'm going to miss her too but I'll be back to see her and you too Jensen."

Shaking the old man's hand, he left and headed back to his car. Making a mental note to return to the auto garage later when it was dark, he drove away towards his apartment house.

All the way home, Aaron digested the startling information that Jensen had given him.

"Unless the old man was mistaken and this was certainly plausible, Jensen had given me some solid leads or clues. Time would tell if the old man was credible but it was a start; a really good start.

"One thing I know for certain, Jensen had confirmed my suspicions that Reverend Kubelik was indeed alive and well on the afternoon of our meeting because he said he'd seen him and Jensen had even confirmed seeing me enter and leave that same bar. Father Andrecki had lied to me but why?"

Pausing for a stop light, Aaron continued thinking aloud. "What in the name of Mike is really going on at *St. Simeon's* and why is Father Andrecki pretending Reverend Kubelik died six months ago?"

***

Realising that he had about four hours before he was to meet Maiya, he decided to have a nap. Unsure if he would sleep, Aaron lay down to try to make some sense of the labyrinth he found himself in.

***

Jensen opened his front door and stepped across as Giselle followed him. A little unsteady on his feet, the old man navigated around his living room and into the kitchen.

From beyond a voice called out to him. "Is he gone yet?"

Sighing, Jensen nodded. "Yeah, he's gone. I invited him back another day though."

"Did you indeed."

CHAPTER SEVEN

Thomas Fieldstone threw down the termination order for Maiya Emerson from head office. He couldn't believe the details it contained and a part of him wanted to rip it up and toss it into the shredder. Getting up from behind his desk, he stood looking out across the street.

"Why had this happened? Why was head office fabricating false statements about a valued employee such as Maiya Emerson?" Thomas Fieldstone muttered under his breath.

Images of Maiya filled his insides with an unquenchable longing, he had never experienced before. No one woman had filled him with such torrid desire and drive to do all and anything he could for her.

Taking a deep breath, Thomas Fieldstone willed himself to cool down and defuse his burning loins. With each encounter with her although completely professional, Thomas only wished and ached for them to be intimate.

***

Thomas' assistant came towards his office.

Signalling him, he motioned for him to close the door behind him.

"Lock it Warren."

"Lock it?" Warren asked with a puzzled expression on his young and handsome face.

"Warren have a seat and then read this," Thomas said as he handed him the termination order from head office.

Warren did as he was bid then peruse the termination order. Handing it back to Thomas, he shook his head. "They can't be serious. Not Maiya, she wouldn't say or do those things. It's impossible."

Thomas' expression grew even more serious.

"I know it but what the hell am I going to *do* about it? This is a termination order and the company policy states—well you know what it states about this sort of thing."

"I can't do it and quite frankly, I'm going to fight this because it's a load of shit if you'll pardon my saying so."

"No, sir, I agree with you completely and if you'll allow me I also think it is a huge crock of shit and I am also prepared to fight it as well. Now Thomas, I'm not sure what's at the heart of this termination order or who for that matter, but I think we have to look into this. If they'll do this to someone like Maiya, what will they do to someone else? I mean who cares that it's family in my case? Someone isn't playing fair!" Warren speculated with passion in his voice.

"Alright Warren, this stays with us for now. Not a word to

anyone and I mean that and especially you because this *is* family in your case. I have to think about this and I have to figure out something which doesn't get the lot of us axed."

Sighing loudly, Thomas ran his fingers through his thin blonde hair.

Rising slowly, Warren stood for a moment before leaving. "You have my word sir. This absolutely stays in this room and be-damned to whoever thought this garbage up. We've got to take care of our own don't we sir and Maiya is one of our own; our *very best* own."

***

Partially closing Thomas' door behind him, Warren struggled with what he had just heard. Not only did Thomas have to think, so did he.

Heading swiftly back to his own office, Warren turned his computer on.

***

Downstairs at *Lytton's Funeral Home*, Maiya Emerson answered the phone as she walked towards the front of the building, using their portable phone.

"Good afternoon, *Lytton's Funeral Home*, this is Maiya speaking."

Hearing a click on the other end of the line, Maiya said hello once again then hung up the phone.

Shrugging, she went about her duties for the next little while on the main floor then down in the basement where their supplies were kept. Opening the large refrigerator, she retrieved some extra cream and milk for the hot drinks that were often served in the reception rooms after the visitations.

***

From behind, she heard footsteps. Turning, she saw Warren walking towards her.

"Hi Maiya. How do things look for this afternoon? Have we had any family or guests arrive for Miss Prendergast?"

"So far only a few phone calls for directions and that sort of thing. It's still a bit early but hopefully someone will show up soon," Maiya said as she held onto the cartons of milk and cream.

"Okay, well if you need me, just come and get me," Warren said as he continued to look at her.

Noticing his distracted staring, Maiya smiled at him. "Warren, is there anything else you wanted to ask me?"

Recovering from his staring at her, he smiled back. "Oh no, I'm just checking in with you. It is rather quiet today, which is a nice reprieve from our usual craziness. Well, I'll let you get to it."

***

Leaving Maiya to stare after him, Warren walked quickly away. He had been so close to committing an act of blatant unprofessional and ethical misconduct he could scarcely think straight. Just the sight of Maiya alone with him in the basement caused his male hormones to fire into overdrive.

A surge of testosterone blasted through his body as he felt his lower body become physically aroused. Warren gasped slightly as he wound his way through the dark halls of the basement of the funeral home.

"Oh that woman is going to drive me to madness if I don't do *something* about her soon!" Warren whispered under his breath.

***

Maiya shrugged as she returned to her duties in the basement. Something about their interaction had deeply unsettled her. She was no fool; Maiya knew how he *really* felt about her; Warren and Thomas both, but each at opposite ends of the sexual spectrum. One wanted to make love to her and cherish her, the other wanted to dominate her, make love to her and then seize her as if she were his own personal trophy. Of the two, her heart went out to Thomas.

"It is not as though I would ever cheat on Aaron, but if I lost my husband, Thomas would be the kind of man I would turn to. He's a lovely fellow and I do really like him. He's also quite attractive and if I wasn't married I would entertain notions of pairing up with him," Maiya admitted secretly to herself.

A driver who also worked the parking lot came into the funeral home as Maiya was sorting through some brochures and replacing the outdated copies.

"Hello Maiya, "Eugenia greeted her as she wiped her feet on the large mat by the door. "The wind is picking up out there. I think it's going to rain."

Smiling at Eugenia, Maiya looked out the front door for a moment.

Seeing a darkening of the skies and the wind tossing things

around she agreed. "Yeah, I think you're right. Eugenia, are you working the lot and then inside here tonight after I leave?"

The lovely African Canadian lady moved closer to Maiya. "I sure am dear but Rex is also coming by about six-thirty just in case we get busy with tonight's visitation."

"Okay, that's good because I didn't want to leave you in the lurch. I know you can't be in two places at once Eugenia."

"Oh you're too good to me. Maiya, I can always count on you to be helpful and fair. I think they have things covered though but thanks, I really appreciate that. I doubt if I'll be driving anywhere tonight but you never know. Thomas said something about a couple more people that might be coming to the home in the next day or so. Maybe sooner once they're released from the morgue."

"Things will be busy then around here. Good, we can all use that," Maiya stated as she started to walk along the hallway with Eugenia.

***

Hearing foot -steps coming from upstairs, the two women separated for the time being.

***

Assistant Managing Director, Gail Gordon approached Maiya as Eugenia headed towards the side entrance of the funeral home. Gail had just come in the side entrance.

"Have you seen Thomas today?"

Wrinkling her pretty brow, Maiya nodded. "Oh yes, several times. Can't you find him?"

Gail's shiny black hair glowed under the soft lighting of the funeral home. Her café au lait complexion complemented her dramatic dark hair. Gail Gordon was a stunningly pretty African Canadian woman who turned heads wherever she went.

"No, I can't seem to locate him actually. He's not answering his phone. I'll go up to his office and try his door. He might be so busy he doesn't hear his phone although that doesn't sound like Thomas. He usually answers either his cell or his office extension. I guess he had to go out suddenly but I would have thought he'd have told you or someone else. I've just arrived Maiya and I wanted to speak with him about something."

Alarm filled Maiya as she thought about Gail's predicament. It was strange indeed and it was completely unlike Thomas who normally was a stickler for decorum and policy.

"That doesn't sound like Thomas in the least. He must have had an emergency but I hope he's okay or his family."

"Yes, I know Maiya. Okay, who's here tonight other than me?" Gail asked in reference to the number of funeral directors present.

"Well, other than you Gail, we have Warren. I just saw him maybe fifteen minutes ago. I think he went upstairs because I saw him downstairs when I was getting supplies in the basement," Maiya speculated helpfully. "You know how noisy it is in the basement with the furnace, the generators, the washing machine and so on and it wasn't until he was almost right behind me that I heard him coming."

Sighing, Gail nodded. "Well that's something then. Warren can cover as my assistant too but I can't stay here until we close tonight. Warren is more than capable as an assistant funeral director. He's newly licensed but at least he *is* licensed and capable of running things in my or Thomas's absence.

"Maiya, I know you're supposed to leave tonight at six pm but could you stay an extra hour until we see what happens?"

Smiling confidently at Gail, she agreed. "My pleasure. I am very happy to stay tonight as long as you need me. I will just call my husband to let him know but otherwise I am fine to stay longer."

"Oh, that's great Maiya! I'd feel a lot better if you stayed on because you've been here the longest of the support staff and you usually work really closely with Thomas. Eugenia is wonderful but she is fairly new only working here a few weeks so I didn't want to throw her into something before she's ready."

"Eugenia said Rex will be in at about six-thirty tonight but no matter what, I'm staying as long as you need me to."

***

Maiya went into a private room and made the phone call to Aaron.

After she explained their situation, she put her cell phone in her blazer pocket. Wondering about Thomas, Maiya couldn't help but feel slightly uneasy about her supervisor. It wasn't like Thomas to just take off and not say something to someone or to her especially, as she was one of his direct support staff assistants.

Climbing the stairs, Maiya tried to bring her mind back to her immediate duties.

***

Aaron stared at the phone as he digested Maiya's news. Feeling a little disappointed, he resolved to see how things went; the funeral home was obviously more important at that moment and Aaron had to accept it.

Glancing at the clock on the wall, he decided to turn on the TV. One never knew what they'd find on it at that time of day.

Sprawling his legs out on their sofa, Aaron thought about the fact that he hadn't done anything to find work since he lost his job nearly a week ago. His eyes left the TV screen for a moment and landed on the unread newspaper near the front door.

"Ah to hell with it! I'll read the want ads another day. Besides, this mystery about the good reverend has my attention right now. I know I haven't done a damned thing about looking for work but I just can't keep my mind on things like that at the moment," Aaron loudly lamented to himself.

"Shit, I'm bored! Maybe I'll start dinner. Maiya would really appreciate coming home to a hot meal especially after having to work extra hours. Yes, let me take good care of my beautiful wife..." Aaron resolved as he got up from the couch.

Holding open the freezer door, he searched inside for something he could prepare which didn't require thawing out. Sorting through the frozen items, he found a large lasagne. Smiling, he lifted it out and read the directions.

"Okay, it looks like we're having Italian tonight Maiya," Aaron said to himself, as he placed the large lasagne in the bottom of the fridge.

Searching through the contents of the fridge bottom, he found the ingredients to make a Caesar salad. "Wonderful! I love a nice salad with my lasagne."

Whistling as he returned to the living room, Aaron calculated that he'd need to turn the oven on in about half an hour.

In the meantime, he began to hanker for a drink.

Opening their alcohol cupboard, he pushed a bottle towards the empty ice bucket.

***

From outside, the black SUV carrying the goons sat watching Aaron's apartment house.

The larger of the two goons lit a cigarette. "If this job didn't pay so well I'd give it up because it's awfully boring. Watch, watch, watch, that's all we do!"

Shrugging, his partner just kept his eyes pinned on Aaron's neighbourhood and home.

"Nobody's pulling your leg to make you stay in it. Besides, what the hell would you be doing otherwise?"

Laughing slightly, the cigarette smoking goon took a draw as he blew smoke rings. "Not what I'd be doing but *who* I would be doing. Do you know how long it's been since I got laid?"

Shaking his head, the other goon had to laugh. "I'm sure you're gonna tell me. Man you're something else. Look, do you think I like that part of this job but hey, it pays the bills. Look, why don't we knock off early tonight and head over to that strip joint I've been telling you about? Who's gonna know we didn't stay until our designated time?"

Putting out his cigarette and lighting up another one, the other goon agreed. "That sounds good to me! Look, I never see anyone around watching us or driving by so yeah, we deserve some R and R as they say. Besides, it's Friday night and I'm really feeling squirrely to get laid. I mean it man!"

Laughing heartily, the non-smoking goon continued to watch the area as he spoke. "For your sake I really hope you can hook up with someone tonight but you never know. Anyway, no matter what happens just getting out of here and having some cold beer while we watch the hot women will do us both a hell of a lot of good."

Both men laughed and began to feel excited as they thought about kicking back at a strip joint later that evening.

***

One by one family members and friends started arriving at *Lytton's Funeral Home* for the evening visitation of Miss Andrea Prendergast.

By six-thirty pm when Rex arrived for his shift, Maiya was glad to have another helper as the funeral home was becoming quite crowded with family and friends of the deceased.

Assistant Managing Director, Gail Gordon walked back and forth with members of the Prendergast family as well as speaking with specific friends.

From where Maiya stood by the front door, she could see Gail had her hands full.

Newly licensed Assistant Funeral Director, Warren Sinclair went quickly up and down the stairs as he brought paper work for family members and answered questions with regards to Miss Prendergast's interment and service.

"Where is your Managing Director, Thomas Fieldstone?" asked Miss Prendergast's mother. "He's the one we originally spoke with about my daughter's service tomorrow. We had requested a priest from *St. Simeon's* church to deliver her mass."

Warren Sinclair was about to answer when Mr. Prendergast interrupted him. "Mr. Fieldstone promised us they'd be playing *Mozart's Requiem Mass* tomorrow during her service. Do you have it or not?"

Maiya felt sorry for the funeral directors who were run off their feet with questions and errands requested by the family of Miss Prendergast. Although she couldn't hear their conversations, she knew the directors were stressed by the sheer volume of questions and requests but didn't show their emotions.

Watching the smooth and calm manner with which Gail Gordon interacted with the family and friends of Miss Prendergast, Maiya smiled with pride.

"Mr. Prendergast, let me make sure we have *Mozart's Requiem Mass* on site for tomorrow. If Mr. Fieldstone promised it I am certain we must have it," Warren stated helpfully.

Turning towards Mrs. Prendergast, Warren Sinclair attempted to answer her queries.

"Mrs. Prendergast, I have your instructions here with regards to your daughter's mass tomorrow. May I confirm the priest you have requested officiate at your daughter's mass?"

"Why I told Mr. Fieldstone that we wanted Father Andrecki. He's the only priest we were familiar with since that other priest passed away. We never really got to know Father Kubelik but I'm sure he was good. Oh well… sadly he's passed on himself so that's that," Mrs. Prendergast acknowledged as she held a tissue in her hand.

At the mention of Father Andrecki and Father Kubelik, Maiya's ears perked up and her attention was immediately honed in on their conversation. Straining to hear every word she could, she moved slowly closer to them.

"Mr. Fieldstone has been called away this evening however we have your instructions and they will be carried out to the letter," Warren Sinclair assured Mr. and Mrs. Prendergast as they stood holding tissues in their hands.

Sighing loudly, Mrs. Prendergast shrugged as she began to walk towards *Lytton Room* where her daughter was resting. Mr. Prendergast followed behind her, as did other family members.

Twenty minutes later the volume of family and friends had slowed down as most were already inside the largest of all the visitation rooms; the *Lytton Room*.

From beyond the French doors, Maiya could see the large

number of family and friends gathered around Miss Prendergast or near her. Feeling slightly emotional, Maiya wiped a stray tear from her eye as she thought how deeply loved the young girl had truly been.

Mr. Prendergast closed the doors to *Lytton Room* as the group began to pray.

Maiya moved away from their sight and down towards the front door.

Hearing footsteps coming behind her she turned to find Warren approaching.

"Well that was something wasn't it? I can't figure out what happened to Thomas."

Maiya studied Warren's expression as he had been speaking. He appeared sincere. "Warren, may I ask you when you last saw him?"

Slightly startled by her question, he moved closer to her. "Why do you ask?"

"Well it's quite simple really, Gail wondered and I just thought you could help us track his movements from earlier this evening. Myself, I think I last saw him around four-ish or sometime after perhaps."

Warren's sultry good looks crinkled a little as he thought for a moment. "I really wasn't watching the time but it might have been around five pm or maybe later. Yes, probably closer to five-thirty perhaps."

"I believe Gail arrived at five-fifteen or so. I suppose Thomas left before she arrived then," Maiya speculated as she glanced down the hall towards the *Lytton Room*.

"Oh really? Well I guess I must have seen Thomas at around five pm then. I could have sworn it was much later," Warren stated as he shifted his weight to his other leg.

At that moment, Gail Gordon rushed towards them. "Warren, if you think you can cope with things I have to leave now. Darned if I can figure out what became of Thomas though. I'll keep trying him tonight at home and hopefully I'll get an answer."

"Sure Gail… I think I can take things from here. I believe the worst of the questions and errands are over with so hopefully the family and friends won't have anything major to ask me tonight. If I get stuck I'll call you okay?"

"Warren you keep trying Thomas too okay? Between the two of us we're bound to locate him."

Glancing at her watch, she smiled at them. "Maiya, I can't thank you enough for helping us out this evening; you're a real life saver!"

"You're very welcome Gail and I'm really glad to be here to help us out. Have a good evening."

Waving as she turned to head out the door, Gail smiled once again at them before leaving for the night.

"Well I better get upstairs and sort out some of that paperwork. If you need me, you know where I am," Warren said as he began to walk towards the staircase. Turning back for a moment, he looked at Maiya.

***

Eugenia came towards Maiya as she stood near the front door watching Warren.

"All quiet on the outside and by the side entrance. Rex is back there just in case. Whew, that was a very large gathering of family and friends."

"Yes it was but I've seen larger gatherings. Eugenia did you see Thomas Fieldstone leave this evening?"

Eugenia thought for a moment while she moved closer to Maiya. "Actually I don't recall seeing him leave here but I was in the parking lot for most of the time in the beginning then I switched to the side entrance and was there until Rex came at about six-thirty."

"I see, yes that makes sense. It's strange though about him tonight. No one seems to recall seeing him leave and no one seems to be able to locate him," Maiya shared as she looked at Eugenia.

A very puzzled look came into Eugenia's lovely dark brown eyes. "I had not known that Thomas was missing this evening. I could have sworn I saw him earlier when I arrived around three pm today. I just assumed he had left a bit later or when I was busy.

"You're right though, Maiya, it *is* very strange and it is completely out of character for Thomas to suddenly leave without mentioning this to anyone or if he did mention his whereabouts why haven't they been forthcoming with that information?"

"Why indeed," Maiya said quietly as she regarded Eugenia next to her. Strangely, her mind went over to Warren who had seemed a little nervous that evening before Miss Prendergast's family had arrived.

Hearing the phone, Eugenia went to answer it.

Remaining like a sentry by the front door, Maiya continued to speculate as to the whereabouts of her supervisor, Thomas Fieldstone. A strange thought came to her mind as she stood looking out towards the street. *Had anyone checked his office?*

As Eugenia returned to her, Maiya suddenly decided something. "Eugenia would you cover me while I go and speak with Warren?"

"Sure thing honey. You do what you have to do and I'll watch the fort so to speak."

"Thanks Eugenia! I shouldn't be long. I just have to ask Warren one question," Maiya replied as she moved quickly towards the upper stairs.

***

Taking the stairs two at a time, she quickly arrived at the top and headed towards Warren's office. Seeing the light on and the door open she approached then knocked.

Looking up, Warren smiled invitingly. "Yes Maiya do you need me for something?"

"Warren I have one question for you. Has anyone checked Thomas' office?"

Receiving a blank look, she had her answer.

"Not that I know of but I can't swear to it. What is your idea? Do you think he left us a note in there on his desk or something else to explain his whereabouts?"

Maiya was nonplussed as she pressed on. "Warren, what about his car? Is it in his usual parking space or has anyone looked?"

Warren's eyes narrowed slightly as he regarded her. "Maiya, I'm not sure I like your tone."

Reeling slightly, she was immediately on her guard. "What has my tone got to do with Thomas' whereabouts? I've just asked if anyone has looked to see if his car is in its usual place. I don't see the problem with my questions. This is getting serious Warren, Thomas appears to be missing. I'd just like to make sure we've covered all our bases."

Recovering himself, Warren tried again. "You're right and I apologise. I have no idea if anyone has checked to see if his car is in its usual place. This place has been pandemonium tonight so I doubt if anyone has had time to use the washroom let alone go looking for Thomas' car. I would assume that Gail checked as she left here recently. However, if you want me to I can take a look now."

"Warren perhaps Eugenia can take a look or Rex might be better. Getting back to my original question could we perhaps have you check Thomas' office if you have a key to it?"

"I wish I could help you with that Maiya but I don't have a key to it. Only Thomas has the key or maybe Gail does but certainly not me. I am a lower man on the pole so to speak," Warren explained with a slightly acid tone of voice.

Maiya was surprised by Warren's lack of professionalism with regards to their interaction that evening. Thanking him for his time she headed downstairs and went to speak with Rex.

"Hello Rex, would you do me a big favour and see if you notice Thomas Fieldstone's car in his usual parking space?"

Smiling at her kindly the older man was agreeable. "I'd be happy to Ms. Emerson ma'am. If you'll just keep an eye on my post for me, I'll slip out there right now. It won't take a moment."

"Certainly Rex, my pleasure," Maiya said with a warm smile.

Within five minutes, the older man returned to Maiya. "Yes Ms. Emerson ma'am, Mr. Fieldstone's car is parked in the staff lot but not in his usual place. I almost missed it. I found his car near the back. Perhaps someone took his place earlier by mistake?"

Breaking out into a cold sweat, Maiya dreaded the conclusion of the whereabouts of Thomas Fieldstone. "Thanks Rex, you're a dear to help me in this way. I'll go let Gail know as she was wondering about this too."

Tipping his hat, Rex smiled again at Maiya. "My pleasure Ms. Emerson ma'am."

***

Quickly locking herself in the women's washroom, Maiya dialled Gail Gordon's private phone number.

"Hello Gail, I'm really sorry to disturb you but we have a problem. Thomas' car is out in the back of the staff lot. Rex just found it."

"Oh my Lord! Thanks Maiya... I'll be right over and tell no one else about this. I'm serious. I won't be long and then I'll take charge of things," Gail promised as she hung up and quickly got herself ready for work again.

***

Hearing some of the family members of the Prendergast family begin to leave the funeral home, Maiya focused her attention on them.

***

Aaron had once again fallen asleep on the sofa while he was waiting for his wife. He'd left the baked lasagne on low in the oven to keep it warm for them.

***

Outside the SUV, carrying the two goons pulled away and drove towards the nearest strip joint. Their absence left Aaron's apartment house complex and street fairly deserted at that time of night. Most of the residents were already at home or just out at the local malls doing some shopping.

***

Waking up suddenly, Aaron rubbed his eyes and looked at the clock on the console near the sofa. It registered nearly eight-thirty pm. Surprised, to see that his wife was not home yet, he debated on calling her then realised if she was busy she would not answer anyway.

Lying back down on their sofa, Aaron decided he would just close his eyes. Before long, he was audibly snoring away in their living room.

CHAPTER EIGHT

Gail Gordon hustled herself out of her car and into *Lytton's Funeral Home* for the second time that day. Running on adrenaline, she couldn't move fast enough to match the speed of her mind that was running at the pace of an Olympian sprinter.

Bursting open the doors, she fairly ran full-tilt down the hallways and up towards Thomas Fieldstone's office. Passing Rex and Eugenia on the way she was relieved to see there were no family or friends of Miss Prendergast still lingering in the home that night.

Coming to a full stop outside Thomas Fieldstone's door, she was glad Maiya stood sentry at its entrance. Speaking in hushed tones, she spilled her comments. "There you are Maiya. I'm *so* glad you're up here and not downstairs. Where's Warren?"

Moving slightly aside for Gail, she spoke softly. "Warren left here some minutes ago. He said he had something to do of a personal nature. That of course, left us completely uncovered in as far as a funeral director is concerned."

Gail was hopping mad at that point.

"Oh that bastard! That's possibly grounds for termination. He better have one hell of a good and pressing excuse or he'll find himself in the unemployment line.

"I'll deal with him later. For now, let's try to find out what we can about Thomas. Are you ready Maiya? I have no idea what we'll find in here. It could be an empty office or a gory death scene."

Maiya took a deep breath as she resolutely moved closer to the door. "I've been trying to prepare myself for this ever since I called you."

Fumbling with her keys, Gail could hardly keep her hands from dropping them. "Oh my God, Maiya, I can hardly open his door, I'm so nervous! I've got to get a grip!"

Taking a deep breath, Gail closed her eyes for a moment then slowly inserted her master office key into the lock. Hearing the lock click open, she hesitated before turning the handle and opening the door.

A draft blew in under the bottom of the door to Thomas' office.

Both women felt it and heard it. Looking at each other, they gulped.

"Oh shit, this is not going to be nice!" Gail remarked with fear and repulsion rising quickly within her.

Slowly Gail Gordon began to turn the handle to the door of Thomas Fieldstone's office. Her heart pounded mercilessly inside of her as she squinted her eyes, not wanting to see the potential horrors that lay within.

Maiya stood just behind Gail and to one side as she also found herself squinting her eyes and not wanting to see what could be inside.

Immediately, a bad smell met the noses of both women as they also were engulfed with a strong breeze that fluttered papers around on the floor and desk surfaces.

Pushing the door open all the way, Gail finally opened her eyes widely and gasped loudly as she focused on the bloody figure of Thomas Fieldstone lying slumped across his chair.

Immediately feeling nauseated, Gail could hardly summons her voice to work. "Oh dear God, this is worse than I thought!"

"*Mon Dieu*! Oh *Mon Dieu*!" Maiya called loudly, as she held Gail's arm following her closely from behind.

Unable to stand the sight of her former supervisor in such horrible condition, she quickly grabbed her phone from within her blazer pocket. Dropping it then picking it up again, she frantically dialed 9-1-1. Turning away from the gory carnage, Maiya felt as if she would throw up.

***

Ten minutes later, three police cruisers from 22 Division in Toronto, arrived and began to take charge of the situation. The coroner was called; a crime scene team and an ambulance arrived just after the three squad cars.

Several police officers moved around the funeral home taking statements while members of the criminal investigation team took photographs of the crime scene and began collecting evidence and isolating fingerprints.

For the purposes of their investigation, all employees were fingerprinted that evening. During the crime scene investigator's initial evidence collection, the body of Thomas Fieldstone remained slumped over in his chair awaiting the coroner.

***

Staff Sergeant John watched as he spoke with one of the officers. "There'll be a million finger prints to sort through. This building will be a friggin nightmare to process. Between that and the bio hazardous waste and other materials, jumping jeepers, it could take weeks before they have anything useful."

Shaking their head, the officer standing next to Staff Sergeant John agreed. "I sure wouldn't want to be processing his place."

***

About ten minutes later, a Toronto coroner arrived at *Lytton's Funeral Home* to begin her preliminary findings and to officially pronounce the victim dead.

Dr. Grace Chong mounted the stairs with her medical kit as she wove her way through the activity of the funeral home.

Noticing Dr. Chong arrive, one of the police officers led her to Mr. Fieldstone's office and the hub of all the activity.

"This way Dr. Chong," directed Constable Amir as he showed her into the office of the deceased.

"Thanks, that just saved me from getting lost in here," Dr. Chong said with a smile.

All eyes were on Dr. Grace Chong as she entered the room and immediately saw the slumped figure of Thomas Fieldstone.

Moving out of her way everyone allowed Dr. Chong to make her examination with ample space.

"Wow, this is nasty," Dr. Chong, said as she opened her medical kit to take out several instruments and gauges. Fully gloving her hands and placing a disposable coverall with apron around her disposable zip up outfit, she moved closer to the victim.

While those in attendance watched with great interest, Dr. Grace Chong proceeded to examine the deceased, taking his liver temperature and gently shifting his upper body and head to assess his wounds. Finding several gun-shot wounds to his upper body and head, Dr. Chong noted her findings as she spoke quietly into a small microphone, attached to her zippered outfit.

Some minutes later, she rose to her full height and spoke. "I'll know a lot more when I give him a full post mortem examination and do an autopsy but according to his liver temperature readings, I'd say he's been dead for about four hours, maybe a little less. Rigor mortis is barely starting to set in so I could still manipulate him. Due to the coldness of the room, rigor has been greatly slowed down.

"I'm not seeing any post-mortem lividity as yet but it could be that it is either too soon or he wasn't moved after death but I also wasn't able to strip him and examine his posterior either. I've pronounced him dead for legal purposes so his death certificate will reflect that.

"He bled out from the majority of his wounds although one of the shots probably nearly punctured his heart. Arterial spray is evident around the room and on the desk and chair surfaces.

"Judging from the shattered glass window, it would appear that he might have been shot from outside but the position of the body isn't consistent with that and I don't think any of the glass attributed directly to his death but it certainly attributed to some of his wounds which aggravated him bleeding out."

Pointing to several large shards resting on the floor with no apparent blood on them, she continued. "I've noted that he has a lot of small bits of glass embedded in his body particularly his upper body and one side of his head but otherwise it is fortunate that he didn't sustain catastrophic damage from shards of flying glass."

Staff Sergeant John moved closer to Dr. Chong. "Thanks doctor. Please keep us apprised of your findings and conclusions. We need to act quickly once we know what exactly happened to him with regards to his injuries. We'll have him transported immediately so that his full post-mortem and autopsy can be performed."

"Sure, my reports will be forthcoming," Dr. Grace Chong, replied, as she handed her examination materials to the crime-scene investigation team as evidence.

***

Downstairs in one of the visitation rooms, Maiya, Grace Gordon, Rex and Eugenia sat on sofas with police constables nearby. Someone had sent out for coffee and tea for them.

Staff Sergeant John approached the group huddled on the sofas. "I know you'd all like to go home now so once you are ready, we'll have someone drive you back. You can pick up your cars tomorrow."

Turning towards Grace Gordon, Staff Sergeant John sat down next to her.

"Ms. Gordon thanks for the contact information for Warren Sinclair who we are now searching for. We only want to get his statement for the evening leading up to his disappearance from the funeral home prior to Mr. Fieldstone being found.

"To your knowledge can you think of why he might have left work suddenly before the end of his shift tonight?"

Drying her eyes with her tissues, Grace Gordon studied the middle-aged police officer who sat next to her. "None, Staff Sergeant John, I haven't a clue as to why he did what he did, because for one thing I wasn't even here. I had already left work earlier this evening and I had made sure at that point that Warren was here so he could cover us in case someone needed to speak with a funeral director.

"You see it is our policy that we always have at least one licensed funeral director on the premises at all times during business hours. I think you'll find all funeral homes do the same. Anyway, because of this I knew it was safe for me to leave as I hadn't been scheduled to work today.

"When I couldn't locate Thomas, I was concerned but felt that he must have had a darned good reason for not sticking around because he is the managing director and a real stickler about policy and decorum."

Jotting down her comments, Staff Sergeant John waited. "So you have no information that could help us with why Mr. Sinclair left suddenly tonight?"

Searching his face, Grace once again answered no.

"Alright, because this is now a crime scene it is my understanding that you have contacted another funeral home in the area to take the incoming persons and to transport Miss Prendergast to their facility," Staff Sergeant John stated as he waited for her confirmation.

"Yes, that's right. I had to take care of those details so at least we have those loose ends tied up. Under no circumstances could we have family members or friends coming here tomorrow in view of what's happened here tonight. The staff at *Ingersoll Funeral Home*, that's who we've made our arrangements with have very kindly offered to take care of contacting the family and friends of Miss Prendergast.

"It should go off seamlessly I should think because *Ingersoll* has an excellent reputation for service and excellence," Grace Gordon added as she shifted on the sofa. "Naturally I've also been in touch with head office about this incident. They are greatly shocked."

"I think there's nothing more at this point so we'll have everyone taken home. If we need anything further, we'll be in touch. With regards to tomorrow, it could be several days or longer before the crime scene investigators have finished collecting evidence so I wouldn't expect to come back to work for some time.

"I'll be in touch with you either way and let you know so you can contact staff and make your necessary arrangements," Staff Sergeant John said as he got up from the sofa.

***

Thankfully, Maiya had been dropped at home by an officer in an unmarked car. During her ride, she said little except to acknowledge their condolences expressed for her loss.

Watching the officer drive away, Maiya stood looking around her. The street was unusually quiet and solemn appearing. It was as though the residents mourned her loss as well.

Fitting her key inside their door, she slipped inside to find her husband fast asleep on the sofa. Not wishing to wake him up she passed by him and went on upstairs to bed.

Curling up in the fetal position, Maiya began to shed tears for Thomas Fieldstone. All through the evening, she'd stoically held off crying. Shock had played its part but most of all, she wanted to mourn him in solitude. Wrenching tears of sorrow burst forth as Maiya cried into her soft pillow, quickly dampening its surface.

***

Aaron Emerson woke up suddenly as he was jolted by a nightmare he'd been having. Wiping his hand over his face, he saw that he'd been sweating. Slowly he sat up and realised how late it was.

"Past midnight! Where the hell is Maiya?!" Aaron exclaimed with panic in his voice.

Quickly he got up and was about to try her cell phone when he saw her shoes by the front door kicked to one side. Raising his eyebrows, he knew that his wife never just kicked her shoes off. Maiya was neat and tidy and orderly and she always placed her shoes carefully by the front door on the small grey mat.

"Maiya must have had one hell of a night! I better go see if she's asleep or how she's doing," Aaron stated with grave concern in his voice.

Quietly Aaron came into their bedroom to find his wife lying to one side holding a pillow close to her chest. Slightly alarmed to see her position, he came immediately over to her.

"Maiya, baby, are you okay?"

Opening her eyes, she looked at him in the dusk of their bedroom.

All at once, she sat up and threw her arms around his neck and shuddered with more tears. "*Mon Dieu*, I will never forget it as long as I live!"

Folding his strong arms around his wife, he pulled her closer to him. "Oh babe, in your own time tell me what happened. My goodness but I was worried about you just now. I'd fallen asleep on the couch but am I glad you're finally home safe and sound."

Slowly Maiya wound down her crying and sat in front of her husband as he switched on a small light next to their bed.

"There now I can see you better baby. Whew, you look as

though you've had one hell of a night. What's been happening at the funeral home tonight?"

Taking the tissues he offered her, Maiya composed herself and then began her story recounting the horrific events of the evening.

Aaron sat stunned in silence as he listened to his wife's gruesome account of them finding Thomas Fieldstone's badly shot up body in his locked office.

Shaking his head slowly, he was at a complete loss for words. "I just don't know what to say Maiya. I really don't. This is greatly disturbing and shocking doesn't even begin to describe it. I am *so* sorry that you had to be one of the persons to find him and see him in that condition."

Pulling her close to him again, Maiya continued crying as her soft heart wrenched with sadness for her deceased supervisor.

Some minutes later, she attempted to dry her eyes and compose herself. Sitting on their bed next to her husband Maiya waited as she held the wad of tissues in her hands.

Aaron studied his beautiful wife as his heart reached out to her in her moments of sorrow. "Sweetie, I don't know if you're hungry but I made us dinner tonight. It's still in the oven on low. Do you want me to make you some tea or give you anything to eat?"

Laughing slightly, she reached out to touch her husband's handsome face. "You are one in a million Aaron. I do love you my dear and I really would like a little something to eat and perhaps some tea. Oh Aaron you are such a good husband. I really love you and I am the luckiest woman alive because I have you.

"You know honey; I guess its times like this that we tend to appreciate what and who we have more than anything else. My goodness I wouldn't trade you for the world!"

Aaron felt like a million dollars after hearing his wife's words. Tears came to his eyes as he held her close to him. "Oh Maiya, my beautiful loving Maiya, my God, how I love you and I absolutely couldn't function without you. Baby, you are *the* perfect wife and thank God, you are *my* wife!

"Come on sweetie, let's go get a snack!"

Laughing slightly Maiya agreed. "I'm with you baby!"

CHAPTER NINE

The next morning came early which ushered in Saturday.

Maiya and Aaron slept in quite late but eventually they woke up nearing onto noon.

Heading downstairs, Maiya began to clean up from the night before and prepare a brunch for them. She had slept a lot better than she had expected, but she felt it was due in part, to her taking some painkillers before she went to bed.

Looking upwards, she saw Aaron descending the stairs looking tousled but rested. "Good morning sweetie. How do you feel today? Wow, it's nearly lunch time!"

Laughing slightly, Maiya ran her fingers through her long dark hair. "I know baby that is why I am making us brunch. Actually, I feel pretty good and a lot better than I had expected to feel today. Maybe I'm more resilient than I had originally thought."

Aaron stood next to his lovely wife adoring her. "Sweetie you're an incredible woman. Can I give you a hand or at least make the tea for us?"

Smiling widely at him, she nodded. "I'd like that. Okay, yes please make us a nice big pot of tea and I'll continue making our omelettes. If there is one thing most French women can prepare, it is a great omelette. Today I'm making us a mushroom Swiss-cheese omelette."

Aaron grinned as he set about making their pot full of tea. "I can hardly wait!"

Their phone rang and Aaron went to answer it while Maiya kept her eye on their omelettes.

"Hello?"

"Hey Aaron, its Don. How are you doing? How's Maiya?"

Sighing loudly, Aaron brought their phone into the other room away from his wife while he brought his friend up to date.

***

Whistling on the line as he digested the news, Don hardly knew what to say. "Where's Maiya now?"

"Oh she's making our brunch but I'm in the den because I didn't want her to hear me going over all that horrible stuff again," Aaron explained as he looked towards the doorway.

"Okay, I get it. Listen the reason I called is to invite you and Maiya over for a barbeque tonight. But maybe this isn't the time?"

Taking the phone back in the kitchen, Aaron came towards his wife. "Honey, that's Don on the line and he's calling to invite us over for a barbeque tonight. How do you feel about that?"

Maiya nodded and then set down her cooking utensils. "Actually Aaron, please tell Don that I would love to come with you for a barbeque tonight. It might do us both a lot of good."

"That-a- girl! Okay, Don I guess you heard Maiya and I have to agree with her. I think it would do us both a lot of good. We'll pick up some wine along the way. What time?"

"Oh that's wonderful! Sure, bring some wine. Be here around six pm give or take. You know us, we're casual. Okay, see you and Maiya then," Don Fenway said with a smile.

"Right, we'll be there around six-ish. Thanks Don!" Aaron said as he hung up his phone.

***

"That's awfully nice of him and Cynthia to invite us over for a nice barbeque. I do love their cook outs!" Maiya said with relish in her voice.

"Our tea is ready so it looks like we can eat," Aaron said as he watched his wife serving their brunch on big plates.

Before she began to eat, Maiya felt the urge to bless their food. "Aaron, let's say a blessing okay?"

Taking her hand in his he agreed. "Yes my love I think we really should say a prayer this morning."

***

Later as Maiya and Aaron got ready to head over to Don and Cynthia Fenway's home for their barbeque, she began to speak about the tragedy again.

"Aaron I guess you're wondering why I thought we should accept Don's offer to go to his barbeque tonight?"

"Not really sweetie. I can completely understand you wanting to start to put some distance between what happened yesterday,"

110

Aaron said as he pulled a golf shirt over his head.

"Yes that's it precisely and I don't think Thomas would want me or us to go around moping and feeling sorry for ourselves. He wasn't that kind of guy but he would have wanted us to find out who killed him and why but that's for the cops to do not us," Maiya explained as she put on her best gold filigree earrings.

"Yes that's right but we can try to help their investigation dear and I think once the dust has settled you might find that you remember something helpful," Aaron suggested gently.

Turning towards her husband, she nodded. "Yes love but not yet. I just want to enjoy my life and feel so alive because that is so precious to do so is it not?"

***

Aaron always loved how his wife expressed herself. He knew her command of the English language wasn't perfect but he also knew she tried her best. More often than not, he felt her sexy French accent was a real turn on.

Maiya had been born in the south of France in the area of Antibes which was in the *Cote d' Azure*. Coming to Canada at the age of fourteen, she had lived in Quebec but later her family moved to Toronto.

Aaron blessed the day he had met his wife. He'd been smitten by her exotic beauty as well as her other remarkable and sweet traits. Sometimes Maiya was a little quirky but that was one quality about her he really admired.

Taking her hand, he led her downstairs. "Baby you are the

most precious part of my life and I just want to celebrate you and us!"

***

Blushing, Maiya felt her heart sing with joy. She really did love her husband Aaron and secretly she considered him one of the best-looking men she had ever met. Sometimes he was a bit clumsy and awkward but those qualities were so endearing she found herself loving him more because of them.

Although she knew she was a terrific looking woman, she drew the line at fooling around. Maiya was a one- man-woman. Thankfully, she also knew her husband was a one-woman-man.

Kissing him on his lips she whispered to him, "Aaron and that is exactly what I want to do each and every day of my life from now on. I want to celebrate you and us and I'm going to do all I can to make our life together a constant joy!"

Hugging her, he led her out their door. "Sweetie if we don't get going, we might just turn back and head upstairs and you *know* what that means."

Maiya grinned playfully as they locked their home and headed towards their car.

***

From down the street, the two goons watched the couple as they left in their car.

Both men were hung over but the one man was feeling extra frisky because he had been able to meet up with a certain woman to take his frustrations out on.

Lighting yet another cigarette, the frisky goon began speaking. "Looks like the two love birds are out for an evening. How pleasant."

Glancing over at his partner, he nodded. "Yep, it sure does look that way. See, nothing happened last night and we had a rip-roaring good time because of it. Say, tonight is Saturday night so what do you say we do it again?"

Laughing, the frisky goon agreed. "I say, press repeat!"

Following along behind Maiya and Aaron from a distance, the two goons laughed as they planned their evening out again.

***

Glancing in his rear view mirror, Aaron was sure they were being followed. "Honey, can you see those jerks in that dark SUV a little ways behind us? Can you read their licence?"

Holding up her compact, she looked in her mirror then read the licence backwards.

Flipping it around in her mind, she nodded. "Yep, it's them again. Oh Aaron those are the same thugs who were following me before!"

"You've got that non-emergency police number haven't you and the case number right?"

"I'm already dialling it now honey," Maiya said as she flipped her phone open and into action.

Leaving a message for the constable at the number, they gave her and quoting the case identification number, Maiya kept her phone on in case they called her back. "Well, I've reported it once again so hopefully they can do something more about it this time."

***

Arriving in the neighbourhood of Don Fenway, Aaron decided to drive back out again and then stop his car and get out. He watched as the SUV went by and then around the corner.

Quickly, Aaron got back in and headed over to Don's house and right into his open garage door. Hitting the garage door opener, they closed it before the goons had a chance to know where they went.

***

Over the years due to weather uncertainties, Don had always made it a habit to leave his own car out on the driveway allowing his guests to drive into the garage. That was the type of man Don Fenway was. As it turned out his hospitality more than paid off that evening.

Entering Don's home from the garage door, Aaron and Maiya came into the basement of Don's house and then out onto his back lawn and patio.

Seeing his friends, he waved them over. "There you are! Pull up a chair and join us!"

Cynthia, Don's wife got up and hugged Aaron and kissed Maiya on the cheek. "Oh it's been forever! Welcome back and let me get you a drink! Don, they brought wine!"

Flipping thick steaks and ribs on his large gas bar-b-que, Don smiled widely. "So I see; that's great because with our steaks and ribs tonight we have some pasta as well so wine will do nicely!"

"Yes, I made some nice pasta from scratch, imagine that and so I'm serving it with a salad. How does that sound?" Cynthia asked as she held the bottle of wine the couple had brought.

"It sounds wonderful Cynthia, "Maiya agreed as Aaron held her waist.

"You're a fantastic cook Cynthia so no matter what you serve it will be perfect!" Aaron stated honestly.

Blushing she waved her hand, "not so as you'd notice but I do try. Anyway, you're two of my favourite people and I just love you both!"

Hugging Cynthia, Aaron and Maiya began to walk towards Don who watched with great admiration on his features.

Cynthia was the veritable well-bred lady. Always the perfect hostess, she was also very stylish and elegant in her 'Forest Hill' sort of way. Handsome features framed Cynthia's golden blonde hair. Although fairly short in stature, Cynthia liked to wear high heeled and 70's style wedge shoes.

Coming up alongside Don, Aaron whispered casually. "We had a little excitement coming over here tonight."

Turning serious, Don held his steak flipper in his hand. "What happened?"

While Aaron filled him in, Maiya wandered over to help Cynthia.

Shaking his head, Don couldn't believe it. "So they're at it again and after your wife phoned the cops on them the first time in the grocery store. Do you think they saw you drive in here?"

"Not a chance but I will go and take a look to be sure," Aaron said as he excused himself and went inside Don and Cynthia's house.

***

Turning out of Don Fenway's subdivision, the goons finally gave up.

Rapping his hand on the steering wheel, the cigarette smoking thug was angry. "I can't believe it but that loser gave us the slip!"

Shaking his head, the other goon spoke. "We're the losers here literally. Ah… forget about him and let's get ready for our night out again. I know another great strip joint you just gotta see…"

***

Aaron looked in all directions as far as he could see and found no evidence of the dark SUV parked or circling around in pursuit of them. Smiling, he felt good. *At least I out-foxed them this time!*

***

Dr. Grace Chong finished the post-mortem examination and autopsy on Thomas Fieldstone, aged forty-nine.

Cleaning herself up, she went to phone Staff Sergeant John. Not finding him answering, she left him a message.

"Staff Sergeant John, its Dr. Grace Chong. I've completed my post-mortem examination and autopsy and without getting into the technical jargon let's just say that Mr. Thomas Fieldstone sustained six shots to his upper body and three to his head by a small calibre bullet. I've got them here. It's from a 22-gauge hand pistol so that rules out someone like a sniper shooting him from outside. It would appear it was a precision shooting.

"The broken office window is a decoy. Time of death has now been established at three hours + or − so that puts it at approximately, six pm. When we found him, I had first estimated he'd been dead for about four hours but now I know it was much earlier.

"As I said, at the time, the coldness of the room slowed down the rigor mortis but now we know why. Whoever did this wanted it to appear that he died much later than he did which likely will coincide with someone's alibi.

"Nothing else significant to report. The victim wasn't moved so it appears he was seated at his desk when he took the shots. Get back to me when you can for more details."

***

An hour later Staff Sergeant John listened and re-listened to Dr. Chong's report. Making notes, he called her back.

"Dr. Chong, thank you for such a fulsome report without getting technical. I know you've already sent down your official report with all of your findings and conclusions. I just had one question at this time. Among the items the victim had on him, was his set of keys found?" Staff Sergeant John asked as he held his pen poised to write.

"Ah let me see, yes his keys were on him. They were in his pants pocket. Now which keys these fit I wouldn't know but *a* set of keys was definitely among his personal affects," Dr. Chong answered as she held her report in her hands.

"Okay, thanks doctor, I'll wait to read your report and if I have any more questions I'll get back to you," Staff Sergeant John stated as he made a note in his file.

"Right, call me if you need to," Dr. Chong replied as she hung the phone.

***

Grabbing the volume of information and reports collected from the Thomas Fieldstone case thus far, Staff Sergeant John began reading through them. No one had been able to locate Warren Sinclair despite the police having a squad car drive by his home frequently. His family had no idea where he was nor had his usual hang outs turned up anything. Because they only wanted to talk to him, they couldn't put out a warrant for him. Warren Sinclair might be as innocent as a child.

***

Sighing loudly, Staff Sergeant John put down his reports for the moment. Taking the series of crime scene photos, he searched through them carefully. Something triggered in his mind about some discarded personnel paper that had been on the desk of Thomas Fieldstone.

Strangely, it had not been blood spattered. Using his magnifying glass, Staff Sergeant John examined the photo showing the discarded personnel paper. He could just make out some writing on it.

***

Getting up quickly he went to the lab to have the photo

enlarged. He needed to read that personnel paper. Something told him it was an important piece of evidence.

"Staff Sergeant John, what can I do for you?" Lab Assistant, Richard Kelley asked as he put down his slide he'd been working on.

Showing the photo to Richard, he pointed. "Please have that enlarged. I need to be able to read the writing and the notations on it. I know the original is in evidence with our CSI's but by the time they look for it, this is faster."

Nodding, Richard Kelley agreed. "Yes, I can have this blown up within twenty minutes. I'll call you as soon as it is done."

Smiling, Staff Sergeant John thanked him. "That's great Richard. Call me."

***

Grabbing a coffee, Staff Sergeant John was just returning to his office when his phone rang. Seeing Richard's extension, he picked it up. "Yes Richard?"

"Sir, I have that photo you wanted enlarged. I'll have it brought over to you."

"Thanks Richard. I really appreciate this," Staff Sergeant John said as he hung up his phone.

***

One of the administrative staff dropped off his photo in a brown envelope.

Opening the envelope, Staff Sergeant John slid the newly enlarged photo out. Taking it in his hands, he turned it around and then using his magnifier he was finally able to read the words printed on it as well as the hand written notations:

'Termination notice for Ms. Maiya Emerson from personnel manager, Alicia Winters. Grounds for termination: rudeness to clients, unsatisfactory work habits and insubordination. Effective immediately, dated October 2nd, 2016.'

Reading the top of the form it displayed the company logo and head office address. Below the identifying information, Staff Sergeant John read in hand written notation: 'Left message for Alicia, 5:18 pm. going to fight notice. Told Warren- said he'd do the same and support me. Conspiracy? Who else knows about this and why? Something going on at head office but with whom and why?'

Looking up at the wall of his office, he thought about what he had read. Was this a motive for someone murdering Thomas Fieldstone? Recalling that Ms. Maiya Emerson was one of the two ladies who had discovered Thomas Fieldstone's body, he wondered about her. According to the termination notice, Mr. Fieldstone was going to fight her termination so obviously he didn't believe it and he also must have considered her a greatly valued employee.

Attaching the photo to his other reports, he went back to reading them.

***

Maiya and Aaron could not remember when they had had such a great barbeque dinner with their friends. The wine flowed as well as the conversation.

Holding her wine glass, Cynthia Fenway spoke. "Don has been telling me about the strange case of the missing priest. Have you learned anything new?"

Realising he had not even brought his own wife up to date, he began telling his friends and Maiya about his conversation and visit with old Jensen.

"Wow! Well, that cinches it! Now we know Reverend Kubelik is alive and he must be in hiding somewhere," Don stated as he poured himself and everyone else another glass of wine.

"Remember though what Aaron said about some people who Jensen referred to as *them*, taking Rev. Kubelik out on a covered stretcher? Old Jensen confirmed it wasn't some of the EMS ambulance staff, he called the persons *them*.

"Now this is really interesting to my mind because first of all it tells us that clearly Rev. Kubelik wanted people to assume that he was removed on a covered stretcher from his home above the auto garage. It was as though he was making a point by having those persons take him out in this manner," Maiya speculated, while she glanced at her audience.

"Now consider how they weren't official EMS staff so who else does that leave? Funeral home or funeral service staff or I guess it could be some persons impersonating those individuals. The other point that I think is interesting is that it was done in daylight and in front of Jensen who Rev. Kubelik talked to and knew, he would note every part of the charade.

"And remember Giselle, it was as though she was a prop cat too. No, something is very much staged about this entire affair," Maiya explained, as she reached for one of Cynthia's homemade butter tarts.

Aaron smiled at his wife in great adoration and appreciation. She never ceased to amaze him. "Babe, I think you've nailed it again! Your logic is wonderful!"

Cynthia and Don agreed and smiled at Aaron and Maiya.

"Yes, I couldn't agree more, "Cynthia said as she also reached for one of her butter tarts. "I love how Maiya put it, it does sound staged and especially sweet little Giselle. What do you think Don?"

Clearing his throat, he spoke. "Following up on what Maiya said, let's take this a bit further. I think old Jensen was leading you Aaron. He kept dropping leads and clues but in specific directions, such as he confirmed it was some kind of a funeral car and he also dropped the bomb about the country club woman doing him in.

"Now that in its self is really suggestive. How could an old codger like that know so much detail from across the road?"

Don looked at his friends and his wife then continued speaking. "Aaron, I'm not trying to make you feel bad like you should have figured this guy out. It's just that now that we are going over all of this, it really seems like he was trying to plant certain ideas in your mind."

Aaron smiled at his friends and his wife, then, set down his wine glass.

"Oh no, I agree Don and Maiya and Cynthia, absolutely old Jensen planted very specific seeds into my mind and seeds he or the good reverend wanted to grow. I don't feel offended in the least rather I think this is really helpful."

Don grinned at his friend. "That's the spirit Aaron. Okay, so what else can we get from Aaron's conversation with old Jensen."

Recalling the day he had spoken with old Jensen, it occurred to him that there was one other inconsistency. "I remembered him saying that he couldn't see the name on the funeral car but he gave a lot of detail about the country club woman."

Nodding his head, Don and the others agreed.

"That's right!" Cynthia said as she sat back in her lawn chair. "How could the old guy know so much detail about a lady from the country club but he couldn't seem to see the details painted on the side of a funeral home car. There is a contradiction if ever I heard one!"

"Yes and all of a sudden he didn't want to say anything more about her. He was reluctant to give a good solid description of the woman. Why?" Maiya asked as she folded her elegant hands in front of her.

Aaron was so proud of his wife and his friends as he regarded them and their suppositions. Their observations made sense and he believed them because they were a mirror of his own theories.

"I'm not sure where any of this gets us, "Aaron said as he sat back and looked at his wife and friends surrounding him. "We still don't know what became of the good reverend but we do know that he isn't dead. What I don't understand is why Father Andrecki has been lying to us; that is if he has?"

"I think it's clear that Father Andrecki is either lying or he is actually in the dark. For whatever reason, Father Kubelik wants people to think he's dead. The only reasons that come to mind is because he's in hiding from something or someone. Aaron and I thought maybe he heard something in confession that has got him into trouble or made him a marked man," Don stated, while taking another sip of wine.

Maiya poured herself another drink. "What if Father Kubelik isn't really a priest but someone pretending to be one? What if he is, perhaps, a person in some witness protection program and he's got some new life and now he's afraid his cover has been blown."

All eyes were on Maiya as she drank her wine.

"Sweetie whatever is in that wine keep drinking it!" Aaron said as he laughed. "But seriously, my love I think you've nailed it yet again! I like it and you know what, it makes an awful lot of sense. It explains why there is some staged story about Father Kubelik. That's what a person would do if they wanted to establish some new life and circumstances for themselves."

Everyone agreed with Aaron, while they kept the wine flowing.

"You know what we need to do?" Aaron said as he was beginning to feel drunk. "We need to go over to that auto garage and check that place out; see if it houses a residence and if so, what's there."

Cynthia remembered how she could help.

"Damn it all, why didn't I think of that!? I've got my real estate licence so I could go there with the purpose of checking out some commercial/residential listing."

Don shook his head as he laughed. "Baby, you're right, why didn't we think of this before? Okay, that's something you could do Monday as they likely aren't open tomorrow, being Sunday."

"Hell yes, even though I don't often work at my chosen occupation I do from time to time list certain properties if they seem to be worth my while," Cynthia explained as she too, started to feel somewhat tipsy.

Maiya joined in by saying, "this one you'll make sure is worth your while!"

As the evening wore on, the group became more intoxicated until finally Don and Cynthia offered Aaron and Maiya a bed in their spare room. Gladly the overly tipsy couple sauntered up to the spare room, while knocking into walls and doorways and laughing as they did so. Don and Cynthia headed rather wobbly but happily towards their own bedroom for the night.

CHAPTER TEN

The next morning, Aaron woke up to find his wife stark naked across the bed. The sight of her like that surprised him. Not wanting to wake her, he gently pulled some covers over her.

Before long Maiya woke up to find Aaron smiling at her and watching her. Feeling a little cold, she looked down at the blanket across her.

"Oh my goodness how did I get like this?" Maiya asked as she realised she had no clothes on under her blanket.

Slowly moving towards her, Aaron grinned as he answered her. "I haven't the slightest idea but I tried to keep you warm."

"Thanks baby. I guess I was so drunk that I forgot where I was and I just started to strip down," Maiya speculated as she pulled her covers over her tightly.

Sighing, Aaron rolled over on his back. "We should get up but I feel so lazy today."

"Mm...I know what you mean. I am having a hard time getting up too. Oh well, if we must, we must."

Taking their turns in the adjoining washroom, the couple

showered and dressed. By that time, they had started to hear sounds from other parts of the house.

Maiya removed the sheets and made up the bed as best she could. Taking their damp towels, she added their lightly soiled sheets to the bundle. "I'll take this down to the laundry as soon as I can."

"Sounds like Don and Cynthia are up. Shall we head downstairs?"

***

Finding their hosts in the kitchen, Maiya and Aaron smiled at them.

"How do you feel this morning kids?" Don said with a smile on his face.

"Yeah I guess we were kind of like teenagers last night weren't we? Oh but it was great fun wasn't it?" Aaron said as he held Maiya's hand.

Winking at them Cynthia offered them coffee. "I've also got some bacon and eggs on the way and some toast with orange juice and I think I've got some fruit we can have too."

"Let me help you Cynthia," offered Maiya as she walked towards the counter.

Don and Aaron strolled out onto the back lawn.

"Got a hangover this morning Don?"

"No, I feel great actually, "admitted Don while he studied his friend's face.

"How about you?"

"No, Maiya and I feel sensational this morning. We really slept well last night."

Don chuckled, "and how about this morning? For some reason I woke up feeling lazy as hell."

Aaron grinned as he looked towards Don's house. "Us too! What did those vineyards put in our wine? Geez Louise I couldn't get out of bed this morning!"

Don laughed loudly as he moved closer to his friend. "I haven't been that lazy in years. Cynthia couldn't believe it but boy did she love it! I usually have her up early but I think we both needed a really good sleep in."

Aaron smiled and then laughed as he said, "you know Don, I think it was just us being here with you two and enjoying such great company, food, drink and the ambiance. Strangely last night made all of us feel lazy as cats this morning."

Glancing back at his house, Don spoke. "It looks like the girls are ready with our breakfast. Man am I hungry! We've all worked up quite an appetite from last night didn't we?!"

"You can say that again! Partying is hard work isn't it!"

***

The goons were parked outside Aaron and Maiya's home a bit later than usual that Sunday morning. Both were greatly hung over and not very talkative.

"I don't see their car today unless it's parked somewhere else. Maybe they got up early and left for some place, or they never came back last night."

Lighting his fifth cigarette for the morning, the one goon replied. "You know this job is really starting to piss me off. Why the hell are we always watching these two? They haven't led us nowhere except on a wild goose chase last night. They haven't been anywhere near that priest so what is the point I ask you?"

Shrugging his shoulders, the other goon just kept drinking his coffee.

"How the hell should I know? Look, it's too early for debates right now and I've got one bitch of a hangover. All I know is the boss says to watch them so we do. It pays well enough so what's your beef?"

"Who exactly *is* the boss? Everything is so cloak and dagger. Money left for us, no faces, just voices. Well I'm getting a sore arse from sitting here all the time watching them and besides like I said, they never go near that priest guy wherever he is. Sometimes I think the whole thing is just made up."

Taking a long draw on his cigarette, he continued. "What I want to know is who it was that spilled on him in the first place? I mean who goes after a priest I ask you? It's a sacrilege."

"How do you know a word like that? Anyway, it was someone who felt that priest was a real threat to them, that's who would go after a man of the cloth as they say. I'll tell you they sure got a great racket going on with that stuff those coffin lovers do. Man I wouldn't have thought of any of this in a million years. They're geniuses," the coffee drinking goon stated as he took another sip.

"Yeah but did you hear the news this morning? Someone

popped that guy at that funeral home where that sweet looking French broad works. Who the hell did that and why?" the cigarette smoking thug asked as he rolled down his window to flick his cigarette out from.

"Damned if I know, but obviously he must have been too close to the heat. You know what they say. Which reminds me, if we don't watch ourselves we could be next?"

***

A police patrol car rounded the corner and immediately headed over to the dark SUV.

"Ah shit! We're screwed now!" the coffee drinking thug said as he frantically began searching for his wallet.

***

Warren Sinclair woke up late Sunday morning. He had tossed and turned all night thinking he heard people outside looking for him. He knew he was being neurotic but it didn't matter; he was on the run and it wasn't just from the cops.

Hearing his friend stirring in the other room, he finally got up out of bed. Opening the door of the spare bedroom, he poked his head out.

"Hey there you are dude. I thought you were never getting up. Do you usually sleep this late?"

Running his fingers through his short dark hair, he looked at his friend. "Not usually no, but today is Sunday and this wasn't my day to work, so I guess I took advantage of that. Got anything for breakfast?"

"Yeah, there's some stuff out there. Help yourself. Listen, I wanted to talk to you about something," Warren's friend began as he stood up.

Stopping in front of his friend, Warren nodded. "Sure Steve, what is it?"

"I heard on the news something about a funeral director being murdered at that same place where you work. Do you know anything about it?"

"What do you mean do I know anything about it? I know as much as you do. I left the office there before he was discovered so I wasn't involved," Warren replied a little too defensively.

"Hey look, I wasn't implying that you were actually involved. I just meant that I wondered if you could shed some more light on what happened and why? I mean was the guy involved in something?" Steve asked carefully.

Sighing, Warren sat down on one of the large leather chairs in the living room. "I don't know what was going on at that place to be honest with you but I do know that something was and I mean something rotten and conniving. I shouldn't tell you this but what the hell? Actually, that same evening, Thomas Fieldstone was murdered, he'd asked me to come in and talk to him. He showed me some termination notice for one of the employees there.

"Now this lady, head office was firing, was excellent. She was an incredible lady and certainly not deserving of the ludicrous infractions head office had dreamed up. It was a total crock of shit and I told him so. He said the same and it seemed that he was going to fight her termination.

"But after that I left him to it and then I got a call from my mom saying my dad was ill but when I got home, he was okay so I just stayed home at that point. It was a false alarm thankfully."

Steve nodded as he came and sat down near Warren. "Okay, I guess that's reason for some of this but like you said, there must have been something really nasty going on at that place. Are you going back there after the cops leave?"

"I don't know. They want to speak with me, the cops I mean, but I don't want to speak with them. But it's more than that or them; I'm thinking I should just disappear for a while," Warren admitted as he got up to get something to eat.

Steve followed him into the kitchen. "I guess I'm just a little concerned that the cops will come here and blame me or say I'm accessory to some shit but I don't know anything and neither do you so you say."

"Well I don't Steve but if I make you nervous I can go to a hotel. Really man, I don't want you to feel threatened or uncomfortable."

Standing by his friend, he shrugged. "Warren I don't mean for you to leave but I just feel a little uncomfortable about all of this."

"Hey, dude I get it so no worries. Listen, let me eat something and then get ready and I'll go and get some motel room okay? No problem and I'm grateful as hell for the bed you gave me last night at such short notice," Warren said honestly, as he looked at his friend.

"Alright Warren, I guess if you're okay with that. I feel like shit though about it all," Steve admitted as he turned towards the living room.

Warren came after him. "Look Steve, it's okay and I really don't want to involve you in this shit whatever it is. You're right about what you said earlier. I've been selfish and that's going to stop."

A short time later, Warren packed up his things and said goodbye to his friend. Heading out to his car, he looked all around him. Feeling nervous, he quickly got inside and started his car. Unsure of where he was going he just started to drive.

***

On their way home that Sunday afternoon from Don and Cynthia Fenway's home, Maiya and Aaron decided to stop in at *St. Simeon's Church*.

Mounting the steps, Aaron held the heavy wooden door for his wife. As soon as she entered the lovely old church, Maiya crossed herself and then slowly walked inside past the second set of doors leading into the sanctuary.

Aaron watched his wife and did the same, feeling he should have some respect. His eyes were ever watchful for any priest that happened to be inside the church.

Coming alongside of his wife, he whispered to her. "Shall we find a pew and sit down for a while?"

Maiya agreed and sat with him silently as they looked around the church. At mid-day there were a few parishioners still lingering from the Sunday morning services.

From across the sanctuary, sat a woman who was very well dressed. Everything about her was polished and pampered looking. Aaron wondered who she was and then his mind returned to old Jensen's description of that woman who had the 'country club' look.

Leaning forward in his seat, he strained to get a better look at the overly elegant woman. Maiya noticed her husband's actions and followed his line of vision.

"Do you know her Aaron?" Maiya asked quietly, while still keeping her eyes on the lady.

Shaking his head, Aaron was about to speak when the lady got up from her pew and began to stroll towards them down the central aisle of the church.

Not wishing to stare at the elegant lady, Maiya and Aaron tried to take unobvious looks at the woman as she fluttered and glided down the aisle.

When she had reached their pew, she dropped something then hesitated before continuing out of the side entrance of the church.

Immediately, Aaron shifted across his pew and bent low to retrieve the object the elegant woman had dropped. Maiya's eyes were glued on her husband to see what he had in his hand.

It was a strange geometric drawing of something resembling a maze!

Passing the strange paper drawing to his wife, she tucked it safely in her purse. Glancing at each other, the couple hardly knew what to say.

Moving closer to her husband, Maiya broke the moment. "That woman deliberately dropped that paper right at our pew. It has to be a message but what could it mean and who is it from?"

Keeping his voice low, he shrugged as he spoke. "You read my mind exactly. It's obvious she knows who we are and has something she needed to give us. Maybe old Jensen told her about me and she recognised me from his description? I don't know. What I do know is that it was not random, she meant to drop that paper right at our pew like you said and she meant for us to get it."

Maiya had a wild idea come into her mind. "Aaron, maybe that message came from Rev. Kubelik. Remember what old Jensen said? He told you about a 'country club' lady who spent a lot of time with him. Well she surely fits that description.

"We need to figure out what this strange drawing represents then follow it and maybe it will lead us to him."

Aaron nodded slowly as he considered the possibilities. "Yeah...this might be from the good reverend after all and here we are in the church where he used to be the main priest. I just wish one of the other priests or any priest would come along so we could speak with them.

"I wonder how we could send word to them that we want to talk."

Maiya looked around and saw the old style confessional cabinets lining the west wall of the sanctuary. "The confessionals appear to be empty so we can't just sit in them and expect a priest

MERLAINE HEMSTRAAT

to come along. Let's wait for a few more minutes or walk around a little.

"I want to pray and light some candles. I especially want to light a votive candle for Thomas Fieldstone. I want to pray for him and ask for intercession for his soul."

Aaron agreed and followed his wife as they moved closer to the metal votive candle racks flanking the bye-altar in the bay of the nave of the church. The beautifully ornate central High Altar was at the front of the church behind the chancel. In the very centre of the sanctuary stood an ornately carved wooden credence table where the clergy celebrated the Holy Eucharist.

Standing away from his wife, Aaron gave Maiya space as she lit a votive candle for her former supervisor and knelt on a kneeler or hassock offering silent prayers on his behalf.

Still looking around the people inside *St. Simeon's*, Aaron walked over towards one of the large stained glass window panels. Studying the brightly illuminated designs and Biblical stories portrayed in the panels, he was delighted and intrigued.

Hearing footsteps, Aaron expected it to be his wife. Turning, he saw Father Andrecki walking towards him.

"Mr. Emerson, isn't it?"

Glancing towards his wife who was still on one of the kneelers, he smiled at the priest. "You sure have a good memory, yes, that's my name; Aaron Emerson. Actually, my wife, Maiya is just over there praying on one of the kneelers."

Father Andrecki turned to see Maiya with her head bowed in

prayer. "Ah yes, well I'd like to meet her when she is finished praying. Perhaps you and your wife would like to join me for tea in say half an hour?

"I'm actually going to the café just across the road. Just find me when you're ready. There will be another priest here in my absence so we can take our time."

"We'd be delighted and I know my wife wants to meet you. Very well, we'll see you in about half an hour at the café just across the way," Aaron promised as he smiled at Father Andrecki.

"Good, well I'll leave you to it," he said as he walked down towards the back of the church near the front doors.

Noticing Maiya was now up and standing by the votive candle rack, he moved closer to her. Finishing her prayers, she crossed herself and then looked for her husband.

"Ah Aaron, there you are. Do you want to stay longer or are you ready to leave?"

"Actually, we have an invitation for tea with Father Andrecki in about twenty-five minutes at a café across the street."

"That's interesting. Well, well, so I finally get to meet the illustrious Father Andrecki. This will be quite a revelation," Maiya said with a smile.

"Won't it?" Aaron agreed as he led his wife towards the back of the church near the front doors.

***

At the designated time, Maiya and Aaron presented themselves at the café across the street. Seeing Father Andrecki sitting at a table for four by the front window, they approached him.

Standing up, Father Andrecki, smiled as he extended his hand to Maiya and then to Aaron. "I am very pleased to meet you Mrs. Emerson. Please join me. I haven't ordered yet as I was waiting for you.

"They have great sandwiches here and salads but I really enjoy their deserts."

Smiling, the couple sat down with him.

Handing the menus to them he waited as they read them.

"Oh I know what I want," Maiya said enthusiastically. "I'll try their chocolate mousse and I'll have a green tea with it."

"Great choice Mrs. Emerson!"

Placing down his menu, Aaron looked up at them. "I'm feeling a little hungry. I think I'll add an egg salad sandwich to the green tea and chocolate mousse."

"Actually, why not? I think I'll join you Aaron," Father Andrecki said as he got up to place their orders.

Aaron joined him and then paid for his and Maiya's snack.

Watching her husband and Father Andrecki, Maiya was thoughtful. *He seemed to play the part of a good priest but was he really?* Feeling slightly contrite, she turned her attention to the window and the outside world.

Setting down their orders, Aaron and Father Andrecki joined Maiya again.

Blessing their food, the group began to eat.

"This chocolate mousse *is* delicious! So chocolaty! Mm... I love it!" Maiya said as she slowly spooned the luscious desert into her mouth.

Smiling widely at her, Father Andrecki was enchanted. "You really seem to be enjoying that! I'm so glad I invited you here, Mrs. Emerson and Aaron."

"Yes, thank you for such a tasty café choice," Aaron said as he bit into his thick egg salad sandwich.

"My pleasure! Yes, their food is very good here and the location is perfect; well for me it is," Father Andrecki admitted as he bit into his sumptuous egg salad sandwich.

During their meal, the trio spoke of general things but once the food was consumed and the tea remained, Father Andrecki got down to business.

"I've been hoping you would return here because I did want to speak to you. I know you left me your phone number Aaron, but what I have to tell you is not something you say over the phone."

Glancing from Aaron to Maiya, he continued with his story.

"If you cast your mind back to the day nearly a week ago when you first came here looking for Father Kubelik, you'll recall that I told you he passed away, six months previously."

"Yes, I'm not likely to forget that moment when you dropped that bomb-shell Father Andrecki," Aaron replied with intense interest.

"Yes, well, the thing is I might as well just spill it out for beating around the bush won't help. I have since learned that

Father Kubelik is indeed alive. Now you might wonder why I told you he was dead. I thought he was dead. I even officiated at his funeral mass. The Diocese also acknowledged his passing. The casket was closed so I wasn't able to look in and confirm with my own two eyes that the man contained therein was in fact, Father Francesco Kubelik."

Maiya cleared her throat and then spoke. "Father Andrecki, pardon me, but if Father Kubelik isn't deceased then where has he been all of this time?"

Aaron smiled as he thought; *trust Maiya to get right to the heart of the issue.*

Father Andrecki's piercing blue eyes penetrated her as he struggled for an answer.

"Mrs. Emerson, you're right, your question is a good one and I regret I have no answer for it. I have my own theories but that's all they are."

"Try us," Maiya said as she sat back and considered the priest. "My husband and I also have some rather interesting suppositions."

Aaron came to his wife's defence as he spoke. "Father Andrecki, that is to say, if you *will* share your ideas with us. We'd love to hear them and quite frankly, I think we should all work together on this."

"Now that you put it that way, I believe you are right and in earnest. Very well, I will tell you what I think or suspect rather. But, and I caution you, these are only theories or suppositions as you said Mrs. Emerson and without evidence, we can't prove a damned thing," Father Andrecki stated seriously, while looking from face to face.

"Agreed and I would also like to add that only one other couple knows our theories. The police aren't aware of our suspicions," Aaron clarified as he waited for Father Andrecki to share his thoughts with them.

Leaning forward, he surveyed the couple sitting across from him.

"I've done some checking; Father Kubelik is an ordained priest but there are some information blackouts on him. Now ordinarily that wouldn't be the case unless it was something related to sexual impropriety. I've spoken to my area Bishop and that is definitely *not* the case, of it being sexual in nature.

"Bishop Radmuller won't say what the information black out is in reference to or what it is due to but there it is. Now that isn't even the best of it. No one has a photo of him nor can anyone seem to get one. I am very much inclined to believe that either the person who was here for some time as our incumbent priest actually wasn't Father Frank Kubelik or he was but his physical identity might have been altered," Father Andrecki explained as he fingered his teacup.

"Father Kubelik was an excellent priest and he knew his stuff, inside and out. There is no question that the man who served as our incumbent was educated in all aspects of being a priest. He had to have been a graduate with a Divinity degree, most likely his

M.Div. or Master of Divinity, which is the basic education all priests, must have in Ontario in order to be an Anglican priest.

"I would imagine it is country wide as well. Be that as it may, this man was educated and there is a record of his ordination, at least under the name of Francesco Kubelik. Those factors I have checked and verified so they can now be considered facts," Father Andrecki, said pointedly.

"As I alluded to earlier the one fact we haven't been able to verify is the physical description or photo of the Reverend Francesco Kubelik."

"My wife and I have wondered about a lot of the same points although we obviously weren't privy to the inside information you were," Aaron explained as he glanced at Maiya.

"But here is the real issue which is the most singular of all; your wife alluded to it and it is the one point which stands out among all other points. Let me go back a little in history first. Last week, on Sunday, Father Kubelik delivered the homily or sermon at the ten o'clock service and I delivered the homily at the eight-thirty am service.

"Now he was in the church for about another two hours after the mid-morning service and then he left the church for where I don't know. His work was done so no one inquired as to his whereabouts.

"The next day was Monday and it was usually our day off although sometimes either one of us came in to do some work or take care of something pressing. From time to time, we have also had funeral services or mass on a Monday but it is not the norm shall we say," Father Andrecki remarked as his eyes flitted from Maiya's face to Aaron's face.

"The next day which was Tuesday, you came to see me and you asked about Father Kubelik. Well at that point, I had no choice but to tell you the story, which I used to believe myself. Aaron, the point I'm trying to make is this is the second time Father Kubelik has gone missing from this church.

"The first time was six months ago when I and many others believed he was dead. The second time was last week on Monday night or Tuesday. I haven't seen nor heard of his whereabouts since then," Father Andrecki explained in a serious tone of voice.

Maiya and Aaron sighed loudly as they struggled to keep the facts straight in their minds.

Wiping his face with his napkin, Aaron began speaking. "Let me see if I understand you. Father Andrecki, you're telling us that Father Kubelik had twice disappeared from *St. Simeon's*, once six months ago and then again last week? My question to you is this; where did he go the first time and for how long? When did he return to *St. Simeon's* from the first time he was away?"

Father Andrecki gazed directly into both their eyes as he hesitated for a moment. Leaning closer to the couple, he formulated his answer.

"Father Frank Kubelik returned to us on Sunday morning last, as if he had been resurrected from the dead. It was as if our Lord Jesus had gone to his tomb and called him forth as he did with

Lazarus, from the New Testament in the Bible."

Aaron and Maiya both verbally exploded. "What!" they called loudly, in unison.

Looking around them, they felt embarrassed, as they had attracted the attention of others in the café.

Nodding his head slowly, Father Andrecki agreed. "I know, I know, it is definitely something for the history books if it actually happened that way. Now, I'm not saying that our Lord Jesus wouldn't raise Reverend Kubelik from the dead, oh he absolutely would, no, I just don't believe that Father Frank ever actually died the first time.

"If I had actually seen our good Father in the coffin and knew he was in fact dead, then I would be blasting his miracle resurrection around the globe.

"Initially, I did believe he died. For virtually six months, I lived with that belief and accepted it and then last Sunday or a week today he came waltzing into our church like nothing had happened and I can tell you none of us knew what to make of him or what had happened to him. The people who didn't know him previously weren't affected but the Wardens and those who knew him nearly passed away on the spot from the shock of it."

Maiya and Aaron exchanged glances and hardly knew how to answer. Father Andrecki's account was more bizarre than they had originally thought.

"So what did he give for his excuse? I mean how did he cover his absence and his funeral and all of that stuff?" Aaron asked with incredulity.

"It was the most incredible thing; he simply didn't give or offer any excuse or account of his whereabouts but he simply said, *Pax et Bonum*, which is Latin and it means 'peace and good'. It was the motto of St. Francis of Assisi."

Laughing slightly, Aaron was astounded.

"That is the most intriguing thing I've ever heard. It does seem brazen of Father Kubelik to just show up that way and then say nothing and then leave or disappear again."

Shaking his head, Father Andrecki agreed. "I know it is like something out of a cheap novel isn't it?"

"Father Andrecki, where do you think Father Kubelik went for the last six months and where do you think he is now?" Maiya asked as she drained her teacup.

"Ah now that is *the* question!" Father Andrecki said as he also drained his cup.

"So, you have no theories or even a guess?" Maiya asked him, surprised at his answer.

"I didn't say that Mrs. Emerson but I'm not sure how much more I should divulge at this time."

Aaron and Maiya were a little surprised at his answer but let it go at that.

The rest of their time together, the trio spoke of other things and eventually Father Andrecki got up.

"I should go now. I do really want to thank you for sharing this time and this intriguing conversation with me. I felt I had to tell you some of my theories. I guess I owed you that much," Father Andrecki said as he got out his car keys.

Standing before him Maiya and Aaron also said they should get going too.

"We better head out now but we really enjoyed this as well Father Andrecki. Please do let us know if you hear of anything else or you just want to bounce some more of your theories off of us," Aaron offered amicably.

"Sure, I will and thank you once again for today."

***

Father Andrecki put in a CD in his car as he drove along. Turning up the volume, he listened to one of his favourite CD's; featuring a Benedictine Abbey, singing a Gregorian Chant compilation. Currently he heard the heart-wrenching rendition of *Kyrie Eleison.*

As he listened, tears began to form in his eyes as he felt such profound longing, which was unquenchable by human means. Imagining the monks who sang *Kyrie Eleison,* were the very voice of Jesus Christ singing to him, he felt utterly overcome with powerfully divine emotion and intervention.

'*Kyrie Eleison, Kyrie Eleison, Kyrie Eleison, Christe Eleison, Christe Eleison, Christe Eleison ...*' the monks repeated in threefold, Lord, have mercy, Lord have mercy, Lord, have mercy, Christ, have mercy, Christ, have mercy, Christ, have mercy, ...'

Finally having to stop driving, Father Andrecki pulled over and shuddered with anguish as he cried until it hurt his insides, shedding his long held emotions, contrition and repentance.

Recalling the day he had been to the confessional, he profoundly remembered his words. "Bless me Father for I have sinned…"

Father Andrecki's mind recalled the words of the priest. "I absolve you of your sins, in the name of God, the Father, the Son and the Holy Spirit…"

Staring straight ahead in his car with his Gregorian Chants flowing in the background, Father Andrecki knew he had made a good and sincere confession at that time. What happened next would be the turning of the tide.

CHAPTER ELEVEN

During their drive home, both Aaron and Maiya were preoccupied with their own thoughts, questions and theories.

***

Mixing some drinks for himself and Maiya, Aaron sank down on their sofa in the living room. "Well, what do you make of all that Father Andrecki said?"

"I'm not sure what to say about Father Andrecki. Honestly Aaron, there is something unsettling about him. I can't put my finger on it but there it is," Maiya confessed pointedly, as she held her drink.

Raising his eyebrows, Aaron was surprised. "In what way? I mean, does he creep you out or do you wonder if he's telling the truth?"

Holding her drink in her hand, she studied its color. "No babe it is more so, the way he did most of the talking and then he seemed reluctant to say where he thought Rev. Kubelik was now. I thought it was strange that's all. Now I believe him from a religious sense but there was just something not believable about his story of Rev. Kubelik just coming back so suddenly like that. Did you believe him?"

"I don't know. I don't know. I agree with you about him being in control of our meeting. He did do the majority of the talking and yes, other than from a religious perspective, I am inclined to not believe the good reverend would just show up like that out of the clear blue without an explanation and then quote some Latin verse? What did he think that would do; fix everything?"

***

All at once, it hit her! *It was a message, just like the maze-like paper dropped by our pew today!*

Maiya sat up and nearly tipped her drink. "Aaron, I've got it! What did Father Andrecki say Father Kubelik said when he returned?"

Thinking for a moment, Aaron couldn't recall the exact words. "I don't know honey, something in Latin and something about St. Francis of Assisi."

Maiya gasped as she set down her drink.

"Oh by golly but this is it! Look honey, I remember it now! Father Andrecki told us Father Kubelik came in and said, '*Pax et Bonum*', which meant 'peace and good'. He also said it was supposed to be the motto of St. Francis of Assisi! Well what is Father Kubelik's first name?"

***

Aaron slapped his forehead as realization hit him. *Could it all be really that simple!?*

***

Maiya had sprung up to get the phone book. She was quickly flipping through the yellow pages as she searched the local churches.

Running her finger down the extensive list, she finally called out the church name. "Here it is! *Our Lady of Good Peace, Roman Catholic Church* and guess what Aaron, it is *very* near *St. Francis of Assisi, Church, Toronto*!"

"But honey, Father Kubelik isn't a Catholic priest, he's an Anglican priest," Aaron gently pointed out.

"I know that babe but maybe those are the places he takes refuge in or someone there is helping him?" Maiya speculated as she put their phone book back.

Refilling their drinks, Aaron was excited. "Sweetie, I think you've made a huge discovery! Do you want to bet that Father Andrecki knows this too? How could he not? I mean we figured it out and we're not priests so he had to have figured this clue out long ago. Maybe that's why he didn't tip his hand; maybe he wanted to see how smart we were?"

Shaking her head, Maiya wasn't so sure. "I don't really think Father Andrecki has considered whether we're smart or not. I sense that he's preoccupied with something much deeper than that. You know, I got the feeling that he needed to go to confession. I felt that he had some big weight on his shoulders and he needed to purge himself of this enormous weight.

"Now obviously I'm not a priest to detect this kind of thing but from a human perspective, that is what I felt. I also think he gave us those messages from Father Kubelik, or at least he gave them to you because he doesn't know me."

Aaron sat up straighter and studied his wife carefully. "Oh really? You think Father Andrecki knows where Father Kubelik is and he purposely gave him the messages for me. But why? What does Father Kubelik think I can do for him?"

"I don't know Aaron but you do know he reached out to you last Monday when you met him. Now he did that for a reason. He came out of hiding for a reason and he reached out to you. Now we've been given two more messages; the maze-like design on the paper and the message about those two churches.

"They have to lead somewhere and I believe they lead to him. I also think that Father Andrecki didn't tell us where he thought Father Kubelik was directly because he told us *indirectly*," Maiya reasoned as she sipped her second drink.

Aaron held his drink not even seeing it. His mind searched all that Father Andrecki had told him and Maiya as well as casting his memory back to last Monday when he'd shared lunch with the good reverend. What was he missing? Aaron knew that something very big and very useful was staring him right in the face but he couldn't seem to focus on it. He needed clarity but he didn't have it and he wasn't sure how to get it.

"Sweetie I know you're right but I just can't seem to focus on the one thing which I know is staring me in the face and that I need to remember. Maybe it will come to me," Aaron hoped as he finished his drink.

"Of course it will. In the meantime, I'm going to see what we can eat for dinner tonight," Maiya stated as she got up and went into the kitchen.

"Maiya, you're off tomorrow aren't you? Let's go over to *Our Lady of Good Peace Church* and *St. Francis of Assisi, Toronto,* church. If what you said is true and they do appear to be messages, we better get over there before those messages are lost.

"We should also try to figure out what that maze-like design on that paper means or where it comes from and you know honey, I wonder if it is a maze or a labyrinth. What's the difference?" Aaron asked Maiya as he watched her in the kitchen.

"I think the difference is in the configuration of the design. I think a maze is like a series of winding paths that might end in walls with no way out. On the other hand, a labyrinth I think has an opening and then it winds around and eventually leads to an inner central place but there aren't any blank walls? I don't know but we can check. How do feel about flash grilled steaks tonight?"

Smiling at his wife, he concurred. "I'd say I feel wonderful about them! Maiya, I think you're right about the difference between a maze and a labyrinth. The more I study this paper it does look like the latter to which you described."

Smiling, Maiya nodded. "There you have it my love. Now to supper!"

＊＊＊

Staff Sergeant John entered the interview room where the one goon was being held. His partner was in another room being questioned by another officer.

"I brought you some more cigarettes. From your identification, your name is Robin Bantry. It appears this is your first time being hauled in by us. That's good and it might be worthy of a much lesser charge, maybe even knocked back to some misdemeanours. Now then, are you ready to talk Mr. Bantry?"

"I told you I don't know anything about those charges you want to slap on me. That person who claimed we were following them is mistaken. I've already told you I was looking for a buddy of mine but he wasn't home. That's why we were parked on that street; he owes me money.

"I was just going to try to get my two hundred dollars and then go about my business. I was going to be real nice and reasonable and just try to get my money back. Nothing more I tell you. Look, maybe I better speak to a lawyer."

***

Hearing him lawyer up, Staff Sergeant John ended their interview. "That's your right. I'll have duty counsel contact you."

Shrugging his shoulders, the goon just kept smoking.

***

Leaving an officer with Robin Bantry, he left to contact duty counsel for him.

***

On his way back, Staff Sergeant John stopped in to see how things were progressing with the other goon they had brought in for questioning.

Coming inside and sitting down, he listened to the thread of conversation.

"Look, we never know who pays us; we just get paid. All we do is surveillance. You know like those investigators do. Nothing more, just surveillance. There's no law against that is there?"

"Actually there is. You don't have a private investigator's licence. You aren't on official business and you can't even tell us who is paying you to conduct 'surveillance'. You are considered stalking people and that carries a criminal charge. Following someone the way you've been doing it is considered stalking them. What is your intent? It could be stalking with intent to injure them, to rob them or to hold them against their will. You see what I mean; all of those activities carry criminal charges.

"We already have police reports filed by persons about you and your licence number was provided. You know you don't have a leg to stand on. Now I figure, you're just a small part of a much bigger wheel. So, if you can just wrack your brain and tell me who you are working for and what their game is we might be able to help you out by reducing some of this."

Getting up from the second interview room, Staff Sergeant John returned to his office. He wanted to re-read the reports and look at the photos from the Thomas Fieldstone crime scene.

Spending the next twenty minutes re-reading and studying the photos, Staff Sergeant John got up abruptly. Returning to the first interview room where Robin Bantry was being held, he opened the door. Motioning to the officer inside, they left the room.

"I've got to return to the crime scene of Thomas Fieldstone at that funeral home. When duty counsel arrives for Mr. Bantry, just see what they say and then maybe knock the charges back a little. We don't want to waste too much time with these guys if they won't sing for us. Set the bail at a low amount so we can get rid of them.

"Use your discretion and see but my hunch is that if they're released on bail they'll lead us to the real operator."

"Alright, I'll see you when you get back."

***

Entering *Lytton's Funeral Home,* Staff Sergeant John moved around carefully upstairs. The crime scene unit had finished collecting evidence and photographing the scene in the upstairs office so he was free to walk around and touch things if he needed to.

Meeting with one of the crime scene investigators working on the main floor, the young man accompanied him up to Thomas Fieldstone's former office.

"You know Randy; I've got to take another look at this room. Something occurred to me earlier when I was studying the crime scene photos," Staff Sergeant John said, as he glanced towards the young man.

"Anything I can help you with?" Randy Oakes, asked while standing next to the police officer.

"I'm not sure Randy," Staff Sergeant John replied, as his focus travelled around the room.

Surveying the room at large, Staff Sergeant John stood at the doorway and looked at the desk where the victim had been shot.

"Thomas Fieldstone had been slumped over facing the doorway. I had originally wondered if the night of the murder, the victim hadn't been shot standing at the window or near the window and then fallen back, landing in his chair, facing the doorway. There had been a slim chance that it happened that way but we now know it was not possible.

"According to the reports of the crime scene team, they concurred saying the trajectory wasn't consistent with someone standing. Clearly, the victim had been sitting down when he had been shot. That evidence presents me with several challenges. We have already interviewed everyone present that night with one exception; Warren Sinclair," Staff Sergeant John explained as Randy followed inside the room.

"It is damned difficult to force someone to come in just for questioning without probable cause. No one can prove at present that Warren Sinclair had been at the funeral home during the time of the murder. The consensus indicated that he had left earlier. The trouble is the coroner couldn't pinpoint exactly to the minute or second when Mr. Fieldstone died and collaborate by some security camera that Warren was or wasn't on the premises during the murder.

"Until Mr. Sinclair can be located and asked to speak with us or he comes to us voluntarily, he still has a large question mark over his head."

"Yes, I can see how that would be a huge problem, Staff Sergeant John," Randy admitted while watching the police officer.

Sighing loudly, Officer John continued walking around the office of Thomas Fieldstone.

"One point which bothers me is the fact that no one seemed to hear the commotion upstairs. Obviously, a silencer was used on the gun but the glass breaking in the window would have been extremely hard to muffle.

"It was true that there had been a visitation that evening at the funeral home and it had been a large gathering with a lot of people coming and going but wouldn't someone have heard sounds which they would have felt needed investigating?

"According to the post mortem examination and autopsy, Thomas Fieldstone was killed earlier that evening so there likely hadn't been many visitors or family at the funeral home. That left just staff. Where exactly had they all been during the approximate time of death?"

Randy Oakes stood next to Staff Sergeant John as he began to open a booklet.

Staff Sergeant John consulted his personal notes. "Okay, we can verify the only staff members in the interior of the building had been Ms. Emerson who had been in the lower levels and basement working.

"Ms. Eugenia and Mr. Rex had been outside in the parking lots and watching the side entrances so that only left Warren

Sinclair. His movements could not be collaborated and it appears he had been floating around freely on all levels of the building but especially in the upstairs. Later Ms. Gordon had arrived and this was collaborated."

"So once again, things return to Mr. Warren Sinclair," remarked Randy Oakes.

Sighing, Staff Sergeant John agreed. "Until we can speak to him and clear him, he remains our one wild card and question mark."

Officer John stared at the doorway and the stairs leading up to it. His mind began to consider if someone had entered the funeral home unbeknownst to staff.

He walked quickly along the hallway following its path. "Let's see where this hallway leads. If I can find some staircase or doorway which leads to the outside; that might be a possible entry point from the street or back parking lot."

"Would you like me to come with you?" Randy Oakes asked.

"Well, maybe, I better let you get back to your work downstairs but I'll tell you what, if I need you I know where to find you," Staff Sergeant John said with a smile.

Turning to leave, Randy smiled. "Sure, just come and find me."

Finding a doorway at the end of the hall, Officer John tried the door. It opened freely and it revealed a staircase down the back of the building.

Taking out his flashlight, he scanned the stairs below and the recess around it. "Seems to be deserted. Alright, now let me see where this staircase leads and if I find a door leading outside. If so, what's the condition of the lock?"

Once at the bottom of the stairs Officer John found an exterior door that locked from the outside. The inside handle freely opened. Examining the lock on the exterior door, he found nothing of interest. The lock looked old and scratched but the scratches appeared to have been made some time ago.

"Okay, this still could have been the entry and exit point. The lock doesn't appear to be that secure looking and it would be easy for a pro to pick it and get inside."

Noting his findings, he continued around outside at the back of the building. With the aid of the fully completed reports, Officer John was able to attempt to reconstruct the crime in the victim's office.

"Alright, assailant parks car or comes on foot, then forces lock and mounts staircase. They would have had to know the lay out of the upper offices in order to find the victim so quickly and easily. They couldn't afford to open the door to the wrong room so they either researched the layout previously or they had intimate knowledge of it such as a staff member or former staff member."

Making a note to have the former staff records reviewed, Officer John continued walking around the exterior parking lot. Standing back, he looked up at the windows of the offices and eventually as he turned towards the side of the building, he saw the boarded-up window of the victim's office.

Immediately, he turned to see who might have a clear view to the victim's window from their home or the street. Noticing a small house across the street, he stood in line with the boarded-up window and observed that one could have a clear view to the victim's window and the back parking lot if they were in the front part of their house.

Jotting down this information, he made the note to verify if the residents of that house had been interviewed.

***

Just as he was turning back towards the exterior of the building, an older woman approached him.

"Are you one of those police investigating the murder of that nice funeral director?"

Taking in the older woman's physical description, he nodded. "Yes, I am ma'am. I'm Staff Sergeant John. I assume you knew Mr. Fieldstone?"

"Knew him? Why I used to baby sit him when he was a tot. Oh, he was a really nice man and such a well-mannered gentleman. He was quite suited to his calling. His family lived around the corner back then but not now of course. I'm not sure where his folks are but he lived a way over yonder towards the city I expect.

"I don't believe he ever married poor chap. Still, it breaks my heart to think he came to this."

***

"Yes, that's right, he was a bachelor. His family have been notified and they live in another city. Do you live nearby ma'am?"

Officer John asked as his interest grew. Sometimes these old dears were a fountain of knowledge.

Turning, she pointed to the very house that overlooked the victim's boarded up window. "That's mine. I've lived there since I was married and that was eons ago. Now, it's just me and my cats. I've got two of them.

"Look, officer, I wanted to say something to you but I don't fancy doing it on the street here like this. My back is aching and I have to sit down. Why don't you come inside for a cup of tea? You look like you could use one or something stronger?"

Barely able to keep a straight face, he smiled at the interesting and humorous old lady. "Sure, a cup of tea would be nice."

***

Inside, her neat but small home, Officer John sat down on one of her comfortable but slightly shabby armchairs. Two large Persian cats sat on the other side of the room watching him. One was white and the other was black. Immediately his mind went to the keys on a piano.

***

Bringing in his tea as well as hers, she sat down then spoke. "You're right, just like a piano, that's why I call them ebony and ivory. Here you are officer and some cookies I did make yesterday.

"Now then, the reason I called you here for tea with me is to report that there have been all kinds of strange happenings at that funeral home in the night. Now this is well after they close. I know this because I asked Thomas about it once."

Taking a bite of her cookie, she thought for a moment. "In fact, the last time I spoke with Thomas was about a week before he was killed. I told him straight off that there were shenanigans going on after closing time and did he know about it?

"Naturally poor well-mannered Thomas said that he did not know about them and wanted me to tell him more so I did. I told him point blank that some people were loading and unloading coffins into the back of the building after they closed for the night. Thomas was quite concerned and said he'd be looking into this."

Officer John sipped his tea and listened to the elderly lady with great interest. It was obvious the old dear was as sharp as an axe. "Ma'am could you see any other details?"

"Oh I should have told you my name shouldn't I? Well I'm Rosemary Hench. I know; a weird kind of name but blame my deceased husband. Anyway, I told Thomas that those hooligans always came in a black hearse and then they offloaded some coffins and they loaded up some more coffins sometime later. They always came around the same time and left approximately the same time.

"It was a black, unmarked hearse, the same kind they used many years ago so maybe it was some kind of an antique car but the point was, had Thomas known about this? He claimed he didn't and I am inclined to believe him and well after what happened it's obvious he didn't know anything about the activity but it probably got him killed just the same."

Officer John considered the intriguing information Rosemary

Hench had provided him. She definitely had a point; his newly acquired knowledge of the nocturnal activities could have mitigated his murder.

Setting down his tea, he made some notes. "Mrs. Hench, do you recall when the people left and when they arrived in the hearse?"

"Sure, it was always three am and always four-twenty a.m. Now you likely are wondering how I happened to be awake at this time to watch this. I'm a terrible insomniac and I often get up and just read or sit in the living room in the dark with my cats. Sometimes in the summer, I sit out on my porch. All I usually encounter is the odd skunk, raccoons and plenty of cats.

"These characters started coming at night around six months ago. Prior to that I never saw them but like clockwork; they generally came at three am and be gone by around four-thirty am. The last time they were here was the night before Thomas was killed."

"Is that a fact? Well, this *is* remarkable information Mrs. Hench and I want to thank you for it. You've been very helpful and observant. We're going to look into this and obviously since the crime those people haven't been back or have they?"

Shaking her head, she answered. "No I guess even they aren't that stupid. If they do come back, I will let you know. Give me your personal extension and I'll call you."

Laughing slightly, Officer John reached into his vest to retrieve his business card. "There you are Mrs. Hench. You're a remarkable witness and lady."

Handing him more cookies, she beamed. "Anything I can do for Thomas would be my absolute pleasure. I want those hoods caught Officer John!"

"So do we Mrs. Hench and with your help I'm sure we will do it," Officer John stated honestly.

CHAPTER TWELVE

Back at the precinct, Staff Sergeant John added Mrs. Hench's information to the Thomas Fieldstone file along with his own observations while out at the funeral home.

Calling his team together, he reviewed the information he had been given and discovered himself.

***

"I want to know if any other funeral homes in Toronto, the GTA or even Ontario have been experiencing similar activity. At this point, we can't go out and interview every one of them but check the reports and see what's been called in or reported over the past six months.

"That's the timeline we'll operate on at this point. As more information becomes available, we may widen our search parameters. Gals and guys, this could be far-reaching so any kind of reports we get wind of might tie this together."

***

Back in his office, he contacted Assistant Managing Director, Gail Gordon.

"Ms. Gordon, how are you feeling now?"

"Oh, I'm on the mend but I don't think I'll ever forget that night Officer John. Will we be able to send in a team to clean things up and get things rolling again at the funeral home?"

"I was calling you about that and something else. May I get a copy of or have a look at the personnel records for past employees?"

"Ah, sure, but I'd need to check with head office because they keep the records. We forward information to them but they hold the actual files," Gail explained as she wrote herself a note.

"That's fine and whatever your process is; the point is I need to look at them as soon as they can be made available to me. With regards to coming back to work, don't schedule the clean up just yet. I'll keep you posted. I know you are anxious to get things back to normal as quickly as you can."

"Will you want to also see personnel files for current employees as well?"

"Not at this point but I may need them later. Please let head office know about that in advance," Officer John answered as he also wrote himself a note.

"Alright, consider it done. I'll call you once they're available," promised Gail Gordon.

***

Monday morning rolled around and Maiya and Aaron first headed over to *Our Lady of Good Peace, Catholic Church. St. Francis of Assisi, Toronto* was about a block and a half away.

Their plan was to visit *St. Francis of Assisi, Toronto* afterwards.

"According to the phone book, *St. Francis of Assisi, Toronto* is an Anglican church. Do you think we should be visiting it first?" Maiya wondered as she stepped from their car.

Shrugging, Aaron looked across at the impressive old church. "I haven't any idea. Well, we're here now so let's just do this as we planned, okay babe?"

Opening the heavy central doors at the top of the large bank of steps, Aaron held the door for his wife. Upon entering, the couple crossed themselves and then quietly walked further inside to the sanctuary. The high, vaulted ceilings were very ornate with side stained glass windows adorning the bay of the nave.

Almost deserted, the church was very quiet with dark painted wooden pews along the central nave of the sanctuary. Several tall statues adorned the walls on pedestals with Stations of the Cross along the circumference of the church sanctuary.

Taking their seats near the front of the church near the central High Altar, they waited to see who they might encounter.

Noticing a Holy Water fount, Maiya got up and filled a glass vessel with a lid. It turned out to be a baby food jar. Bringing her Holy Water back to their pew, she tucked it into her purse.

Aaron was intrigued by the brilliant stained glass windows flanking the central High Altar. Noticing some symbols he'd seen in the past, he quietly asked his wife about them.

"The large symbol which looks like a P and an X through the bottom of the P is the *Chi Rho* which is Greek letters and the other letters on the left and right is the Greek alpha and omega. I remember this from years ago in France," Maiya explained as she studied the impressive windows. Then, she remembered an additional point. "Aaron, the *Chi Rho* is the first two letters in Greek for 'Christ'."

Smiling at his wife, he was always impressed with her.

"That's wonderful Maiya! I'm glad you remembered and explained those symbols because I'd seen them for decades and now I understand the significance of them. Beautiful…"

"Yes, these symbols of Christianity are very ancient and very beautiful. Their meanings appear mysterious but they aren't once you understand their profound significance," Maiya remarked as she glanced around at the church.

"Well, so far no one has come to see us or made them known. I wonder why we were led here."

"Perhaps the reason is more subtle, maybe something in the building itself? Let's look around more closely and see if anything becomes clear," Maiya suggested as she got up quietly and walked around the stunningly beautiful church.

Aaron walked on the opposite side of the church and inspected the various statues, adornments, church furniture and overall ambiance of the building.

Arriving at the back of the church by the front doors, Maiya noticed some brochures about the church. Taking two, she slipped them in her purse.

Retracing her steps she wound her way to the other side of the church and over to the bay of the nave where the votive candles were situated. Drawn by the candlelight, Maiya looked down and saw the uniquely decorated floor. *It was a small labyrinth design!*

Taking out her paper that the 'country club' lady had dropped by their pew at *St. Simeon's*, Maiya studied the design on the paper then knelt down to study the floor of the church. *The labyrinth design looked identical!*

Rising, she looked for Aaron. Not seeing him, she quickly headed to the front of the church and to the doors. Glancing all around, Maiya could not understand where her husband had gone.

Feeling a wave of panic surge over her, she searched the public areas in the church however, her efforts were in vain.

Wanting to scream out his name, she attempted to calm down.

Coaching herself, she spoke aloud. "Okay, calm down lady. Where could he be? Look outside and maybe he is out there?"

Maiya flew out the doors and into the sunlight. Searching all around, she saw their car still parked. Reassured to see it, she kept walking and running back and forth until she felt weak from her efforts. Feeling the urge to faint, she wobbled slightly, as she stood in her spot.

At that moment, a very good-looking young priest, wearing all black with Collarino or tab collar shirt, came up the steps and noticed her looking distraught.

Changing his direction, he came to her side as his keen eyes studied her situation. "Ma'am, may I help you? You seem to be in perils."

Extending his hand, he continued by introducing himself. "I'm Father Mulhaney. Please, let me help you."

Maiya was exceedingly glad for his assistance.

"Thank you Father Mulhaney. Please, can you help me find my husband? We were in the church just ten minutes ago and we separated to look around and then when I started to search for him he had completely vanished!"

"Does he have a cell phone?" Father Mulhaney asked, while reaching out to steady her.

Shaking her head, she explained. "No, only I use one. Oh my goodness where can he be?!"

"Just one moment Ma'am, I have a cell phone and I'll call for another priest to help me look for your husband. Do you have a photo of him?" Father Mulhaney asked helpfully.

"Oh, yes, I do actually."

Flipping open her purse, she found a photo of her and Aaron taken a few months ago. Handing it to the priest, she waited.

Studying the photo, he remarked, "Ma'am, may I keep this for a moment while we search for him?"

"Yes, of course. I'm Maiya Emerson and my husband's name is Aaron Emerson."

"Thanks Mrs. Emerson. Why don't you come inside and sit in my office? Another priest, Father Obadiah is on his way here now. I sent him a text."

***

The main church doors opened and a marvellous looking

African Canadian man emerged in a priest's black, full collar shirt and cassock.

Quickly rushing forward, he immediately began to assist Maiya. "Please come and sit down. One of the parishioners will sit with you. She's a dear older lady. I'm Father Obadiah, come on in."

"Thank you, I'm Mrs. Emerson," Maiya explained as she was led by Father Obadiah and Father Mulhaney.

"Yes, Mrs. Emerson, thank you for telling me your name. We'll get you some water too or would like some tea?" Father Obadiah offered kindly.

"Maybe a bit later, thanks."

After Maiya was seated with the kindly older woman parishioner, Father Mulhaney and Father Obadiah quickly went to search the grounds and the entire building.

At the conclusion of their search, they repeated it until they were certain Mr. Emerson was not on the premises or the grounds.

Sighing, Father Obadiah got out his cell phone. "I think we have no choice but to phone the police."

When the two priests returned to report they had phoned the police to report her husband's disappearance, Maiya broke down and cried until she thought she could cry no more.

Overwrought with emotion, fear and worry, she was taken into the private office of Father Obadiah and Father Mulhaney.

The kindly older lady parishioner remained at her side. "Dear, the police will find your husband. Can we get you anything else in the meantime?"

Maiya wiped at her red- blood shot eyes. "No, thank you. I really appreciate all of your kindness. I'll try to be strong so I can speak to the police."

Father Obadiah and Father Mulhaney knelt by her as they watched her with concern.

"We'll do as much of the talking as we can. Spare you the effort Mrs. Emerson," offered Father Obadiah with great compassion.

Taking her hand for a moment, Father Mulhaney agreed. "Mrs. Emerson, just leave the bulk of it to us. Try to rest if you can. Was your husband taking any medication or did he have a medical condition?"

"No, Aaron has no medical conditions I'm aware of and he is not on any medicine." Suddenly she had a thought. "Oh, would someone try searching over at *St. Francis of Assisi, Toronto* church? He might have gone over there!"

Exchanging glances, the two priests wondered, but agreed.

"Sure, let me go Mrs. Emerson," Father Obadiah offered, as he got up and took the photo with him."

Father Mulhaney stayed crouched down next to her. "Were you and your husband going to visit *St. Francis of Assisi, Toronto* or are you parishioners of that church?"

Glancing from the priest to the kindly older lady, she nodded. "Yes, we were going to visit that church right after we visited here. That's why I wondered if he might have gone on without me or got excited about something and just headed over forgetting I was still here?"

Raising his eyebrows, Father Mulhaney wondered about her comments. "I see. Well, probably you are right and he forgot himself and just went right over to the other church. It's a lovely church too. It's Anglican, not Catholic."

"Oh I know. Actually, we were looking for an Anglican priest we know. We thought he might be at that church."

"Oh? What is his name Mrs. Emerson?" Father Mulhaney asked as he stood up.

"The Reverend Francesco Kubelik," Maiya said for effect.

Hearing his name, Father Mulhaney started for a split-second then recovered. "Oh, you were hoping to see Father Kubelik?"

Watching the young priest's expression, Maiya continued speaking. "Yes, we were given a message that he might be at that church. Actually we wondered if he might be here too."

Looking directly into her eyes, Father Mulhaney answered. "Everyone is always welcome here but as he is an Anglican priest and this is a Catholic church he might have been visiting us?"

Maiya nodded quickly. "Oh yes, to visit you. Well we might have been mistaken." Then she brought her mind back to her current dilemma. "Oh where can my husband be?"

Smiling at her kindly, Father Mulhaney sat down in a chair next to her and the kindly parishioner. "If you will allow me, I'd like to pray right now for you and your husband."

***

While the priest prayed for her and Aaron, Maiya felt his deep and heart-felt petitions for them. It made her feel strengthened and encouraged. She believed and knew that God heard them and would return her husband to her.

"Thank you very much Father, I really appreciate your kindness."

***

A knock came on the door as the police were shown into the priest's office.

While Father Mulhaney did most of the speaking, the two officers eventually spoke with Maiya.

After she recounted her story, the officers made notes and took down further information.

Constable Singh slowly walked towards Maiya.

"Mrs. Emerson, my partner and I will take a look around for our report. Once Father Obadiah returns if he doesn't have your husband with him, we'll file this report and begin to see what we can do about his disappearance.

"We usually prefer to give it longer but under the circumstances we feel this requires our immediate attention."

"Thank you officers. I really appreciate that. Let us hope Aaron comes waltzing in here with Father Obadiah," Maiya stated with great passion in her voice.

While Constable Singh took a look around accompanied by Father Mulhaney, the other police officer remained with Maiya and the older parishioner lady.

As the minutes passed, Maiya hardly knew what would happen. She prayed her husband would return escorted by Father Obadiah.

CHAPTER THIRTEEN

The priest's office grew more silent as Maiya kept looking at a clock on the wall. *Tick tock, tick tock, tick tock…*

All at once, the door to the priest's office opened and in burst Aaron Emerson accompanied by a beaming Father Obadiah!

***

Instantly, Maiya leapt up and folded herself in his open arms.

While the officer and Father Obadiah and the parishioner looked on, Maiya and Aaron were reunited.

Crying tears of joy on both their parts, the couple were at a loss for words initially.

***

Maiya stepped back and looked at her husband while fresh tears rolled down her lovely face. "Oh my good Lord, I was so worried about you! Thank God, you are okay! What happened Aaron? Why did you leave me here?"

Reaching up onto his head, he brought down bloodied fingers. "Babe, I was hit on the head and dragged over to *St. Francis of Assisi* church!"

Shock registered on Maiya's pretty face, as she held her hand up to her face.

Officer Macintosh strode forward, as Officer Singh and Father Mulhaney arrived in the priest's office. Seeing Aaron, they all encouraged everyone to sit down and allow Aaron to tell his story.

As Aaron sat down next to his wife, Officer Macintosh looked at Aaron's wound.

"How do you feel? Any headache or chills? How is your vision, is it fairly normal or blurry?"

"Yes, I have a huge sore spot on my head if that constitutes a headache but otherwise, I think I'm okay. My vision seems fine, thank God, but may I have some tea?"

Father Obadiah sprung up and apologised. "Forgive me, I should have thought of that. Please Mr. Emerson, continue with your story."

"I would recommend that you stop by a hospital and have your head wound checked. Do you want to go there now? We can get you there unless you can drive Mrs. Emerson?" Officer Singh asked, as Officer Macintosh nodded.

"Yes, I can drive and my license is up to date. I'll take Aaron as soon as he is ready to go," Maiya said as she held her husband's hand.

"Sure babe, but can I just sit here for a while and have my tea?" Aaron said as he looked at everyone waiting for his story.

"Of course, when you are ready. Take all the time you need my love," Maiya said as she wiped at her eyes and nose with a tissue.

Officer Singh smiled at Aaron as he spoke. "Mr. Emerson your wife is right, just take your time. We're not rushing you and if you start to feel unwell, let's get you to the hospital."

Father Obadiah returned with Aaron's tea and one for Maiya too.

Gratefully, the couple accepted the tea as Aaron began his account.

"Maiya and I were walking around in this lovely church and we were enjoying looking at everything when all of a sudden I caught sight of someone I thought I knew who I had been looking for. I should explain. We've been trying to locate Father Francesco Kubelik.

"I'd met him a week ago and ate lunch with him and then discovered that he had gone missing from *St. Simeon's Church*. Father Andrecki, at *St. Simeon's* told me the other priest was missing.

"Anyway, darned if I didn't think I saw him enter this church then quickly leave again, so off I went in pursuit of him. I honestly forgot myself and I know I should have gone and got Maiya but then I figured he'd be gone again and I just risked it."

Taking a drink of his hot tea, he continued with his account. "Well anyway, I know all that now but at the time I just went with the heat of the moment and I tried to catch up with Father Kubelik or who I thought was the good reverend. Once I neared *St. Francis of Assisi, Toronto Church*, I felt this sharp pain and something whacking my head from behind and down I went and that was it. I was out cold.

"The next thing I remember was waking up inside of the church, that's *St. Francis* church. A few minutes later, this wonderful angel priest, Father Obadiah comes towards me and takes one look at the photo in his hand and says, 'God be praised' or something like that. He starts talking to me and asks if I can move and he offers to help me up."

Father Obadiah agreed. "That's exactly what happened from the time I saw him. I wish I had arrived sooner and I might have been able to prevent him from being struck or at least seen who did it to him."

Exchanging glances, both officers wrote their notes.

"Mr. Emerson, why were you so intent on finding Father Kubelik?" Officer Macintosh asked, as he held his notebook and pen.

"Well I just liked him and I wanted to speak to him in a spiritual sense and that's really about it. He had been a very helpful and insightful confidante previously. I guess you could say we really connected and I wanted very much to talk to him again. I was very happy that it appeared I had been presented with an opportunity to do so," Aaron answered cautiously.

"Okay, that's fine then. This man who you thought was Father Kubelik, can you describe him a little better?" Officer Singh asked, as he waited for Aaron to take another drink of his tea.

Thinking for a moment, Aaron began his description. "I'd say this man who was dressed like a priest all in black complete with cleric's collar, was Father Kubelik's height of say 6 feet or better and his hair was dark like the good reverend's and his face, I think it was similar to Father Kubelik's but I can't say for sure.

"It was from a little distance. He must have resembled him somewhat or I wouldn't have felt compelled to tear out of here after him, to try to speak with the priest."

Scratching his head, Officer Macintosh still had his uncertainties.

"I'm still not connecting why you were so adamant to find him and get a hold of him in the manner you did or tried to, I should say."

At this point, Father Mulhaney spoke up. "Officer, maybe I can help out here. In the ecumenical community, we have all learned of the strange absence of Father Francesco Kubelik. Naturally when Mr. Emerson just happened to meet him a week ago and then fancy that he saw him, he would have tried very hard to connect with him. Any of us would have done the same. I am sure you have in your files a record of his disappearance."

"So, it is because of him learning that he went missing that Mr. Emerson hotly tried to pursue him. Okay, I see it now. And you heard of his disappearance from whom did you say?" Officer Macintosh asked.

"From Father Andrecki, over at *St. Simeon's Church*," Aaron replied as he took another drink of his cooling tea. "Yes naturally, I was very pleased that I had been lucky enough to meet him quite by chance today, or so it appeared."

Maiya finished her tea and then spoke. "Officers, if you need more information I am sure Father Andrecki can help you with that. My husband and the priest took an instant liking to each other and became friends. He merely wanted to see Father Kubelik again and receive spiritual guidance from him."

Officer Singh nodded as he spoke. "I think that covers that part of this story. Mr. Emerson, if you recall anything else that can help us please do give us a call. Here is our non-emergency number. Please quote the case number. How are you feeling now?"

"I'm much better but I should let my wife take me to the nearest hospital or walk in clinic."

"We're really glad this ended as well as it did. We are sorry you got hit on the head and moved into the church but at least you are safe now and that's huge," Officer Singh stated as they prepared to leave the church.

Walking out with the two priests, Aaron and Maiya thanked them for all they had done and their immeasurable help.

"You are welcome anytime. Please do come and see us again Aaron and Maiya. You'll always have friends here," Father Obadiah said as Father Mulhaney agreed.

"Yes, please come back and let us know if you do find Father Kubelik," Father Mulhaney requested warmly.

Maiya turned to him and spoke. "Why Father Mulhaney, we thought we were directed here because of this." Holding out the labyrinth drawing, she waited.

Both priests looked at the drawing and exchanged glances.

"May I ask you where you got this drawing?" Father Mulhaney inquired in hushed tones.

Quickly, Maiya brought them up to date regarding the 'country club' lady dropping the drawing by their pew.

Making a decision, Father Mulhaney spoke in earnest. "Would you be willing to return after you've been seen to by a doctor or after you have rested? There are some things we need to speak with you about in reference to that drawing."

Aaron and Maiya exchanged glances.

"If my husband is up to it, shall we come back tonight or tomorrow?"

"Why not join us for dinner? I usually cook and Father Mulhaney is staying with me now so we usually dine together. Please join us and if you can make it for seven p.m. that would be great," Father Obadiah invited as the other priest smiled in agreement.

"Yes, the sooner the better," Father Mulhaney added mysteriously.

"Alright, it's settled. I'd love to and I know Maiya would enjoy it too. May we bring anything?" Aaron asked as he held his wife's hand.

"Just yourselves. Here is the address," Father Obadiah said as he held out a slip of paper.

***

Later at the hospital, Maiya and Aaron waited for his

assessment. Thankfully, the emergency ward had been much quieter than usual.

Shaking his head, Aaron rubbed his tired eyes. "What a day! I mean, who would believe any of this? Honey, I *really* am sorry for scaring you as I did. Please forgive me."

Smiling at him, Maiya reached over and kissed his cheek. "Baby you know I can't stay upset at you. Besides, you didn't do anything wrong. You just thought you'd go get Father Kubelik or talk to him and then come back to me. You never bargained on getting a whack on the head.

"Who do you think hit you? I mean who could it have been? It must have been someone that was watching us from within *Our Lady of Good Peace Church*."

"Yeah I wondered about that too babe. I have no idea and I obviously didn't see them because they whacked me from behind. It beats me who did it but one thing is for sure, it wasn't the man I was following whoever that guy was," Aaron replied as he studied his wife.

"Who do you think you were following? I mean, do you really think it *was* Father Kubelik?" Maiya asked as she massaged his shoulder.

At that moment, Aaron's name was called, for his examination by a doctor.

An hour later, Aaron was released from the hospital. Thankfully, his injury was superficial and the x-ray showed his skull was normal with no fissures or indentations. His wound had been dressed and he'd been given a prescription for some painkillers.

"Boy I got lucky eh babe? That could have been much worse!" Aaron said with relief in his voice.

"Darling both priests and myself prayed for you. I *knew* you'd be fine," Maiya shared as she walked along holding her husband's waist. "In fact, there have been many 'Divine' elements lately. I believe these are signs; we should pay attention to them."

Taking his wife in his arms, he kissed her fiercely. "I love you so much Maiya! Thank you honey for praying for me and always taking care of me."

"Oh Aaron, I would perish if anything happened to you. I love you too my darling. We take care of each other don't we?"

"Yes we do!" Glancing at his watch, he spoke. "Sweetie, it's nearly time to head over to the priest's apartment. Let's go there now and wait in the car if we're too early."

"Agreed."

CHAPTER FOURTEEN

Staff Sergeant John's team had keyed in the search parameters for any reports involving funeral homes. Most had been a disturbance in nature; some fight or tussle that had occurred due to overly emotional family members or friends.

Surprisingly, there had been no hits involving reports of strange activities occurring at the funeral homes during the hours they were closed. While the reports were ongoing, Officer John was disappointed with the results so far. He knew that the report could change at any moment but so far, it was discouraging.

Officer John still had the personnel reports to review once they arrived from the head office of *Lytton's Funeral Home*.

Holding the enlarged image of the staff member termination order, he read it again and this time he focused on the name of the corporation; *Labyrinth Green; a Division of Respectful Pastures Memorial Group.*

Thinking about the corporation name, Officer John wondered about it aloud. "That name doesn't seem to fit the activities of a funeral home service chain. To my mind, it sounds more like a landscaping company or an arborist company."

Shrugging, he put the enlarged photo back in the file with the rest of the evidence from the Thomas Fieldstone murder case.

Recalling Rosemary Hench, he wondered about what she had witnessed.

"Rosemary's description said the people were offloading coffins and then re-loading them again into an old hearse." Staring at his notes, he wondered how credible her story was. Admitting to be an insomniac, had she been suddenly dreaming?

"Mrs. Hench had told Thomas Fieldstone about the 'shenanigans' in the night and she said he had been concerned and appeared serious about the reports. That meant he believed her or at least it was a credible sounding story to him and one in which he said he was going to look into. Not long after Mrs. Hench had spoken to him about the strange occurrences in the night, he had been killed. Were the two related or completely separate?" Staff Sergeant John mused aloud.

Getting up from his desk, he went in search of a cup of coffee.

"Oh Sarg, I wanted to let you know that duty counsel has helped arrange for those two guys to get bail, pay some fines and do some community service. We dropped their charges to misdemeanours and their duty counsel explained to them that they were misdemeanour first timers so luckily they were only summary offences.

"They have been warned and if it's repeated or escalates their charges will likely go way up to indictable offences," Constable

Amir reported, as he caught Staff Sergeant John returning with his coffee.

"When is their bail hearing?"

"Lucky for them, it should be next week," Constable Amir answered as he walked next to Staff Sergeant John.

"Okay, that's fine, thanks," Officer John replied as he carried his coffee back to his office.

***

From time to time, Officer John recorded his thoughts then had the tapes transcribed. Taking out his voice recorder, he pressed 'record'.

"How often do funeral homes order new caskets? How large is the show room at *Lytton's Funeral Home*? Ask Gail Gordon about the early morning coffin exchange. See what her comments are. Look further into the business activities of *Labyrinth Green; a Division of Respectful Pastures Memorial Group.* Are there other names for the chain and if so what are they and how do they differ province to province or city to city?

"Why was there a termination notice for Ms. Maiya Emerson? She was one of the two women who found Thomas Fieldstone's body; is this significant or just a coincidence? Ask Gail Gordon if he can get Ms. Emerson's personnel file. Check for hidden security cameras both on site and in the area. Someone else may have seen something on the day the victim was murdered and the nightly coffin exchange."

Putting his voice recorder down, he felt he had some good

points to pursue. Looking at the clock on the wall, he was now off-shift. Sighing, he got up to leave for home.

***

Aaron and Maiya sat outside the apartment complex of the two priests.

Looking over at the lit windows and doorways, Aaron felt their choice of residence was pleasant enough. "Nice place eh sweetie? I'm sure on the inside it will be equally decent."

Maiya agreed as she also looked at the lit windows and doorways. "Yes, it's an older complex but well maintained. Aaron, what do you think they'll tell us tonight? Do you think anyone else will be there with them?"

"Like you mean Father Kubelik?" Aaron asked as he mirrored his wife's thoughts.

"It had occurred to me yes. I don't know; there are so many strange twists and turns in this entire affair it is rather capricious isn't it?"

Laughing slightly Aaron agreed. He always felt his wife put her finger on the essence of the matter.

"Well put my love; things are rather capricious and actually so are some of the priests in this strange tale. Well especially Father Kubelik; he's the most capricious of them all."

"Who else has been capricious?" Maiya asked as she kept her eye on the clock in their car.

"Well Father Andrecki for sure right babe? I mean he is the one who admitted to lying to us in the first place. He's been very

THE LABYRINTH OF THE CAPRICIOUS PRIEST

changeable so ergo; he's been capricious."

"Yeah, I'd forgotten about him. I think we can go up there now?" Maiya said as she started to get out of the car.

Locking their car, Aaron held his wife's hand as they entered the building where the two priests shared a residence.

Pressing the two priest's door buzzer, they waited.

Music was heard from beyond the door but no one came. A few minutes later, Aaron pressed their door buzzer but still no one came to the door. Exchanging puzzled glances with Maiya, they continued to wait. Moving closer to the door Maiya placed her ear to the wood. Straining to hear, she shook her head.

Aaron decided to try rapping and calling to the men. "Father Obadiah- Father Mulhaney; its Aaron and Maiya Emerson. Are you guys okay in there?"

Giving her husband a strange look, she tried. "Father Mulhaney, please can you come to the door? Father Obadiah, please will you answer? We're starting to get a little worried about you."

All at once, a door opened further down and an older man peered out. "I say, who are you two looking for?"

Moving towards the older man, Maiya started to speak. "Sir, hello, we are trying to speak with Father Obadiah and Father Mulhaney. The two priests invited us for dinner tonight."

Looking closely at the couple, the older man shook his head. "I don't know who you're talking about. You must have the wrong apartment. Try the management office downstairs. They might still be open."

Aaron stood nearest to the older man as he spoke. "Thank you sir, we'll do that. Can you tell me who does live there in that apartment, number 214?"

Laughing slightly, the old man smiled as he was about to close his door. "Sure I can tell you that, my daughter lives there with her son."

Aaron and Maiya were stunned as they began walking away from the older man's apartment.

Taking the stairs this time, Aaron began to speak rather passionately. "What in the name of Mike is going on here!? You know babe, I'm getting a little tired of being led around by the nose by some priests!"

Maiya held his arm as she navigated the staircase. "Shh, Aaron, don't say that! Maybe we made the mistake and went to the wrong address or maybe something happened. Please don't blame them, they're priests and they were very good to you and me for that matter!"

Aaron stopped as he waited for his wife to get to the last step. "You're right honey but doesn't this seem rather strange? I mean really; how could we have made the mistake when they wrote their address down for us?"

Searching her husband's face, Maiya nodded. "Oh yeah, I forgot about that. May I see the slip of paper they wrote their address on?"

As Aaron handed her the paper they walked out to the lobby.

"Babe, I'm going to check with the management office."

Still holding the slip of paper, Maiya agreed. "Okay, I'll wait here. Actually-no! I'm coming with you!"

Catching up with her husband, the couple entered the management office of the apartment building complex. Seeing an older woman at a desk, they came towards her.

"Excuse me ma'am, but we were wondering if you could help us," Aaron asked amicably.

Rising to stand before them behind her desk, the older woman smiled. "Well that depends on what it is. If you are interested in renting an apartment I can show you one or two units that have just become available."

"Madam, we are trying to locate some friends of ours. Could you tell us if a priest by the name of Father Obadiah and Father Mulhaney live in this building?" Maiya asked evenly.

Wrinkling her brow, the older lady put on her reading glasses. "The names don't ring a bell but they might be new. Let me take a look at my computer." Reading her screen for a few minutes, she looked up at them. "No, sorry, I can't say they live here. Never heard of them and I think I would have remembered if two priests rented from us."

Aaron ran his fingers through his hair. Taking the slip of paper from his wife, he plunked it down on the desk in front of the older woman. "I just can't understand this! Here is the address one of the priests gave us just this afternoon. They invited us to dinner. How could they not know their own address!?"

"May I see that slip?" the older woman asked as she turned it towards her. Reading the address silently, she thought for a moment. "You know, I just had a thought. From time to time, we get mail that is mixed up and if my memory serves me, it is for this particular building you have on this address. The postal code is slightly different. The address reads: 100 Battery Road, Apt 214. The address here at this building is 100 Battery Road and we have an apartment 214 but our postal code is different. What you want is 100 *Old* Battery Road, Apartment 214.

"It's just possible the priest forgot to write the word 'old' which would make a lot of difference. Here, if we look that address up on the internet, it is actually on the other side of town. Don't ask me why but there it is."

Both Aaron and Maiya looked at the computer screen and saw that the older lady was right.

"Well that has to be it! We can't thank you enough! We better get going as they'll wonder what happened to us this time!" Aaron said as he took Maiya's hand.

***

Putting the car into drive, the couple headed over to the neighbourhood on the far side of the city.

Reading the dashboard clock, Aaron began speaking. "Boy Maiya, this is one crazy bunch of circumstances! The more we have dealings with these people the stranger things become. I suppose they could have forgotten the word 'old' but really, who does that sort of thing?"

"Aaron, there you go again passing judgement on those poor priests. Please darling let them be. They were upset by what happened to you so we should cut them some slack," Maiya chastised as she looked out the car window.

Sighing, he began to feel contrite. "I guess you're right. I am being rather callous aren't I? Well hopefully this time we'll find them because if not, that's it, we're going to a restaurant after this!"

CHAPTER FIFTEEN

Pacing back and forth, Father Obadiah looked out their large living room window, which fronted the parking lot. "I just can't understand it. I hope nothing else has happened to them. Well, let's give them another twenty minutes then I'll try calling them."

Father Mulhaney joined his friend at the large window. "Did we give them the right address? I mean with all the commotion we might have written something down wrong?"

Turning towards his friend and colleague, Father Obadiah began to wonder. "There is that. Maybe we did mislead them. Oh my, that wasn't very nice of us was it?"

"Well let's see. Hopefully they'll be along soon. How is dinner, will it keep until then?" Father Mulhaney asked as he turned towards the kitchen.

"Oh things will keep for a few more minutes. Say, I think I see them now! Oh God be praised if it's them!"

***

Opening their door, Father Mulhaney welcomed Maiya and Aaron inside. "We thought you got lost. Did you have trouble finding us?"

Maiya nudged her husband as she knew he was about to tell them what really happened. "Oh yes, we got turned around. Some of these streets aren't marked that well at night. You have a lovely home and something smells wonderful!"

Aaron grinned as he knew his wife was the diplomat. "Yes, dinner smells so aromatic!"

Father Obadiah beamed as he stood beside the other priest. "Oh I hope you'll like it. I made some South African dishes tonight. They are from my family as I was actually born there."

"Is that a fact? Well I'm sure my wife and I will enjoy your family recipes immensely," Aaron remarked as he followed his wife into their living room. "We're sorry we're late. We hope dinner isn't spoiled."

"Please have a seat and make yourself at home," Father Mulhaney invited as they all sat for a few moments together. "I take it the hospital gave you a clean bill of health."

"Yes thankfully it turned out to be superficial and more of a nuisance than anything else," Aaron explained as he looked from priest to priest.

"Thanks be to God for that!" Father Mulhaney said as Father Obadiah agreed.

"Please excuse me as I turn things off. We should be able to eat in a few minutes," Father Obadiah said as he hurried out to the kitchen.

"No need to apologise," Father Mulhaney answered as he

regarded his guests. "I suspect we made the error and gave you the wrong address or that is to say we omitted part of our address. You are very kind to have said nothing about it.

"We're delighted you could join us tonight and other than Father Obadiah's excellent cooking, we hope we'll be good hosts."

"Tonight we'll be having South African *Piri-Piri* chicken, South African *Braai* drumsticks and South African Yellow Rice. For desert, I have made some *melkterts* or milk tarts. We also have some fine South African wine. I do hope you'll like it all," Father Obadiah called from the kitchen.

"Excuse me while I give him a hand with setting it out for us," Father Mulhaney said as he got up to help the other priest.

A few minutes later, the group was assembled at the table beholding the bowls and plates of steaming, sumptuous and highly aromatic cooking.

"Shall we join hands as we bless the food?" Father Mulhaney said as he spoke a prayer of blessing for the food before them.

"Alright, please dig in!" Father Obadiah said with a huge smile while starting to pass the food around.

Maiya and Aaron immediately remarked on the delicious and spicy food that Father Obadiah had prepared for them.

"Oh this is magnificent! I want the recipe please!" Maiya said with joy as she bit into her spicy *piri-piri* chicken.

Aaron couldn't help but lick his fingers. "I have never had anything so wonderful! Sorry honey, no offence to your most excellent cooking but this is really outstanding food!"

"No I agree, you should be a professional chef Father Obadiah," remarked Maiya as she continued to savour the spicy and aromatic food.

Smiling at Father Obadiah, Father Mulhaney set his fork down for a moment. "Your cooking is a big hit. I love his cooking and frankly, I could eat it every day. I never tire of it."

Father Obadiah grinned as he spooned a large helping of yellow rice on his plate. "I'm so glad my cooking pleases you! It did turn out didn't it?"

Half an hour later, as the group sat filled and utterly satisfied, they got up with their excellent wine and retired to the sofas and chairs in the living room.

"That really was an astounding dinner. I must say I hope my wife will cook these dishes for me. I believe I've found my new favourite foods!" Aaron admitted as he moved closer to his wife.

Smiling at him, she agreed. "Oh I will with the help of Father Obadiah. It really was a wonderful dinner. I want to prepare some French food for you as well. I hope you'll like it."

Both priests smiled widely as they thought about succulent French food.

"We'd love that and whenever you want to have us over it would be our pleasure," Father Mulhaney said as he took another sip of his wine. "I know you are anxious to hear what we wanted to tell you earlier today."

Maiya and Aaron sat up straighter as they held their wine glasses, in anticipation.

"Yes, well, it all started when you showed us the drawing of the labyrinth. You see we have an identical looking labyrinth design on the floor over near the bank of votive candles.

"I'm not sure how much you know about labyrinths," Father Mulhaney asked as he looked from Maiya to Aaron.

"Well nothing really apart from them being interesting and intricate designs," Aaron answered for them both.

"Mrs. Emerson, do you know anything about labyrinths?" prodded Father Mulhaney.

"Please call me Maiya. Actually, we were discussing the differences between a maze and a labyrinth earlier. We finally decided that we had a drawing of a labyrinth and not a maze. I did notice the labyrinth on the floor near the votive candles earlier today," Maiya said with a smile.

Smiling appreciatively, Father Mulhaney began his narrative. "I thought since you are French from I assume France, you might have known something about them because there is quite a history of their use in that country.

"You see, some of the only surviving labyrinths are in France, for example in the cathedral nave of Chartres Cathedral in Chartres, France which dates to the early 1200's AD. As far as we know the earliest labyrinth used in Christianity dates from 324 AD at the *St. Reparatus Basilica* in Orleansville, Algeria or the area is also known as *Al-Asnam*.

"Anyway, enough of the wherefore, the why is perhaps the most interesting. Over the centuries, pilgrims have been known to walk or reputed to even crawl along the winding path of the labyrinth as it replicates the road to Jerusalem. Years ago and many still do this, but clergy walk the pavement of the labyrinths to celebrate the Easter rituals of Christ's death and resurrection," Father Mulhaney explained as he looked at his audience.

"In a similar way, pilgrims walk the labyrinths before approaching the High Altars to mark the completion of their journey which is obviously more so spiritual. Most walk labyrinths to pray or search for solace and worship God as they do so. These unique formations are tools for prayer, worship and spiritual growth," concluded, Father Mulhaney.

"I see… so, labyrinths are used for devotion to God and are symbolic as a path to God," Aaron stated as he looked to the two priests.

"Well not so much as a direct path to God but definitely a devotional tool and really they might serve as almost a metaphor of life's trials and tribulations. In medieval times, people did think labyrinths were like the hard path to get to God so in a way, you're correct but hopefully people don't still think that because God has always been and is more accessible than ever through the salvation and resurrection of his son, Jesus Christ.

"Interestingly from a pre-historical perspective, labyrinths were thought to have been in service to trap malevolent spirits and they were often used for ritual dances. This is the pagan reference to labyrinths which often makes people shy away from them."

"Thank you Father Mulhaney for such interesting background

regarding labyrinths" began Maiya, "but couldn't you have told us all of this at the church?"

Smiling at her, he nodded. Father Mulhaney felt that Maiya Emerson was a remarkably insightful woman. "You are very shrewd Maiya and you are correct. If it were simply a matter of giving you some historical information about labyrinths, we could have provided this anywhere.

"The truth is, we and some others are on the trail of some individuals who have formed a confraternity which has established some bylaws and rules about who can join. Generally, confraternities are lay persons meaning non-clergy but from time to time, some members of clergy might join or oversee a particular confraternity depending on what it is," Father Mulhaney explained, while shifting his focus towards Mrs. Emerson.

"Indeed there are many confraternities which the Catholic, Anglican and Lutheran churches to name a few, works in harmony with. From our understanding of this strange confraternity, which is, I believe comprised of mainly laypersons or non-clergy members, a particular labyrinth design is their focal point as a means for favours they believe they will earn in the afterlife. I suppose they think of it as a kind of portal."

Father Mulhaney paused for a moment as he regarded his guests. Glancing at Father Obadiah, he continued with his narrative.

"That is why I gave you some background so you would understand what is considered generally acceptable use for labyrinths in Christianity today and over the years. Now I come to the tricky part. It is our understanding that Father Francesco Kubelik was either propositioned by this new confraternity or he was privy to some of its details or worse, their activities, under the seal of the confessional.

"Now you might wonder what the big deal is if he heard something in confession or these individuals wanted to attract him and elicit him into their group. The crux of this issue lies with a couple of points," Father Mulhaney stated pointedly.

"No one to our knowledge outside of their own confraternity, with the exception of Father Kubelik knows the details of what was told to him by someone or some persons. That includes the bylaws and rules of the confraternity and I suspect their activities.

"It is further our understanding that this organization shall we say, has some strange, mysterious and dark rituals which we are very concerned about.

"As a result, Father Kubelik has gone into hiding and it has been our solemn vow to protect him and confound anyone who is looking for him. Until this matter is resolved in a satisfactory manner no one will divulge where he is nor allow anyone access to him."

Pausing for a moment, Father Mulhaney took a sip of his wine. Setting down his glass, he continued speaking as he watched his audience, rapt with attention.

"There is a second point which we need to share with you. It is further to our understanding that a certain business organization has some involvement with this strange confraternity. We think they could be members or maybe they are the heart of the confraternity."

Father Obadiah sat forward as he spoke. "As Father Mulhaney said before, confraternities are supposed to be of a pious and goodly as well as Godly nature. They are often consistent with some principals of the Bible and can involve some historical aspects of some of the lives of some of the saints. Miracles have also been attributed to some of these goodly and Godly confraternities.

"However the organization which Father Mulhaney speaks of and that which Father Kubelik has been elicited by is considered not likely a goodly or Godly confraternity. In fact, they would appear to be more of the opposite end of the spiritual side, meaning evil spirits to which they absolutely have nothing to do with God, the Bible, any saints or anything good and Godly."

Maiya and Aaron hardly knew what to think, as they attempted to digest the details they had been given by the two priests.

Finally, Maiya leaned forward as she placed her empty wine glass on the coffee table. "This might seem silly but why are you sharing this with us?"

Father Mulhaney looked her directly in the eyes as he spoke. "Father Kubelik trusted your husband enough to reach out to him. Therefore, you are considered safe or accepted into the circle of friends who are helping him and who are on the trail of these persons in this mysterious confraternity. Not only that, but also repeatedly you and your husband have proven your fidelity and devotion to him. This has not gone unnoticed."

"I see... thank you and you're right. We only want the best for Father Kubelik," Aaron said as he glanced at his wife. "From the beginning my heart has yearned to find him and to help him. Now, that I know this new development I will never do anything to jeopardize his safety wherever he may be.

"Father Mulhaney and Father Obadiah, how else can my wife and I help you and him?" Aaron asked earnestly.

Getting up for a moment, Father Mulhaney closed their curtains. Turning around he stood before them all. "Pretend you never met Father Kubelik but keep your eyes and ears open. If he wants you to do anything for him he'll send you a message."

"Just like the messages that he already sent us," Aaron stated as he reached out for Maiya's hand.

Nodding their heads, both priests agreed.

"What about that elegant 'country club' woman; who is she?" Maiya asked as she crossed her long and shapely legs.

Father Obadiah answered this time. "Mrs. Emerson or I should say Maiya, that lady is Father Kubelik's sister. She is married to a very wealthy man and they have a large home near *Monk's Abbey Golf and Country Club*."

Hearing the name of his country club, Aaron started for a moment. "I'm a life time member of that country club. Maybe I know this lady and her husband. If they're members, I'll likely know of them at least."

Exchanging glances with Father Obadiah, Father Mulhaney sat down in a large chair opposite his guests and the other priest. "We know you're a member of that golf and country club."

Aaron put down his glass and sat up straighter. "Now how could you know that? I'm sorry guys or sorry Fathers but are you having me followed?"

Putting up his hand, Father Obadiah answered. "Aaron, please, we mean you no harm and no we're not having you followed. That is not who we are. One of our Monsignors is also a lifetime member; a gift from one of his family members. He recognised you. Be a peace my son. All is well."

Aaron sighed, as he received a dark look from Maiya. "Okay, I apologise as this case has me feeling pretty paranoid."

Shaking his head, Father Mulhaney was not so sure. "You have good reason to feel paranoid Aaron so your first instincts are right but truly we and our ecumenical community are not having you followed. As Father Obadiah said that is not who we are. Besides, you and your wife are the good people; you're on our side.

"It might seem like you are being observed but that was only in the beginning to establish your alliances and where they lay. We have long since confirmed you are 'one of us' so to speak. Everything is to protect Father Kubelik you see."

Shifting in her seat, Maiya began to speak. "I have a couple of questions. How does Father Andrecki fit into all of this? He used to work closely with Father Kubelik. He told us some similar information in that he said he purposely lied about Father Kubelik's whereabouts.

"But and I think my memory is correct in saying that he seemed to wonder where Father Kubelik actually was and it was as if he wanted proof he was a real priest. He wanted a photo of him and couldn't find one anywhere.

"He also had some bizarre story about him going missing about six months ago then coming back and people had to wonder if he was actually resurrected from the dead like Lazarus in the Bible."

Thinking back for a moment, Maiya continued her account. "Father Andrecki also said when Father Kubelik waltzed into the church, and those were his words, on that last Sunday before he disappeared again, he said to those in attendance *Pax et Bonum* and that was all he gave as an explanation. What do you make of all that?"

Both priests exchanged surprised glances.

Father Mulhaney spoke this time. "Now I don't think anyone knew any of that. His account seems strange and yet perhaps in his own way he's doing what we are. Interesting…"

"Please could you return to my question? How does he fit into all of this?" Maiya asked patiently.

"Yes, you're right Maiya and I'm sorry. How does Father Andrecki fit into all of this? He doesn't that's how. We always assumed he was on our side and with us as we've kind of joined forces. A group of concerned clergy and laity have joined forces to protect Father Kubelik and flush out these strange ones in the confraternity.

"But to get back to Father Andrecki; we weren't aware of any of this strange account you've given us. Perhaps I should set the story straight. You said he told you Father Kubelik went missing six months ago then surfaced recently and walked into the church as if nothing happened and then said *Pax et Bonum*, which means peace and good in Latin. That's ludicrous! For one thing, Father Kubelik never went missing until just recently," Father Mulhaney reported with a tense expression on his handsome face.

"Something doesn't smell right about this," Father Obadiah said as he got up. "Would anyone like some more wine or tea or coffee?'

Everyone agreed that tea would be welcome so Father Obadiah put on the kettle for a pot.

"To tell you the truth, my wife and I wondered about what Father Andrecki had said but what could we say? Also strangely, we thought it was a message from Father Kubelik because it led us to you and your church," Aaron explained, as he sat holding onto his knees.

"Father Andrecki showed us his death notice and leaflet from his funeral mass he officiated at for him. There was also a link on the Diocesan website about Father Kubelik's death."

"What?!" Father Mulhaney and Father Obadiah exclaimed in unison.

"Wait a minute, you mean to tell me you weren't aware of this?" Aaron said with surprise in his voice and registering on his face.

Maiya also looked like she had never heard anything more bizarre in her life.

Both priests stood next to one another and nodded.

"Yes that's right," Father Mulhaney said as he looked to Father Obadiah.

"Aaron, neither of us knew a thing about these developments. Maybe it would be a good idea if you told us everything you know or learned from Father Andrecki."

"There's not a whole lot more to tell you except that it would appear Father Andrecki is living in some kind of a dream world. I hate to say it and obviously I'm not qualified to do so but he must have gone bonkers all of a sudden," Aaron replied as he looked down at the coffee table.

"The death part is what is really disturbing," Maiya said as she studied the two priests. "It appears that he actually believed what he told us then said he now believes Father Kubelik is still alive but the crux is that he seemed to be indicating that he actually lived this out six months ago.

"He heard of the car accident death caused by a drunk driver and it was on February 19th, 2016 and then he said he officiated at his funeral mass. So he must actually believe that happened. How could he be so mistaken or so confused?" Maiya wondered as she wiped a hand over her face.

Getting up to help prepare the tea, Father Mulhaney spoke solemnly to Maiya and Aaron. "I swear to heaven, Father Kubelik did not pretend to die or actually die six months ago and there was no funeral mass for him at his church or any other. The Diocese would not be a party to a lie like that or another for that matter."

Shaking their heads, Maiya and Aaron were once again at a loss for words. Beginning to feel as if they were mired in some kind of strange labyrinth of innuendoes, deceit, cover-ups, dangerous alliances and fantasy, the couple sat back and felt tired and more confused than ever.

After both visited the washroom, they returned to find the two priests looking puzzled as well.

"I've been thinking," Maiya began as she re-seated herself next to her husband. "Maybe we should try something which might be kind of mean spirited but under the circumstances I don't think we have a choice. I propose we test Father Andrecki and see just exactly which side he is on."

Everyone was intrigued by her suggestion.

"What did you have in mind?" Aaron asked his wife as he glanced at the two priests.

"Unless anyone has a better idea, I think we should pretend that Father Kubelik wants to meet him; something like that. Then we can see what he does and who he brings with him and who is watching from a distance. Kind of like a sting operation."

Aaron smiled at his wife's idea. "Babe, your idea is fantastic. How do others feel?"

"I agree with it," Father Obadiah said as he poured himself more tea. "If Father Andrecki is innocent then he won't mind. I really hope he is because there is a part of me, which just can't believe any of this about him. He must be a lost soul under the circumstances and I will pray for him. There is one other consideration though."

All eyes were on Father Obadiah.

"Father Andrecki might be testing us and he might have been testing Aaron and Maiya."

"What do you mean he might be testing us?" Father Mulhaney asked as he turned toward his friend and colleague.

"The same way we felt the need to test him. All I'm saying is Father Andrecki might be completely innocent and sane and very clever as well as cautious," Father Obadiah proposed as the group considered his idea.

"Excuse me for a moment," Maiya interjected. "Do either of you have a photo of Father Kubelik or Father Andrecki for that matter? I've wondered before if maybe Father Andrecki was some person posing as a priest. Maybe he's working undercover?"

The two priests sat still and seemed greatly surprised by Maiya's question and her supposition.

Aaron waited with bated-breath. He congratulated his wife silently on her practical, great thinking. *Trust Maiya to always put her finger on the crux of the issue! She's a one in a million!*

Laughing slightly, Father Mulhaney shook his head. "I can't believe it but why didn't we think of this before? Maiya, I share your thoughts, the man posing as 'Father Andrecki' might very well be someone quite different than who we know to be 'Father Andrecki'.

"Of course we have photos of all of us because we took some of the same classes together for our Divinity degree. Often, someone took photos of us as a group and we formed the Divinity class as a whole although we graduated from different colleges but it was all under the same university.

"Just wait a moment and I'll go and fetch them," he said as he got up still shaking his head.

Feeling rather proud of herself, Maiya took a long drink of her tea then set down her cup. *At last we'll be able to see photos of those priests and ensure they are who they claim to be.*

CHAPTER SIXTEEN

Warren Sinclair prepared himself for that evening's meeting. As a newly inducted member, he had to watch himself. Through one of his new, 'friends' Warren had secured new accommodation which proved to be safe and secret; two of the elements he needed most.

Leafing through the handbook, he placed it in his jacket pocket. He knew that the robes would be provided for all members so his would be forthcoming. Feeling slightly apprehensive, he looked in the mirror of the bathroom of his new accommodation.

Staring back at himself, he recalled something that he wished he could forget. Closing his eyes, it shut out his image but not the memory. Burned in his psyche, Warren shuddered.

Opening his eyes, he glanced at his watch. It was time to go; he had best not be late especially for his first official meeting.

***

Assistant Managing Funeral Director, Gail Gordon's dinner was interrupted by a phone call. Seeing the call display number was from head office she was surprised.

"Hello, Gail Gordon."

"Ms. Gordon, its Wanda from head office. As you know, I'm Mr. Radcliffe's assistant. He wants to meet with you tomorrow in his office. Please be there for ten a.m."

***

Gail was about to speak when the line went dead. Still holding the phone, she set it down.

"Now what the hell is going on here? Why did they call me with a mandatory meeting? Just like that; no opportunity to respond or do anything. That's not their usual way of dealing with management at the funeral homes."

Gail's husband came into the room as she was staring at her cell phone and still mumbling to herself.

"Honey, what was that you were saying? Who called at this hour? Come and finish your dinner."

Turning to her husband, Gail immediately filled him in on the strange phone call.

Frowning, as the couple sat down at the table again to eat, Gail's husband hardly knew what to say. "When have they ever called and demanded a 'command performance'?"

"I know! I just can't believe it. That Wanda, the executive assistant of Mr. Radcliffe sounded so snotty when she called and then she just shot off her marching orders and then hung up. It's bloody rude and I'm going to tell him that tomorrow. Oh this makes me *so* mad!" Gail called out as she struggled to control her temper.

Sighing, he tried to calm his wife. "Gail maybe they're really getting the heat because of Thomas' death? Maybe customers are really upset and demanding to know when they can have services at Lytton's again."

"Ian, I'm sure you're right but is that any reason to treat me like shit?!" Gail lamented as she picked up her fork.

Ian Gordon shook his head. "No, it certainly isn't a reason to treat anyone badly. Well I hope you do give them what for because this irritates me as well and it disrupted our dinner which pisses me off."

"I'm so mad I could just spit right now," Gail said as she tried to focus on their dinner together.

"Honey, when and where is Thomas' funeral?"

Thinking for a moment, Gail answered Ian's question. "His body hasn't been released from the morgue yet but once it has been I'm told they will be contacting me. At that point, I will be conferring with Thomas' family to see what their preferences are. I've left a message with them already indicating all of this."

Taking a mouthful of his dinner, Ian Gordon nodded.

***

Father Mulhaney returned holding two photo albums in his hands. Seeing the intense expressions of curiosity on the faces of his guests, he smiled at them.

Opening the first album, Father Mulhaney began flipping through the pages quickly until he found the first photo he'd been looking for. Holding open the page, he handed the album to Aaron.

"Please see if this is the image of the man you met and had dinner with over a week ago."

Aaron studied the photo intently as Maiya looked at it with great interest.

"Well, he's much younger looking here and his hair is different but I'd know that priest's face anywhere. Yep, that's our good reverend, Father Kubelik." Passing the album to his wife, he waited.

Maiya held the album in her hands as she closely scrutinised the photo. "So that is Father Kubelik at what age?"

Father Mulhaney thought for a moment. "I'd estimate him to be in his early thirties in this picture, maybe thirty or so."

Father Obadiah waited until the album was passed to him. "From the looks of you Father Mulhaney, this photo had to be taken when you were around the same age. I think you and Father Kubelik are very close in age aren't you?"

"Yes it was second year Divinity class so we were both likely around thirty-ish. I'm only a few months older than he but yes that is the earliest photo I have of him."

Reaching out for the album, he turned some more pages until he found some graduating photos that he passed over to Maiya and Aaron.

"Now he's looking a bit more the way he does at present," Aaron remarked with a smile as he handed the album to his wife.

"Ah, yes, I see this photo shows him looking a bit more mature. He's a fabulous looking man. I am surprised," Maiya said with a serious expression.

Aaron felt slightly jealous by her comment. "Why are you surprised he's so good looking? I told you what he said to me didn't I?"

Glancing from Father Mulhaney to Father Obadiah, Maiya shrugged. "You did tell me but I'm still surprised he's so beautiful looking. This could be a real problem for him being a priest."

Father Mulhaney smiled. "Actually Maiya's right. I remember Father Kubelik confessing many times how he had a lot of women after him. He really was a lady killer as they say and yes for a priest that isn't the best thing. Fortunately, as he was and is Anglican, he can marry if he wishes. However being Catholic we don't have that option."

Maiya studied Father Mulhaney's expression. "I get the feeling that maybe there are times you might wish you were Anglican too?"

Blushing slightly, Father Mulhaney smiled at her. "My... but you *are* perceptive. Oh, I remember now, you wanted to see a photo of Father Andrecki."

Taking back the album, he flipped through the remaining images then opened the second book. Turning these pages, he searched for the picture he wanted. Reaching over, he handed the book to Maiya.

Immediately her gaze fell upon photos of a man she had never seen before. Studying the pictures closely, she passed them to her husband. "See what you think Aaron."

Aaron glanced from one photo to the other and then looked over at the two priests. "Why, this can't be Father Andrecki. He doesn't look at all like this." Pointing to the photos, Aaron continued his observations. "Why, this fellow in the photos appears to have brown hair and his eyes are different than the man we met. Also, this fellow has a wider face and he looks completely different. I don't get it."

Both priests exchanged glances.

"We don't get it *either*. It's possible there are two Father Andreckis. Our Father Andrecki we went to Divinity classes with had brown hair and blue eyes but they weren't piercing but rather they were kind of dark blue or navy really. He was stocky and not six-foot-tall but closer to around five foot ten inches although sometimes people think that someone that height is around six feet tall.

"His name was Stanislav Andrecki before he was ordained. We all called him Stan and he was originally from Poland. He came to Canada when he was a child if I'm not mistaken. I think the name of the city he was from was called *Łódź*," explained Father Mulhaney.

"Well we have no idea what our Father Andrecki's name is or where he's from but it's obvious he couldn't have grown a few inches and changed his face," Aaron remarked as he kept looking at their Father Andrecki.

"We can easily check his given name on the Diocesan website," Father Obadiah said as he got out his tablet and launched the internet browser. Within a few moments, he had the website in front of him.

"This will straighten the entire puzzle out about our two Father Andreckis," Father Mulhaney stated as he watched his colleague search the clergy list.

Gasping slightly, Father Obadiah handed his tablet over to his colleague and friend.

Father Mulhaney read the tablet results and shook his head in disbelief. "Oh now this *is* ridiculous! I can't believe this! The search results show there is no Father Andrecki listed as a member of clergy in this Diocese at least. Let me try again."

Maiya and Aaron were once again shocked and had no explanation for the results.

How could there be no Father Andrecki at St. Simeon's Church! Who is that man posing as a priest and why isn't his identity questioned?! Aaron's mind raced around like an Olympian, while trying to piece together some semblance of logic.

Handing the tablet back to his friend and colleague, Father Mulhaney sighed loudly as he began speaking. "I'm so sorry Maiya and Aaron for all of the shocks and strange, puzzling facets to this series of mysteries. We had wanted to help clear the air with regards to some issues and yet we have done nothing but fill it with smoke and haze.

"I think the only thing left to do is visit *St. Simeon's Church* and find out who this man is that is masquerading as a priest referred to as Father Andrecki. For whatever reason, the man posing as Father Andrecki has to be a real priest but he isn't using his real name to you and your wife and who knows who else which makes no sense and I can't understand how he gets away with it." Father Mulhaney lamented, in slightly frustrated tones.

"Wait now; let me see your tablet again. Who are the incumbents listed at *St. Simeon's Church*?" Father Mulhaney queried fuelled by his sudden thought.

Setting new search parameters, Father Mulhaney brought up the details for the church name and not the clergy members. Clicking on the details of the church, it showed Father Francesco Kubelik as the rector or main incumbent and Father Royce Carlton as assistant priest. Another name was documented below the two priests. Rev. Helena Albertson, Deacon Associate.

Sharing his findings with his guests and Father Obadiah, he waited.

"Well it's obvious Father Andrecki's name is not listed but he could actually be this priest named Father or Reverend Royce Carlton," Aaron said as he sighed. "Either way it looks like we're going to have to go to *St. Simeon's* and find out."

Looking at the clock, Maiya and Aaron felt they were growing weary and needed to go home and rest.

"I like your idea Father Mulhaney. Let's agree to meet at *St. Simeon's Church* on a day that is convenient for everyone," suggested Maiya as they headed for the door.

After thanking the two priests for the wonderful dinner and hospitality, they left their home with promises to connect and go to

St. Simeon's in the very near future.

***

Flopping into bed, Maiya and Aaron fell fast asleep quickly. The evening and day had worn them out. Both hoped that the next day would begin to clear up some of the obscurity of the previous days.

Sometime in the night, Maiya woke up to find a shadowy figure in their bedroom. Quickly clamping a rough and strong hand over her mouth, a cloth was held to her nose and she passed out before making a sound. While Aaron snored away, strong arms lifted a chloroformed Maiya Emerson out of her bed, down the stairs and into a waiting van outside their home.

Silently driving away with an unconscious Maiya Emerson in the back, the van headed for a secret location in another part of town. The two men sitting in the front of the van exchanged glances. While they navigated the streets of Toronto, they kept silent.

Some hours later, Aaron woke up and instinctively reached out for his wife. Feeling around with his fingers, he only found sheets and a pillow. His eyes opened and as they adjusted to the light of the room, he glanced at the digital clock near their bed, '*9: 25 a.m.*

Sitting up quickly, he swung his legs out of bed and listened for sounds in the washroom or downstairs.

"Maiya!?" Aaron called out loudly. Hearing silence, Aaron was slightly surprised.

After using the washroom, he headed downstairs and was further surprised to find no breakfast cooking nor smell of coffee or his wife sitting reading. Aaron's growing sense of dread heightened as he went from room to room searching for his wife.

Sinking down on the sofa, he ran his fingers through his dishevelled hair. "Where in the name of Mike can she have gotten to and why didn't she leave me a note?"

Suddenly recalling that he thought he'd noticed her purse still hanging from the chair back in their bedroom, Aaron flew up the stairs to confirm. Seeing her purse where she had left it, he felt a huge wave of panic surge over him. Looking out the windows, he saw no sign of his wife outside.

Quickly throwing some clothes on, he ran downstairs and began to dial his friend Don Fenway's number.

"Don, look I'm sorry for calling you so early in the morning, but I think Maiya's gone missing!"

***

Don Fenway held a glass of orange juice and nearly tipped it as he struggled with the shock of his friend's words. "Aaron, please try to stay calm, is her purse there? What about her clothes and the car is it still in your parking space?"

"Yes, Don, all of those things are in place but her clothes I don't know what she'd be wearing Maiya has so many of them."

Glancing at the chair where Maiya usually folded her nightgown from the night before, he saw it was empty. "Don, her nightgown isn't on the chair where she usually leaves it once she gets dressed. Oh, shit! I just *know* something has happened to her!"

"Okay look, Cynthia and I will be right over and we'll help you look for her. Failing that, we'll have to call the police."

***

An hour later as a greatly dejected and worried Aaron Emerson returned with his friends to his home, the trio came into his kitchen. Don Fenway took their house phone and began to dial 9-1-1.

After explaining the nature of their emergency, they waited as the 9-1-1 operator told them a police unit had been dispatched to Aaron's address.

***

Cynthia's face was haggard looking as she watched Aaron's expression. "Aaron, would you like me to make you some coffee or tea?"

Looking up at her, he shook his head. "No, thank you Cynthia, maybe later."

Don and Cynthia Fenway remained sitting around the kitchen table with Aaron as they waited for the police to arrive.

Patting his friend on the shoulder, Don began to speak. "Aaron, we've done everything we knew to do and now the rest lies in the hands of the police. They'll find her."

Aaron felt sick to his stomach as he sat waiting for the police. All at once, he got up and headed quickly into the washroom. From within, his friends heard him retching and being sick to his stomach.

Tears filled Cynthia's eyes as her heart went out to Aaron. "Oh my God, Don, we've *got* to find her or I mean the police have to find her. Aaron won't last without Maiya."

Nodding his head, his expression remained thoughtful and worried.

Hearing and seeing a police car arrive, Don got up to let the police in.

After explaining that he and his wife were Aaron's friends and that he was in the washroom being sick to his stomach, they waited while taking notes.

Finally, Aaron emerged from the bathroom and saw the two police officers standing in his kitchen with Don and Cynthia.

"I'm sorry but I needed to throw up. I'm Aaron Emerson and my wife Maiya Emerson has disappeared from our home sometime this morning or in the night."

"Mr. Emerson, I'm Constable Riet and this is Constable Li. Please tell us what happened as near to the facts as you know them."

After Aaron explained the exact sequence of events as he knew them, Constable Li began speaking. "Mr. Emerson, to your knowledge would your wife have gone to a friend's home or elsewhere but leaving behind her purse as an oversight. Had she been upset or had you two fought recently about anything?"

"No, to all of your questions. In fact, last night my wife and I had had dinner with two priests in their home and enjoyed ourselves thoroughly. We got back here around eleven-thirty last night, and then we just flopped into bed because we were so tired and that's all I know.

"The names of the priests are: Father Mulhaney and Father Obadiah and I can give you their address," Aaron said as he moved towards the note pad on their kitchen countertop. Scribbling the address, he handed it to Officer Li.

"Thank you Mr. Emerson. Could you give us a photo of your wife and any other descriptive features which might be helpful?" Constable Li asked as she held the slip of paper.

"Sure, yes, excuse me while I get a photo of my wife," Aaron said as he hurried off towards the staircase.

"Officers, while Mr. Emerson gets the photo, I can tell you that Mrs. Maiya Emerson works at *Lytton's Funeral Home* as a receptionist. She's quite tall probably about 5 feet 10 and she is slim," Don Fenway volunteered.

Taking notes, Officer Riet looked up at Don Fenway. "She isn't at work this morning is she?"

"No, or at least I doubt it because of the funeral home being a recent crime scene as you surely have records of. All the employees were waiting for clearance to return to work. Aaron, that's Mr. Emerson, he'd know more about that."

Officer Li spoke as Aaron came down the stairs holding a couple of photos in his hand. "Mr. Fenway, we are aware of the recent crime at *Lytton's Funeral Home* but we thought that perhaps the employees had been instructed to return to work by now."

Seeing Aaron arrive, Officer Li turned to him. "Mr. Emerson

would your wife be back at work today?"

Handing the photos to the two officers, Aaron stood by his friends. "Not yet. Maiya, that's my wife, she was waiting to get the word to return to work. It hadn't come down yet from head office I guess. No, I can't see her suddenly getting word to return to work this morning and leaving her purse behind and heading off to work with her nightgown under her clothes and not leaving me a note."

The two police officers continued taking notes.

Officer Riet spoke as he placed his notebook in his pocket. "Thanks for the two photos of your wife. She's a lovely looking lady. Is it alright if we look around for our report? We'll also need to send in a crime scene team to check for finger prints or other evidence in the event your wife was taken forcibly from her home. Please stay down here while Officer Li and I look around."

Aaron nodded as he joined his two friends at his kitchen table.

Hearing the police officers radio for a crime scene unit to come to his address, they continued up the stairs to his and his wife's bedroom.

Don and Cynthia Fenway stared at the kitchen table while Aaron fiddled with the napkin holder on his table. Looking up at his friends, he smiled. "I can't thank you enough for helping me today and always. It seems like I'm always in some shit about something."

Cynthia blew her nose as she tried to smile at Aaron. "Dear, you and Maiya are our best friends. We love you both and there's nothing we wouldn't do for you. Besides, you'd do the same thing for us in the reverse."

Don agreed and added, "I can't help but thinking this has something to do with all of the stuff we've been involved with lately." Lowering his voice, he continued. "Remember those goons who were watching you and Maiya, well that's what I mean."

"I guess I had better tell those constables about those goons. They'll have the reports and actually we have the report numbers or Maiya does in her purse."

At that moment, the two officers came downstairs.

Aaron got up and told them about the goons that had been watching him and his wife previously. "I know we have the reports or incident numbers around here somewhere. Maybe my wife has them in her purse? Can I go and get it?"

Officer Li smiled and said, "I'll grab it for you. Is it that purple leather purse hanging on the back of the chair in your bedroom?"

"Yes, it is," Aaron said as he waited.

"Mr. Emerson, do you mind if I look in it first?" Constable Li asked while she held Maiya's purse.

"Be my guest."

After Constable Li looked inside, she handed the purse to Aaron. "Okay, you can look in her wallet or elsewhere."

Aaron held his wife's purse in his hands and then brought it up to his nose. Smelling the slightly exotic and deeply feminine scent of the purse and leather, he dropped his hands as tears began to fill his eyes. "I'm sorry," Aaron said as he turned away for a moment.

Everyone gave him space as he had his moment. When he recovered, he felt inside and brought out her wallet. Opening compartments and looking in hidden folds, he finally located the various incident numbers for the reports made regarding the goons.

"Here you are. My wife and I reported these incidents a couple of times. The reference numbers are here."

"Thank you Mr. Emerson," Constable Riet said as he took the slip of paper and wrote down the numbers. "This will be helpful."

Handing it back to Aaron, Constable Riet looked out the window to see the crime scene unit arriving.

"Mr. Emerson and Mr. and Mrs. Fenway, now that the crime scene unit is here, you'll need to come outside and stay out of their way. We apologise, but they need to do their work alone. Once they finger print you in order to clear your prints you're free to go about your business. We'll have a constable posted while they are here and then when they are through you can return later.

"Is there somewhere you want us to take you?" Constable Li asked as she glanced from face to face.

***

Officer Riet met the team at the door and let them enter as they spoke together and looked around.

***

"Constable Li, we'll take Aaron to our place or somewhere else. If you need him, this is our phone number," Don Fenway offered.

Getting the finger printing out of the way, the trio were

preparing to leave Aaron and Maiya's home.

"Before you leave Mr. Emerson, do you need to get anything like your wallet or house keys or jacket?" Constable Li asked him kindly.

"Yes I guess I better get those things."

"I'll come up with you just so you don't touch anything you don't need to and I can document it," offered Constable Li.

***

After he had secured his keys, his wallet and a jacket, he left his home with his friends. Glancing back, it felt strange leaving his home to the police to go through and document.

Aaron sat in the back seat of Don and Cynthia's car. Looking out the windows he hardly saw his surroundings. His mind was completely on his wife. *My dear God, where is Maiya? I need her back with me now! I love her so much and I can't live without her!*

***

"Aaron how about some breakfast? We can either go to our place or a restaurant," Don offered as he drove.

Realising it was nearly noon and he hadn't eaten anything he smiled slightly. "Yeah, maybe I do need to eat something. Sure, let's go to a restaurant. Your choice."

"You got it buddy!" Don said as he navigated their car towards one of their favourite restaurants.

CHAPTER SEVENTEEN

Maiya Emerson woke up in a darkened room. Feeling groggy and disoriented, she moved slowly and in an uncoordinated fashion. Struggling to see her environment, Maiya realised she was bound to a chair and she was sitting up. Her bindings were however not tight but strangely rather loose.

Gasping slightly with terror, Maiya wondered where she was and most of all why she was in the place she found herself. Foggy images floated piecemeal back into her awareness as she fought to recall what had been her last memories before she awakened.

Setting about the task of trying to remove her bindings, she felt around and tried to find a way to bring herself back to freedom. Still finding the ties and cords too hard to remove, she waited.

Discovering she had no tape or cover over her mouth she tried to speak. "So those bastards kept my voice free. I wonder why? Well at least I can hear myself speak which is something."

Feeling a headache coming on, Maiya sighed heavily. "Oh what I wouldn't give for some pain killer right now."

Slowly her recollection returned to her as she thought of her husband. Feeling anguish surge over her, Maiya began to cry. Her heart broke wide-open with thoughts of Aaron and their last moments together.

Hearing noises in another room, Maiya listened intently as the tears continued to roll down her cheeks. Murmuring voices were heard from beyond but their words were unintelligible.

Realising she needed to use the washroom, Maiya began to yell.

"Hey! I need to use the washroom! I know you're out there!"

Almost immediately, the door began to open but Maiya couldn't see who was coming inside. As more light shone into the room where she was held, she saw with horror that the person was a hooded figure. In their hand was a knife.

Maiya's heart pounded in her chest as she felt her skin break out in a cold sweat. Her bladder was full and she felt as if she might lose her control at any moment.

The hooded figure approached her slowly holding the knife as they began to cut her ties. Quickly, they grabbed her arms, as they held the knife to her side and led her towards the door where a hood was placed over her head.

Stumbling along, Maiya was led to a room, which turned out to be a washroom. Being pushed inside, the hooded figure shut the door on Maiya.

Quickly she tore off the hood from her head then she saw she was indeed in a washroom. The room looked clinical like in a hospital and devoid of any charm or personal touches.

After she had finished her toilet, Maiya came towards the door and spoke. "I'm done now. What do you want me to do?"

From beyond the door came a strange and raspy voice. "Put on your hood and you can come out again. Do not attempt to try anything as we have our knife ready and a whole lot more."

Maiya was tempted to disobey but thought the better of it. "Okay, here I am. I'm coming out with the hood on. I'm hungry and I need a drink too."

While Maiya was once again led with her hood on back to the holding room, the raspy voice spoke to her from behind. "Your food is ready and it will be brought in once you are bound again."

As Maiya was being bound, again she spoke to the hooded figure. "Why are you doing this? What have I got to do with you?"

Hearing a raspy chuckle, the voice merely answered her. "But my dear, you have ruined *everything*. You will pay with your life. We have our sacrifices but not yet, for we must wait for the grand master. Once they arrive the ritual can begin."

A series of shivers coursed up and down Maiya's body as she felt the sheer terror of the hooded person's words. Fresh sweat broke out all over her body as she gulped and struggled to not scream. *My God, they've planned to sacrifice me in some devilish ritual or ceremony! They must think I'm some kind of a witch or priestess or something. My God, I must get out of here!*

Closing the door, they left her in the semi darkness with her terrifying thoughts.

In a moment, another hooded figure arrived with a tray of

food. They unbound her hands so that she could eat and drink all the while holding their knife at the ready.

Massaging her wrists, she was glad to have a reprieve from the cords that cut into her skin. After the door closed, Maiya tried to look at the food before her.

Smelling the food, she believed they had served her roast beef with potatoes and vegetables. The meat had been cut up for her and the other food was tender so she could cut it with her fork.

Sighing loudly she dug in. "I'm not the least hungry but on the other hand who knows when I'll be fed again. The food does smell good though." Tasting it, she decided that the food was quite good even if murderers had prepared it.

Eating in the semi darkness proved to be a challenge but Maiya managed somehow. Her mind kept trying to think of a way she could escape. All the while listening for sounds out in the other room, Maiya remained alert.

Finding some tea and some cookies on her tray, Maiya continued to eat her dinner. Her thoughts were divided between Aaron and finding a way out of her prison and eventual death. While she ate, her mind returned to the strange title she had heard the hooded figure refer to; *grand master*.

Maiya wondered who or what a 'grand master' was. It sounded like some kind of a cult leader but on the other hand was it an actual title for someone? Maiya kept trying to wrack her brain for a time when she *had* heard the term used. Hazy memories of long ago when she'd been in France drifted into her awareness.

Shaking her head, she gave it up for the moment. Maiya felt she had much more pressing matters like her survival, for one, to deal with.

Attempting to move her tray, she found she couldn't shift it without nearly tipping herself over. Maybe that would be useful Maiya pondered with a surge of hope filling her from within.

Hearing the sound of someone entering, she sat still waiting.

***

Aaron ordered a late breakfast as Don and Cynthia ordered tea and muffins.

After their waiter brought their drinks, they settled back and looked at each other.

"Aaron, it might seem like the wrong time for this but could you tell me what you learned at the home of the two priests and also who were these priests?" Don asked as he stirred his tea.

Quickly he brought Cynthia and Don up to date with the highlights of their evening with the two priests. He also referenced his short assault and abduction the morning before at *Our Lady of Good Peace Catholic Church.*

"So you see we quickly became good friends with Father Mulhaney and Father Obadiah but they wanted to tell us some secret things about labyrinths and eventually Father Kubelik and that was why we were invited over for dinner."

Shaking his head, Don Fenway glanced at his wife. "That is a remarkable story and now apparently this other priest Father Andrecki also doesn't exist. What will it be next? You know Aaron that is why I wanted to bring up this subject. I am sure that all of this is intertwined.

"It started with Father Kubelik going missing and before that he was supposedly dead. Then you met up with Father Andrecki who could be anyone from the sounds of it.

"Next that poor fellow from Maiya's workplace, Thomas Fieldstone is murdered. Then you go to that Catholic Church and are conked on the head and dragged away towards that other church nearby, *St. Francis of Assisi, Toronto* where Father Obadiah finds you and brings you back to his church. Afterwards, you go for dinner at the two priests' home and hear more astounding news and ever more puzzling facts and then your lovely wife Maiya goes missing this morning."

"Yes that's right Don, but what is your point, I'm sorry but I can't see a connection with my wife's disappearance."

"Sorry Aaron, I forgot about those goons who were tailing you and Maiya," Don reminded him.

"So you think they are the link?" Aaron asked as he sipped his tea.

Cynthia was thoughtful as she began to speak. "You know honey, Aaron is right I'm not really seeing the connection either. I know those thugs were trailing Aaron and Maiya, but they could be some isolated situation. We have no proof that they were connected to any of this. What else makes you think there is a connection?"

"I don't know; it's more a gut feeling really. There's just been such a remarkable series of events and happenings lately that I believe these things are all connected somehow," Don replied as he saw their waiter approaching. "May I have some coffee too?"

"Certainly sir and here are your orders," the young waiter said as he placed their food in front of them.

"Aaron, are you going to tell the two Catholic priests about what's happened to Maiya," Don asked as he waited for his coffee.

Biting into his omelette, Aaron regarded his friend's question. "I think I better because for one thing it would appear they have had some ecumenical or other friends keeping an eye on us. In fact, they may already know about this by now. Either way, I want them in on it because they can help us."

"I agree honey, Aaron is right. We need as much help as possible to find Maiya and they know her so let's get them and anyone else we can think of involved," Cynthia suggested as she buttered her muffin.

"Oh I agree and if Aaron wasn't going to do it I would have done it myself," Don admitted as he received his coffee from their waiter.

"How is everything so far?" their young waiter asked as he looked from face to face.

Everyone agreed that their food and drink were fine.

As the young waiter left their table, the trio resumed eating and drinking.

Aaron bit into his home fries and then his omelette as he pondered how he could find his wife.

"You know, I'm certain this all falls into the purview of the priests. I'm certain they can help us find her and figure this mess out. It might be that Father Kubelik has to come out of hiding to do so."

Don's eyebrows rose as he considered his friend's comments. "You have a point there and you know what, something just occurred to me. Maybe that is the plan? Maybe whoever took Maiya did so in order to flush Father Kubelik out of hiding."

Aaron stopped eating as he held his fork midway to his mouth. Staring at his friends, he began to smile slightly.

"Don by golly, I think you've landed on something this time! Yes, that might actually be what this is all about or some of it anyway. Obviously people are watching us, both good and bad, so they know what has happened by now and they also know we went and spoke with the two Catholic priests who apparently know where Father Kubelik is or they know someone who knows his true whereabouts."

"Alright, after we eat, let's head over to *Our Lady of Good Peace Catholic Church* and see who is there. Hopefully one of the two priests will be in attendance. It's Tuesday morning so maybe they'll have a morning mass or something. It's worth a shot and we have to start somewhere," Don proposed as he ate his muffin.

Aaron slapped his head for a moment. "Don, you'd normally be at work long ago. I've kept you from work today. I'm so sorry!"

Smiling, Don Fenway touched his friend's hand for a moment. "No worries Aaron. I forgot to mention that I had a couple of 'personal days' coming to me and today and tomorrow are both my days off this week. The timing is great for me to have these days off as it turns out."

"You can say that again! I'm so grateful that you could be with me today Don and Cynthia. Oh that reminds me Cynthia, did you ever go and look at that auto garage where Father Kubelik used to live?"

"I did try to but the owner wasn't interested in me having a look around; possible commission or not. No, the guys at the auto garage were helpful but they only rent from the owner. Actually, it's some corporation. Let's see, I have the name somewhere."

Searching her bag, she finally found her notebook. Flipping the pages, she began to read from her entry. "The name of the corporation is: *Labyrinth Green, a Division of Respectful Pastures Memorial Group.* Strange name for a company that owns an auto garage isn't it? I thought it sounded more like a landscaping company."

Aaron thought about the corporation name and wondered about it too. Where *had* he heard or seen that name before?

"Thanks a bunch Cynthia. It's weird but that corporation name sounds familiar to me but I can't seem to place it right now. Maybe it will come to me," Aaron hoped as he finished his breakfast.

"Well there it is again that reference to labyrinths. You see Aaron and Cynthia, I really am convinced that all of these loose ends are tied to the same central puzzle," Don stated as he poured himself another cup of coffee. "This is good coffee, I wonder if I should order another pot of it?"

"I think I'd like some too Don," Cynthia said as she moved her empty cup towards him.

After flagging down their waiter and ordering a second pot of coffee, the trio continued with their deliberations.

"I wonder what the police will turn up." Aaron pondered as he played with his fork.

"Whatever they turn up it had better lead to them or us finding Maiya," Don conjectured as he waited for his coffee.

"Well I know a lot of what we come up with is nothing but a conjectural analysis of the situation but what else do we have?" admitted Aaron as he sat back in his seat.

"No, you're right and our theories might be way off base but I doubt it. Someone might consider our conjectures absurd but unless they have something better I say we go with them," Don suggested as his wife nodded in agreement.

"That dreadful shooting of Mr. Fieldstone appears to be isolated but as you and my husband said, I also believe it's connected and interestingly Maiya worked at the same place and she was one of the persons to find his body. Maybe that act alone is responsible for her disappearance," Cynthia Fenway speculated.

Considering Cynthia's comments, both men agreed.

"There is that and even if it isn't the contributing factor it might have been a kind of lever which prompted certain people to consider Maiya potentially dangerous to them," Don suggested as he thought about his wife's theory.

Aaron put down his fork suddenly and moved forward as he looked from Don to Cynthia. "Now I remember! That weird corporation name is the same name of the head office that owns *Lytton's Funeral Home*! I've seen it on correspondence that Maiya had brought home in the past. So that really *does* tie that funeral home corporation into the affair of Father Kubelik! You're right Don; all of this stuff *is* connected!

"Now take that part of their name; *Labyrinth Green*, what does that remind you of? Remember the Catholic church? They had a labyrinth design, which a message was sent to us by Father Kubelik's own sister. It was a message from him so a clue really. And, she and her husband live near *Monk's Abbey Golf and Country Club* so there is *that* connection too!"

***

Assistant Managing Funeral Director, Gail Gordon waited in the outer office of the VP of Operations for *Lytton's Funeral Home and Labyrinth Green, a Division of Respectful Pastures Memorial Group*. Wanda, the VP's secretary or executive assistant sat like a strange little gnome watching her and the office around her.

Gail Gordon had never noticed until that moment how strangely unnatural everything was at the 'head office'. Glancing around at the office furnishings, Gail even noticed how unnatural and out of place or surreal they all appeared to be. Feeling very apprehensive, Gail wished they would just get on with things.

***

Looking at her cell phone clock, she saw it was going onto

eleven in the morning. Gail was beginning to tire of waiting.

"Wanda, you did say Mr. Radcliffe wanted me to arrive here at ten this morning. Well I did and so I was wondering if he is detained somehow. Should I perhaps return another time?" Gail Gordon asked, as she fought to control her temper.

Narrowing her eyes, she pasted on a false looking smile. "Oh I shouldn't do that Ms. Gordon. Mr. Radcliffe will not like that a bit. He'll be seeing you shortly. Please be patient."

Opening her mouth to reply, Gail thought the better of it then formulated her reply. "Oh yes, I am a patient lady there's no doubt about that, but I was only considering Mr. Radcliffe."

"How kind of you to do so. I'll make a note of that Ms. Gordon," Wanda answered with her gnome like smile.

Presently the outer door opened and Mr. Radcliffe stood by the opening. "Ms. Gordon please."

Feeling as if she was being summoned by the executioner, Gail found her stomach tied up in knots. Rising, she followed him into his inner sanctum of offices.

Arriving at their final destination, he closed the doors as Gail stood nearby.

Motioning her to a chair in front of his enormous desk, he came around and took his seat. Shuffling some papers, he looked across at Gail.

"Now then Ms. Gordon, it has come to our attention that there have been some requests by the police for certain personnel files. We will not be complying with this request and the police can obtain a warrant if they want to; it's their right. It is also our right to ask for one before we hand over any access to personnel files.

"Further, it has come to our attention, that Mr. Fieldstone had deliberately ignored our order for the termination of one of his employees; namely Ms. Maiya Emerson. Quite foolishly, he was preparing to fight our termination order. I hope you will not consider being as foolish. When *Lytton's Funeral Home* reopens for business, which I'm told will be shortly, I want you to personally terminate Ms. Emerson's employment with our facility. Is that understood?"

Gail Gordon could scarcely contain her anger. Her blood boiled mercilessly within her veins as she struggled to remain composed. Clenching and unclenching her fists under the lip of his enormous desk, Gail took silent deep breaths. She knew he was waiting for her answer but Gail couldn't imagine what that answer would be. She needed time to think.

Mr. Radcliffe waited impatiently for her answer. "Ms. Gordon? I'd like an answer."

Finally, Gail formulated a response. "It would help if I knew the rationale for Ms. Emerson's termination. She'll want some. I think we owe her that much as a long-time employee."

Mr. Radcliffe waved his bejewelled fingers. "We owe her nothing except by the *Employment Standards Act*. No, it is within our purview to terminate her without cause. End of story."

Gail knew she was treading on thin ice.

"What about from a human perspective? What about from the

perspective of the very name of this organization; *respectful*? Is that what we've become; boiling things down to a mere governmental act and abolishing the human side of employee relations?"

Seeing the veins sticking out in Mr. Radcliffe's neck, Gail Gordon knew she had pissed him off. Unable to back down, Gail waited.

Something shifted in his expression and he suddenly mellowed a little. "Your point is taken. Ms. Gordon, I'll consider your argument and note it accordingly. At first blush, I would say your argument was absurd however, on second thought there may be some merit to it. Leave it with me."

Surprised but still wary, Gail asked him what was to be next. "What do I do about Ms. Emerson? Shall I still enforce her termination notice or wait until your decision?"

Bridging his flashy ringed fingers before his face, he spoke authoritatively. "You... do nothing for *now*. I'll get back to you but...I do want you to keep an eye on her and if one more complaint comes in about her... terminate her immediately."

"Very well Mr. Radcliffe, I'll await your decision and I'll keep my eye on her performance from this point forward," Gail Gordon promised reluctantly.

She knew she was going to do no such thing but she had to play along in order to buy more time for them.

"Alright, thank you for coming in today," he said as he turned towards some papers on his desk.

Understanding she was dismissed, Gail got up and left his inner sanctum of offices. Passing the gnome-like secretary, Gail couldn't wait to exit the building.

Outside, she took a huge gulp of air and exhaled slowly. From that point on, Gail would do all she could to bring that organization down.

Inside her car, she realised Mr. Radcliffe had said nothing about Warren Sinclair. Believing that was a singular point, she digested it further.

"Why would he not ask about Warren Sinclair? His behaviour was far worse than anything Maiya could ever try to do but of course he's family so that makes *all* the difference in the world, the *hypocrite*!"

Something about the entire affair didn't sit well with her. To Gail's knowledge, Warren had not been heard nor seen since the night of Thomas' death. His behaviour was definitely cause for personnel action and yet not a word about him. She was his superior so why hadn't old Radcliffe mentioned him? While Gail thought about it further, she realised that because Radcliffe had *not* mentioned him meant that there *was* a conspiracy going on which involved his beloved nephew, Mr. Warren Sinclair.

Smiling to herself, Gail spoke aloud. "Mr. Radcliffe, it looks like you've tipped your hand." Sighing loudly, she continued to drive home.

Seeing a bar ahead of her, she smiled. "It looks like I'm in need of one of those."

Entering the local bar, Gail saw that the lively lunch crowd had arrived. Wherever she went, she always turned heads. This bar was no different.

After being seated and giving her order to one of the perky waitresses, Gail sat back and took out her pen and small writing pad.

From across the room Gail was being observed unbeknownst to her.

At that same moment, one of her friends noticed her. "Gail! How are you? It's been forever. Do you mind if I join you? Gosh you look *beautiful*!"

Recognising her friend from college, she smiled at the brawny male standing before her. Secretly she'd had a crush on him in her school years.

"Oh yeah, please do! Everett, I am *so* glad to see you again! Sit down and thank you for the compliment!" Gail said enthusiastically.

Grinning at her widely, the great looking man joined her. "What luck finding you here? Are you on your lunch break?"

"Actually I'm not working today but hopefully tomorrow or the next day. How about you, on your break now?"

"No, I'm in between jobs right now. I've got some interviews lined up so I'm sure things will get back on track momentarily," Everett admitted.

"I see… well if I hear of anything I will tell you. Too bad you weren't still in the funeral home business. I could really use your help right now. We're super short-staffed Everett," Gail stated evenly.

Shaking his head, he shrugged. "Not after that episode but if it's non-director work I can do it. I can drive and do anything else but not that of a funeral director. You know I have the training but after that episode, I hung up my funeral director's shingle for good."

Acknowledging his comments, Gail remembered too well his *episode*. Hardly wanting to recall the details of it, Gail grimaced a little.

Everett had been alone at a funeral home in the city. Most of his staff had been down with the flu and that particular evening a depraved individual entered the funeral home and nearly killed him. Barely coming out of the incident with his life, it had scared Everett that he vowed he would never work as a funeral director again.

"Everett, if you did work at the home where I am now, wouldn't it possibly bring back memories?"

Looking up from his menu, he shrugged as he considered her valid question.

"I hope not. If you remember though the suspect had blamed me personally for the mistakes made by another funeral director mixing up his family member for another body. If I was a driver or some other position other than a funeral director how could they blame me for anything as I wouldn't have access to the deceased persons."

"That's true Everett. Well, see what you think. I'm at *Lytton's Funeral Home* now."

Hearing the name, Everett started for a moment. "Oh, that same place where Thomas Fielding was killed?"

Slowly nodding she agreed. "The very same. Look, I wouldn't blame you if you passed this by. I'm going to have the worst time attracting *any* staff to my location in the future. No one will want to work there and I don't blame them. Actually I might even quit."

Everett looked surprised. "Gail, that's not like you. What's been happening?"

Not meaning to, Gail ended up filling him in on the gossip and crap that had been going on at the funeral home. Taking a long drink, she set down her glass. "I think I need a refill."

Everett went to the bar and brought back two more drinks for them.

Looking her in the eyes, he spoke. "Gail, I'm going to accept that job no matter what. I can't work as a funeral director but I *can* work as anything else. You need me and just maybe, I can help you."

Holding her second drink, Gail studied his handsome face. "Everett what do you mean?"

Glancing around him, he brought his vision back to Gail. "I've got a buddy who is a private investigator. This guy's good. If I give him a few details, off the record then he can make some casual inquiries but it would help if I worked there. This would give him cause to be checking into this company. He would say it was done as a favour to me as an employee of this firm."

Gail smiled widely as she held her drink. Using her other hand, she congratulated Everett. "You're hired! Welcome and when can you start?"

Laughing slightly, Everett nodded. "Why thank you! How does the first day they clear you for back to work sound?"

Raising her glass to his she continued to smile. "It sounds perfect! Cheers my new assistant, non-director of course. With any luck it will be tomorrow or the next day we'll get the go-ahead to return to work."

"Cheers!" Everett said as he toasted their new arrangement.

"Everett, I've just found the right position for you; how about being our new operations manager? As you know, these individuals are often not licensed directors," Gail said as she took another drink.

"It sounds perfect and you're right. I can work as an operations manager," Everett admitted happily.

"Now that poor Thomas has passed away I am at the top of the heap so to speak, so I really will need to have a great new operations manager I can trust. Oh I'm *so* glad Everett! This was really meant to be!" Gail said as she looked into his sparkling green eyes.

Noticing her rings on her left hand, he smiled. "I see you didn't wait for me."

Gail lowered her eyes as she looked at her drink. "Don't do that to me Everett. Only you could tempt me but no, Ian and I have been married for five years now and he's wonderful. If I'd only waited for you..."

Taking her hand in his for a moment, he kissed it. "Yes Gail, if only you had waited for me..."

An awkward silence followed Everett's last comment.

Everett looked into her gorgeous dark chocolate colored eyes. "Oh Gail I hope we can work together without any problems. You know I'm still in love with you. However, I'm a nice guy so I won't make trouble for you or us and we have jobs to do."

Hearing his words, Gail felt a shiver run down her spine. Part of her still secretly loved him too. His sparkling emerald green eyes and his soft almond toned skin beckoned for her touch. "Please Everett, I said *don't* do that to me. That's right we do have our jobs to do. If ever things change though, you know you'll be the *first* to hear about it."

CHAPTER EIGHTEEN

Aaron, Don and Cynthia drove over to *Our Lady of Good Peace Catholic Church* in the hopes of speaking with both or either priest.

Entering the solemn church, they found Father Mulhaney walking up the central aisle carrying some books. Seeing his friend, he waved.

"Aaron! Hello, where's Maiya?" Father Mulhaney asked as he neared his friend. Noticing Aaron's friends, he introduced himself. "Hello, I'm Father Mulhaney."

Don and Cynthia introduced themselves then waited.

"Did you leave Maiya at home?"

Taking him aside, Aaron began to speak in low tones. "Could I speak with you privately? My friends can come in of course."

Seeing Aaron's tense and troubled expression, he nodded. "Certainly. Please come into my office everyone."

Don and Cynthia shook their heads.

"We'll wait out here for you Aaron," Don said as Cynthia agreed.

"Alright, thanks for waiting for me," Aaron said as he followed Father Mulhaney into his private office.

Inside, Aaron saw Father Obadiah just leaving the room. Waving at Aaron, he continued onwards.

Sitting directly across from him on the couch, Father Mulhaney prompted Aaron to begin. "Whenever you are ready Aaron."

Hardly knowing where to begin, Aaron just blurted out what had happened after they had left his home the night before.

Receiving a shocked look from Father Mulhaney, he listened further to Aaron's account as he also brought him up to date on what he'd learned or considered.

At the conclusion of his narrative, Father Mulhaney got them both a drink of water.

Sitting next to Aaron, Father Mulhaney was greatly moved and upset. Wiping at his eyes, he struggled to regain his composure. "I am so very, very sorry for your sufferings and for your pain in not knowing where your wife is now. We'll do *all* we can to help you find her. Let me pray with you now Aaron."

After Father Mulhaney prayed a very heart-felt and moving prayer, he sat back and began to think. "Oh my, but where to start. I have to agree with you that this might be a ruse to bring Father Kubelik out of hiding. But what else have we got? Let's see…"

"My friend Don and I were wondering about that place where Maiya works. Remember that strange name for the head office corporation; *Labyrinth Green, a Division of Respectful Pastures*

Memorial Group?"

Facing Aaron, Father Mulhaney nodded. "Yes, that's right and you said that Mrs. Fenway's real estate inquiries turned up the same name for the owners of that place where Father Kubelik allegedly used to live. The aspect that bothers me is the 'labyrinth green' part."

Aaron considered a thought that he had not previously shared with the priest.

"Are you familiar with *Monk's Abbey Golf and Country Club?* Well remember how Father Kubelik's sister lives near there? My question is could there still be some old monk's cells in existence in that building but covered over which would be an ideal place to hide someone or for someone to hide themselves?"

Looking directly into Aaron's eyes, Father Mulhaney smiled for a moment. "You are *very* shrewd Aaron. That is *indeed* a possibility. I have heard that there is a way to access these old covered over monk's cells." Snapping his fingers, Father Mulhaney sat up rigidly. "That's it! Oh, I can't believe I never thought of it before! I've seen this several times but why didn't I connect it?!"

Getting up quickly, he went to consult some old volumes he had in his bookcase. Aaron watched in fascination as the young priest flipped page after page while searching. Finally locating the volume he wanted he brought the dusty old book with him.

Sitting next to Aaron, Father Mulhaney began to study a drawing of an ancient labyrinth that was in a cathedral in France.

Apparently, not still in existence, the labyrinth was often copied and placed in other churches since then.

Holding the book open for Aaron, Father Mulhaney looked at him as he pointed. "You see Aaron; this is a drawing of an ancient labyrinth that was used by Knights Templar and looks exactly like the drawing you had been given by Father Kubelik's sister. The name of the labyrinth was titled, 'Labyrinth Green'!"

Understanding hit Aaron as he whistled. Holding his face with one hand, he stared at the priest. "Are you telling me that the original section of the *Monk's Abbey Golf and Country Club* has this same design somewhere in its building? Like maybe under one of those thick rugs the wonderful old building is famous for?"

Thinking some more, Aaron recalled something else. "One of the sections of the golf course has a sign which says, 'Labyrinth Green'. I used to wonder what the hell that meant, oh sorry Father and now I know."

Nodding his head, Father Mulhaney agreed. "Oh don't apologise and just maybe those old designs are under the rugs in the building. You see there were several photos taken of the old abbey before restoration and I recalled seeing these fantastic labyrinths on the floors. If my memory serves me, there was a series of them in that old building. Aaron, I wanted to draw your attention to something else. Which country keeps coming up in all of this?"

Aaron thought for a moment then burst out his answer loudly. "France!"

"Yes and where is your wife originally from?"

Aaron frowned for a moment. "I can't see how that has any bearing on any of this. Yes, she's originally from France but what difference does that make?"

Sitting back with the old volume on his lap, Father Mulhaney prepared to enlighten him. "Aaron I don't know how much you know about the Knights Templar but if you can spare a few minutes, I might have something which will help you.

"Very quickly let me say that the Templars were formed sometime around 1119 AD and disbanded in approximately 1312 AD. They were formed in France and the monarchy of the day wasn't too happy with some of their powers and their widespread appeal. They were originally formed as a Catholic Military Order that was to principally ensure safe passage for pilgrims to the Holy Land.

"Their motto was *Non nobis Domine, non nobis, sed nomini tuo da gloriam,* which is the Latin meaning for 'Not unto us, O Lord, Not unto us, but unto thy Name give glory.' Pope Clement apparently disbanded the order in 1312 under pressure from the monarchy of France who was the Pope's relative." Father Mulhaney paused then continued speaking.

"The Knights Templar had very specific rules and codes of behaviour and their rule or code book was called, the *Latin Rule,* and it had approximately seventy-two different clauses in it. There were several ranks such as the Noble Knights, Non-Noble Sergeants and Chaplains as well as there were Grand Masters during their time in existence. The Knights Templar had many other names such as the *Poor Fellow-Soldiers of Christ and the Temple of Solomon* and depending on which country you were in, there were other orders stemming from the main order in countries such as Portugal, Scotland and so on.

"Now this might be the wildest long shot in the world but just what if the persons who took your wife were some modern day members of an organization fancying themselves to be modern day Knights Templar? Because you wife is French they might see her as being some direct descendent to some original Knights Templar and they might have fancied that she is some priestess or something wild like that.

"Now I know this sounds absolutely ludicrous but what if I'm right? Can we afford not to consider it seriously?"

Aaron stood up for a moment and then spoke. "I'm still not clear how you arrived at this or worked this out."

"Okay, let's look at a few things. Recalling that the corporation name for the funeral home chain where Maiya works is named *Labyrinth Green, a Division of Respectful Pastures Memorial Group* and we found that several places have these strange labyrinths such as this church and the original in France that was named 'Labyrinth Green'. It has a direct connection to the Knights Templars and they often used these symbols in their lore, your wife is born in France and the Templars were originally French from France. When they were disbanded, there were scores of them tortured and put to death in a most horrible way rumoured to be at the hand of the monarchy.

"These poor souls were charged with unspeakable crimes and treasons, therefore there are some who feel they were treated unjustly and I agree and they might want retribution so they might fancy your wife is some kind of priestess or person who can give it to them because of her origins," Father Mulhaney explained as he monitored Aaron's expression.

"Also, it is just possible that there is this very same labyrinth design named 'Labyrinth Green' somewhere on the floors of the golf and country club and that is a further pointer. We already know that a section of the golf green is so named, 'Labyrinth Green' so there's that connection. I am quite sure that this is all the case. In addition, the old monk's cells are still in the original building that has been boarded up and this is probably where the labyrinth floor or floors are and it could be where your wife is," Father Mulhaney concluded pointedly.

Sitting down, Aaron believed he was finally beginning to comprehend the priest's ribbon of evidence. It was a crazy and winding trail but it made a lot of sense. If Maiya really was hidden away at the *Monk's Abbey Golf and Country Club*, there wasn't a moment to lose!

"Father Mulhaney, if what you say is true, how can we get over there and start to find her? I mean, the management and ownership isn't going to allow us to just waltz in there and start splitting walls open. I figure if they got Maiya in there without anyone seeing or noticing then we can get in too. We just have to find the opening or entrance to their lair."

Smiling at him, Father Mulhaney agreed. "Right! Now here's what I propose we do…"

***

Maiya once again woke up but this time she realised there was someone in the room with her.

Shocked and afraid, she began to pray for help. Praying that she would not be harmed, Maiya placed her faith in God alone.

Hearing slight sounds in the room, she was aware of someone moving nearer to her. Holding her breath, Maiya watched with her eyes slightly open. Only seeing a shadowy figure, she kept listening and watching as her heart pounded in her chest. Moving still closer to her, she strained to hear and sense their every movement.

All at once, she caught a familiar fragrance! Initially unable to place the source of the scent, she held on to the hope that this person was kindred somehow. Inhaling deeply, she realised where she had smelled the scent recently; *it was at the funeral home!* Although not the horribly strong scents of formaldehyde, glutaraldehyde, methanol and other solvents used in the embalming chemicals, Maiya recognised the scent just the same.

Then it came to her! Frankincense! Maiya had smelled the pungent but beautifully calming scent both in church and at the chapel of the funeral home. Whenever clergy had used it to purify the area and the casket prior to the funeral mass, she had smelled the pungent fragrance.

Remembering that baby Jesus was given Frankincense and Myrrh as gifts from two of the Wise Men, Maiya felt elated as tears began to flow from her eyes. Looking up towards the ceiling of the semi lit room, Maiya took it as a sign from above. Silently thanking God, she knew that from that point on, everything would be fine. Courageously Maiya faced the hooded figure in the room with her.

Instead of them bringing a knife, they brought scissors. Deftly untying and cutting her bonds, they laid a finger on her mouth. Slowly, they traced Maiya's beautiful lips with their finger. Hearing their breathing shift, Maiya closed her eyes as she prayed they would not molest her.

A strangely familiar voice spoke near Maiya's left ear. "Do not leave here yet. I will give you a sign... then leave! Run as fast as you can past the great labyrinth for if you don't they will kill you! Tonight they mean to sacrifice you! You are their priestess and with your blood, they will finally have the retribution they seek. Don't let anyone know you are free until it is time. I must go now, wait for my signal."

All at once, they hurried from the room and closed the door behind them. Maiya knew she was free but dared not disobey her rescuer. Still unable to identify the strangely familiar voice, she had a way out! Once again thanking God, Maiya waited in the semi-darkness for the *sign*.

***

Father Francesco Kubelik prepared himself to leave his hiding place of some days. Chastising himself for not leaving sooner, he felt somewhat contrite over his actions of some days ago to move into hiding. *God always protects his children and we are surrounded by a covey of angels. Put on the full armour of God everyday...*

The time had come and it was now an emergency. His friends needed him and his time of protecting himself was over. Father Kubelik knew he could never half begin to protect himself the way God would fully protect him. He prayed before he left and placed the entire matter before God. Stoically, he went out into the night.

From just beyond his hiding place, he saw one of his friends waiting for him. Running into their arms, he was embraced by Father Mulhaney and then by Father Obadiah. Silently they made their way to the waiting vehicle and then drove away under cover of darkness.

Once inside the vehicle no one dared put on a light. Placing a hat on Father Kubelik's head and a scarf around his face, he kept himself shrouded in the dark.

"Thank you for picking me up my brothers. When my sister sent word from you about what had happened, I knew the time had come to face this and defeat the dark ones," Father Kubelik said as he sat in the back seat of Father Mulhaney's car.

"You will be safe with us until this is over. We have a plan and a very good one at that. It also involves your friend Aaron Emerson," Father Obadiah said as he kept looking straight ahead.

"I am very sorry about his wife. Although I had not met her, yet I am certain she is a great woman. Are our other brethren and clerics in place?"

"Yes, all is in readiness and waiting for you to arrive. You'll lead them for it is you who the dark ones want; that and Mrs. Emerson. Since you are both originally born in France, they want both your blood and with the combination, they believe you and Mrs. Emerson will give them true retribution.

"I think this cult is more in alignment with some movement fancying they are modern day ancients for a cause. Their activities are mysterious and they seek ancient wisdom with a modern twist, which sounds almost like the ancient Rosicrucians. They aren't true Rosicrucians but they fancy they are some modern branch of it. I had at first thought of a modern day version of Knights Templar with a twist, but now I think it is closer to some sect which fancies itself to be a branch of the Rosicrucians, but with an evil twist so it might be something else entirely," Father Mulhaney explained as he drove towards their home.

"Where are we to meet?" Father Kubelik asked as he stared straight ahead.

"We think they hold their meetings at the golf and country club; the one near your sister's home," Father Obadiah said as he also stared straight ahead. "The hidden old section which used to be the monastery is where we believe they focus the centre of their secret society activities."

Shaking his head, Father Kubelik spoke heatedly. "Such blasphemy and sacrilege!"

Glancing in the rear view mirror, Father Mulhaney saw that they weren't being followed.

"Francesco, what about 'Father Andrecki'? What do we do about *him*?" Father Mulhaney asked. Then he understood. "He's *the one* isn't he? He's the one who came to confession with his sins."

Father Kubelik merely nodded then spoke. "Yes we must do something about *him* and yes there's *the one*. Let me come to him in my own way."

Father Obadiah spoke as he continued looking straight ahead. "This reminds me of Judas Iscariot. Only Judas never confessed to our Lord. It was the other way around. Jesus confessed to him that he was his betrayer. Somehow this feels similar."

Father Kubelik smiled for a moment. "You are very right Edmund Obadiah. You always were a true visionary. You are our silent but strong one. Yes, I agree and I will be facing 'Father Andrecki' just as Jesus faced the soldiers coming to arrest him at the prompting of Judas' testimony and his betrayal kiss."

Father Mulhaney got into the conversation. "Francesco won't be betraying a confidence either. What was told to him under the seal of the confessional will stay sealed but he will be facing him and pointing him out as *the one*."

"Andrew and I will have my full regiment of clergy and friends with me to back me up. This really does feel like the night when Jesus was about to be arrested only this time we are turning the tables and we'll be getting someone and some many others arrested," Father Kubelik prophesized.

Nearing their home, they ceased speaking.

Father Kubelik's mind wrestled with the tasks at hand and the manner in which he knew he would have to face his adversaries. It was the only way and if he had to be martyred for the greater good then so be it. Feeling a sense of compassion come over him, he vowed he would treat 'Father Andrecki' with kindness and love.

After the three priests had changed and prepared themselves, they set out again in the night. Their mission was an urgent one and all three priests were anxious to get on with things.

**

From beyond the other rooms, Maiya heard a loud bang.

Quickly she got up and stood by the door ready. Watching under the door, she saw everything go pitch black. Grabbing the door handle, she flew out of her prison and into a hallway and beyond.

From ahead of her she could make out a candle lit room. On the floor was a great labyrinth that her rescuer has spoken of. Maiya put on the speed as she ran through the hallways not knowing where she was going.

Nearly tripping over the staircase, she found herself at a doorway and then smelled the outside air. Jerking the door open, she flew outside into the dark of night. Brush and stones hurt and scratched her bare feet but she paid them no heed. Running along a path, she found herself on the golf green. The grass was soft and clipped under her feet. Digging in her toes, she ran for all she was worth towards the main street where she heard cars travelling back and forth.

It was at that point that she saw the car with three men inside.

Fearing the worst, she cried out to God once again as the door opened and Father Kubelik scooped her up and brought her inside their car. Seeing Father Mulhaney and Father Obadiah, she began to cry, as Father Kubelik placed a blanket around her.

Quickly driving away, the three priests consoled Maiya as she wept and thanked them for helping to save her.

"My dear Mrs. Emerson, I am Father Francesco Kubelik and we're now taking you to your husband. He's at his friend Don Fenway's house."

Maiya reached out and hugged the priest, as she cried and sobbed in the back seat next to him. "Oh thank you! Praise God, thank you!"

All three priests were overcome with emotion as they struggled to remain composed.

"We all prayed for you Maiya and here you are! God always listens to our prayers and he surely listens to three powerful priests doesn't he?" Father Mulhaney said as he wiped tears from his eyes.

"I have but one question my dear. How did you escape?" Father Kubelik asked as he replaced the blanket from around Maiya's shoulders.

Smiling and brushing away stray hairs from her face, she began to tell her story. "It was God who sent this kindly person to me. I don't know who they were but they set me free and they caused a commotion and then I was able to run until I literally ran into you."

All three priests exchanged glances.

Clearing his throat, Father Mulhaney began to speak. "Maiya, we were impressed upon by God to wait in this exact spot we were in when you came running. Just prior to arriving, we all three could have sworn we heard a voice telling us to wait at this exact spot and not to leave. It was surely an angel instructing us at God's command."

Turning to face her, Father Kubelik spoke. "Mrs. Emerson, I came here tonight to set you free and to face certain evil ones but when we all heard this voice telling us to stay put, our plans changed and we obeyed and then you came from the darkness like an angel.

"As I watched you running, I saw behind you a magnificent light. It was a heavenly light because there was no place, where this light could have come from in the natural. We all believe it was the heavenly light of an angel behind you securing and lighting your path to us."

As Maiya heard these wondrous accounts, she cried fresh tears of joy and once again hugged Father Kubelik.

***

Pulling into the driveway of Don Fenway's home, the three priests with Maiya came quickly into the open garage of Don's house.

Aaron was waiting for them as he ran to his wife and picked

her up and hugged her so tightly he nearly hurt her.

***

As the three priests and Don and Cynthia Fenway looked on, they watched with great emotion as the jubilant couple were re-united once again.

Maiya and Aaron both cried together as they hugged and he swung her around.

Realising she was not properly dressed he spoke through his tears. "Baby we better get you inside and get you cleaned up and put you into something warm and soft."

While the three priests stayed downstairs with the Fenways, Aaron tended to Maiya and got her into the bath and then some warm clothes of Cynthia's.

Fifteen minutes later, the couple came downstairs as everyone got up and hugged Maiya then brought her some hot chocolate.

While she drank her hot chocolate, she told them her story. Listening intensely, everyone congratulated her for her bravery.

Aaron got up and contacted Constable Li and Riet. Leaving them both messages, he re-joined the group.

CHAPTER NINETEEN

"Maiya, who do you think your rescuer was? You mentioned they smelled of Frankincense and you recognised that smell from the funeral home chapel as well as from church in the past?" Father Mulhaney asked as he regarded her sitting next to Aaron.

***

Holding her mug in her hands, Maiya wasn't sure. "I kept thinking I recognised their voice and their scent somehow and yet I couldn't place it. Maybe when I return to work eventually it will come back to me."

***

Aaron wasn't so sure she should return to work at the funeral home.

"Babe, we'll talk about this later but my thoughts are I don't think you should return to work again at that funeral home. I don't think it's safe for a lot of reasons."

Maiya nodded as she looked around at her friends. "You know when something like this happens it makes you think about everything you have and how much you value what you do have. I had lots of time to ponder those questions. Actually, I think I agree with Aaron. Part of me will miss the place but so much has happened I just don't think I could ever feel safe or happy there again."

***

Father Kubelik smiled at her and then clapped a little. "I am *so* proud of you Mrs. Emerson. Well done! It isn't easy making that kind of decision. I know because I've often had to do the same."

"Please call me Maiya. I really appreciate that and I can see why my husband loved you from the start. You are a wonderful man. All of you are! You are three of the best and most beautiful priests on earth!"

Cheers rang out for Maiya as she continued to drink her hot chocolate. Smiling at them all, Maiya knew that she was in the presence of some of the most special people on earth.

"Father Kubelik, what are your plans now? You've come out of hiding so will you stay out or where will you go?" asked Don Fenway as he regarded the priest with great interest.

"Part one of my missions has been accomplished and that was to rescue Maiya. Now part two waits. This second part could be especially difficult but we might get lucky and it's a breeze. With the help of my friends, we have to bring down this evil order or cult and deal with a certain 'priest' who must be handled carefully and with compassion and understanding.

"As some of you may have already guessed this entire problem started over two weeks ago when I was privy to some

265

especially disturbing information shared with me in confession. The penitent was deeply troubled and they sought absolution. I gave it to them from God. However that was not the end of things," Father Kubelik explained, as he looked at his audience.

"This same individual couldn't believe they were cleansed of their transgressions therefore they unwisely spoke of this to others and I became a marked man so to speak. I was 'marked' because they considered me a liability as they believed I knew their hidden society's secrets.

"What I learned won't be divulged but I can say and I must say that it pertains to a branch of a modern order of a cult following who fancy themselves to be some connection to the Rosicrucians in that they seek ancient knowledge and wisdom but with an evil twist," Father Kubelik stated sadly.

"Originally I and Father Mulhaney thought they fancied they were connected to the Knights Templar and they may still be in some distant way connected. The modern day Templars are a result of the movement that continued unofficially after the disbandment in 1312 AD. It is believed by some that the Templars and Rosicrucians were connected as well." Father Kubelik paused for a moment as he took a drink of water.

"We also suspect and believe that this strange cult following has at its root some connection to the very corporation which Maiya works or worked at shall we say. We aren't sure the length and breadth of this yet but we do know it exists.

"Another puzzling angle of all of this is the *Monk's Abbey*

Golf and Country Club. There are some strange meetings which are held there but where exactly we aren't sure. Maiya was held in one of rooms and we suspect from her account of the words spoken to her, that she was going to be taken to some room with an altar and she was believed to be some priestess," Father Kubelik remarked with a cringe.

"These abominable, blasphemous and terrifying acts are deeply disturbing and illegal in the sense of human sacrifice, imprisonment, forcible confinement with a weapon and that they are being carried out on private property to name a few charges," Father Kubelik concluded, as he reached for his water glass.

"So, we have our work cut out for us and with the cooperation of some of our other friends and clerics as well as the police we'll put an end to all of this evil," Father Obadiah remarked as he looked from face to face.

"What will you do tonight? Or will you spring a surprise attack on them tomorrow instead?" Cynthia asked.

"That's a great question Mrs. Fenway. I think with the lateness of the hour we should rest and consider a new and better strategy for another time and it may be tomorrow. The sooner the better," Father Kubelik admitted.

"Well everyone is welcome to stay the night and I hope they do," Don Fenway invited as he looked at his guests.

Maiya and Aaron smiled as they held each other's hands. "Well we're certainly staying the night."

The three priests all exchanged glances. Smiling at the

Fenways, they agreed. "I can speak for us all when I say your offer is very welcome. I think we'd love to stay the night and we'll sleep wherever you have a spare cot or couch," Father Mulhaney said as he glanced at his colleagues.

"Yes, I must say your home is very warm and comfortable and I am among true friends so yes, count me in, "Father Kubelik said as he folded his hands across his knees.

"I'll help make breakfast," Father Obadiah said as he smiled.

"Wonderful!" Cynthia Fenway replied as she got up to check on the sleeping arrangements. Don got up too and excused himself to help her.

The three priests also excused themselves as they made a phone call that prompted them to make another phone call and then a third phone call.

"This is Father Francesco Kubelik, I want to report a series of crimes which we believe took place somewhere in the old section of the *Monk's Abbey Golf and Country Club*. Mr. Aaron Emerson has already left a message for two constables Li and Riet with regards to his wife, Maiya Emerson. She is now safe and with her husband here at the home of her friends, Mr. and Mrs. Don Fenway.

"We're giving you this tip because we suspect there have been and still are unauthorised meetings held at this golf and country club by members of a secret society. According to Mrs. Maiya Emerson, they threatened death and held her with a weapon against her will until one of the members strangely allowed her to leave.

We found her and brought her to her husband where she is now."

Father Kubelik listened as the police officer spoke at some length then he spoke. "If you find a man posing as 'Father Andrecki' please be kind with him as I want to speak with him myself."

Turning to his friends, he pursed his lips. "It is now done. Let us see how things evolve from here."

***

The gathering of hooded figures stood while their 'grand master' walked among them. Slowly looking at each member, the grand master inspected the members.

Coming to a stop, they began in a strangely piercing voice. "I will ask but once, who let the priestess go? She didn't escape without someone's help. Who was it? If you confess your sins now I may be predisposed to be lenient with you."

No one came forward. This only served to anger the grand master more.

"Very well, you all know the consequences. Step this way and be punished!"

A hooded assistant to the grand master prodded the hooded members out of the room and down the hall to the great labyrinth room. Each member was instructed to kneel down on the floor at specific intervals on the labyrinth drawing.

Several members made sounds of fear as they understood they might be killed for their transgressions. Others remained silent while they waited.

The grand master approached them all and took a large axe from a special holder on the wall. Wielding the axe over his head, he began to speak in some unintelligible language.

Moving closer to the group of hooded members, the grand master prepared to mete out his punishment.

Booming their voice in a threatening manner, they spoke. "Who will be the first to taste the kiss of steel!"

From beyond the mass of hooded figures, a lone hooded figure reached down and pulled out a gun. Taking quick aim, they pulled the trigger and hit the grand master square in the chest. Dropping the heavy axe to the floor in a loud clatter, the grand master rolled to one side bleeding and nearly dead.

Pandemonium broke out as other hooded figures tried to attack the gunperson.

Wielding the gun at the crowd, they called out loudly to the group. "Stop! You saw what I just did now don't make me shoot anyone else. Someone call an ambulance!"

Like lightening, several hooded members pulled out cell phones and began to dial 9-1-1.

Still holding them at gunpoint, the gunperson moved towards the grand master who lay bleeding but appeared to be alive. They moaned and tried to talk in some strange language.

Within minutes, police cars had surrounded the rear of *Monk's Abbey Golf and Country Club* as well as an ambulance.

From outside came the sounds of officers attempting to break into the building.

The gunman motioned for some of the hooded figures to go and assist the police. "Go! Show them the easy way in here!"

Instantly two hooded figures turned and ran down the corridor towards the easy secret entrance.

Within minutes, a brigade of police officers accompanied by several EMS staff ran into the room of the great labyrinth.

The gunperson had already dropped their weapon and was holding their hands up in the air. The other hooded figures were told to get down on the floor, face down.

While the EMS staff attended to the victim, several police officers processed and restrained the hooded members. The gunperson was brought to the side of the room in restraints.

"Who are you!" one of the officers called out to the gunperson.

"Look in my shirt pocket. My badge and my identification are there."

"Your badge!" the police officer said incredulously, as she patted the gunperson down and then retrieved the identification and badge.

***

Taking her flashlight, she read over the badge and identification. Another police officer came and joined her as they looked at the gunperson.

"Detective Paul Andrecki of the R.C.M.P, Toronto, North Detachment (New Market)?"

Nodding, he waited while the two officers satisfied themselves as to his identity.

Removing his restraints and letting him be at ease, the three officers moved away towards one of the empty rooms.

"Sorry about that Detective Andrecki but how could we know? You're working undercover aren't you?" the female officer stated the obvious as her colleague looked on.

Removing the rest of his hooded garb, he revealed regular civilian clothes. "Yes for over four months now I've been working undercover infiltrating this secret society's activities. We first received a report from a civilian and then it was processed through criminal intelligence and finally because it deals with organized crime at a potentially national level, my unit got involved.

"Suffice it to say I witnessed this evening a series of acts which were meant to take a female victim who had been forcibly removed from her home and drugged then brought here and held under duress and with a weapon against her will. Their plans had been to 'sacrifice' her tonight."

The female police officer looked horrified. "Sacrifice her! My God, that's unbelievable! You know this for a fact?"

"For a fact. The victim's name is Mrs. Maiya Emerson and I can tell you that someone cut her loose and then caused a commotion and she escaped with her life. I am hopeful she made it but I can't say for sure. It was horrible not being able to do anything about this while I was undercover but when the 'grand master' had snapped their cap tonight and was threatening to literally take the axe to everyone, I drew the line and shot them. I assume they're still alive?" Detective Paul Andrecki asked as he looked from officer to officer.

Radioing the officers in the other room, the female officer got the report. "Yes he's stable. They are taking him to the hospital as we speak. Do you know who the 'grand master' is?"

"Sure and that is part of our investigation. This network is far-reaching. I should tell you one more fact. As part of my undercover profile, I also needed to temporarily impersonate a member of clergy at *St. Simeon's Church*. I made a confession of some of the facts I'd learned to Father Francesco Kubelik but unfortunately someone learned of this and it inadvertently placed Father Kubelik at risk. He had to go into hiding for some time due to this leak by someone. I'm not sure who.

"I can also tell you there is quite a unique and wonderful network of priests and lay persons who are also assisting us with these inquiries. Interestingly, the husband and wife team; Aaron and Maiya Emerson are also involved although they don't know who I really am; they just think I'm an Anglican priest," Detective Andrecki explained, while glancing from face to face.

Constable Wendy MacPherson smiled as she spoke. "Wow! I can just imagine how much more there is to this. Well for now, let's just leave things as they are and you can fill us in later if you wish to or need to. We better get back out there and help process the scene."

"The crime team will be already at work on the rooms as well so we better get back out there and clear some of this stuff away for them," Constable Ivan Steinbeck said as he began to move into the room of the great labyrinth.

Detective Paul Andrecki brought out his phone and made a report to his office.

***

All guests passed the night without any difficulty and Aaron slept with one eye open to keep watch over his wife as she slept soundly in the crook of his arm.

***

After breakfast, the next morning Constable Li and Riet came to the door for Aaron and Father Kubelik.

Taking out her notebook, Constable Li reviewed her notes. "We wanted to give you a report from the information you gave us last night. The Toronto Police raided the old section of the *Monk's Abbey Golf and Country Club* and brought in the various members of some hooded society for questioning. Their 'grand master' was actually shot but not fatally by an undercover RCMP officer.

"The ownership and management of the golf and country club have temporarily closed the club pending the police inquiries and investigations. We want to thank you both for the excellent and extremely timely tip you provided us with on both accounts.

"Suffice it to say that your quick action along with that of the RCMP officer brought this particular branch of secret society to a halt and it prevented a series of mass murders."

Constable Li's audience was astounded as they glanced from Aaron to Father Kubelik and over to the police officers in attendance.

"Mrs. Emerson we are extremely pleased to see you are well and with your husband and good friends again," Constable Riet said as he smiled at her. "You are an extremely brave lady."

Maiya Emerson smiled back and then spoke. "Thank you, but I have God to thank and his angels, my friends our blessed priests."

The three priests smiled warmly at Maiya as they considered her heart-felt compliment.

"Constable Li, may I ask if a certain 'Father Andrecki' was among the persons in this hooded society?" Father Kubelik asked as he sat down in a chair.

Flipping through her notes, she looked puzzled. "Well not a 'Father Andrecki' but the RCMP officer's name is Detective Paul Andrecki. I don't know if that is who you are referring to but I can't see how."

The two other priests appeared puzzled as they glanced at Father Kubelik while the others also watched his expression. A large smile creased his extremely handsome face as he nodded in acknowledgment and new understanding. "Yes, thank you, I have my answer *now*."

Getting up together, the two constables rose to leave.

"If we hear of any other relevant information we'll let you know. Once again thank you all very much," Constable Riet said as he walked towards the Fenway's front door.

Rising and heading towards the upstairs rooms, the three priests prepared to pack up their things and head back home.

Maiya and Aaron remained downstairs with the Fenways.

Some minutes later, the three priests stood together as they said their good-byes.

Hugging the ladies and shaking the hands of the men, they stood for a moment.

"We can't thank you enough for taking us in and giving us refuge for the night. You are forever in our hearts, prayers and minds," Father Obadiah said as he stood to one side.

Father Kubelik came towards his hosts and said, "Mr. and Mrs. Fenway, never will I forget you and all that you've done for my friends and me. Thank you and please do come see me soon at the church."

Father Mulhaney came forward then said, "I'm not sure how I can outdo what these two priests just said so I'll make it easy. Thank you and God bless you all."

Everyone laughed as they hugged the three priests once again and said their good-byes.

Watching the men drive away, the Fenways returned to Maiya and Aaron.

"Gosh they're lovely men aren't they?" Cynthia Fenway said as she sat next to Maiya.

"They sure are, they're just beautiful inside and out," Maiya commented with brotherly love in her heart.

Aaron looked at his watch then said, "Maiya, maybe we should get going too. We need to give back some privacy to Cynthia and Don."

"You know you're always welcome here and please don't feel you need to rush away. I'm off today too remember?" Don said with a smile.

"Thanks Don old buddy. We appreciate it and ordinarily we would hang out but I better get Maiya back and squared away."

The couple nodded in understanding as Aaron got up to get them ready to leave.

Rising from the sofa, Maiya hugged her friends tightly. "What would we have done without you? I feel so safe and so welcome here with you. But Aaron's right, I have to go home and see my place again. I can't be afraid of it."

"Well dear if things get scary you come back and take it slowly okay?" Cynthia said as she held Maiya's face in her hands. "We love you both."

Tears came into her eyes as she regarded her friends. "We love you too!"

Aaron came up from behind and hugged his wife from around her waist. "Babe, shall we go now?"

Sighing, Maiya said with a smile, "if we must, we must."

Driving home, the couple were quiet.

Glancing at his wife, Aaron spoke with concern in his voice. "Babe, are you okay? I know you're likely nervous to return home but sweetie, we need to do this sooner or later. I just hope I didn't rush you."

Looking away from him, she tried not to cry. "Oh Aaron, I guess the trauma of that horrible time will be with me for a while longer. I'm sorry…"

Arriving home, Aaron hugged his wife and kissed her tenderly. "Maiya my sweet love, I love you more than I'll ever be able to express. The trauma affected us both baby but I'm trying to be strong for us both."

Not realising just how Aaron had been affected she apologised as tears rolled down her sweet cheeks. "I'm so sorry honey I've been only seeing this from my perspective. Yes, you went through hell as much as I did only differently."

Holding his wife and consoling her gently, Aaron kissed the top of her head. "Sweet baby, don't worry I'll be strong for us both. You just take all the time you need to heal and get over this okay?"

Maiya laughed slightly as she thought of something. "Now we're both unemployed. Oh shit; we're really something aren't we?"

"Hey baby don't you worry about that. Something will work out for us both and I have a feeling that between our new friends and our old friends something is about to break."

Later that day, Maiya and Aaron became accustomed to their home again and each other. Both had really needed the intimacy and security of each other's touch. Too much had happened and nearly happened and Aaron and Maiya never wanted to repeat those horrors again.

While Maiya bathed upstairs, Aaron went towards his familiar drink cabinet. Recalling their tender but explosive intimacy they had shared, Aaron felt utterly renewed and reenergised as he thought of how much he loved pleasuring his wife. She had needed a gentle yet loving touch that afternoon. He had given it to her and made sure she felt both perfectly loved and perfectly satisfied.

As he brought out his drink bottle, he stopped. Something within him had progressed and he no longer felt the interest or need to drink as he once had. Just maybe the three priests had influenced him more than he had realised.

Moving towards the kitchen, Aaron sought out different refreshment. Finding the ingredients for making some iced tea, Aaron brought up two tall glasses of mint-iced tea.

Maiya was just dressing as she saw the glasses. "Oh, what is that?"

Smiling widely as he wrapped his arm around her waist he said, "mint ice tea. I hope you like it baby. Non-alcoholic, no less."

"Oh, very nice indeed. It's funny but alcoholic drinks don't seem to interest me the way they used it. Now I think I'll still enjoy some wine from time to time but strangely I just don't feel like anything else alcoholic," Maiya admitted as she finished dressing.

"Baby, it's so strange but I feel the same way. I swear it is those three priests. They're a good influence on us."

"Of course they are my love, they're priests and the best priests alive I think," Maiya said as she took her ice tea and tasted it. "Mm, this is very nice."

"Why thank you baby," Aaron said as he also tasted his

concoction. "Not bad at all."

Sitting on their bed, Maiya took another drink then spoke. "Aaron, what was your idea you had about working with your friends? You mentioned something about it earlier."

Joining his wife, he held his drink as he settled himself. "I had an idea about working with them somehow. Maybe some kind of investigations or some kind of research company. I don't know baby but something where we can use our newly discovered skills. It's become obvious that we all have these skills we didn't know we possessed."

"I see. This idea has possibilities. Well of course we would have to float it by our friends but I like it so far," Maiya admitted as she took another drink.

***

Staff Sergeant John received a phone call from Assistant Managing Funeral Director, Gail Gordon.

"Hello Ms. Gordon, how can I help you?"

"Officer John, I have some information for you." After sharing the details of her strange meeting with Mr. Radcliffe, she waited for his comment.

"That's quite interesting Ms. Gordon. So, Mr. Radcliffe blatantly said the corporation won't cooperate and that we would have to get a warrant for the files," Officer John repeated as he took notes.

"Yes that's right. Even though I'm the acting managing funeral director since Thomas' demise, I still have to follow their protocol. As you know, I received word from your precinct that all was clear to return to work so I am heading into the funeral home for the first time today and I've hired a new assistant, Mr. Everett Logan who will be my operations manager. He used to be a licensed funeral director but after an incident some years ago, he retired as a funeral director.

"Mr. Logan won't be working in the capacity of funeral director. Also, I still haven't heard from Warren Sinclair. I can't understand what's happened to him but he's definitely gone AWOL as they say."

***

Typing into his computer, Staff Sergeant John brought up some newly documented information.

Quickly reading it, he shared some of the information. "Ms. Gordon, I can tell you where Mr. Sinclair is. He's here at the station. He's being questioned in reference to an incident last night. Pending the results of that, we may be letting him go.

"Shall I have him return to his job at the funeral home?"

Digesting this bit of news, she replied without much confidence. "Yeah, please have him report here as soon as he can. I need him! He is my only other funeral director who is licenced."

"Okay will do," Ms. Gordon.

***

Maiya picked up the phone and dialled Gail Gordon's number.

"Gail, its Maiya Emerson. Listen Gail, I need to tell you something but it will not be easy. I have decided to leave the

281

funeral home. So much has happened and I really can't feel safe and happy there any longer. My husband also doesn't want me working at the funeral home any longer.

"There is one other thing. Over the past few days, there was an incident, which involved the police, and it also involved some others but needless to say, I simply can't return to work there. I'm sorry."

Gail Gordon wanted to shout. "Sorry as hell Maiya! I really wish I wasn't hearing this because you have always been the one person I could count on. Now I don't know anything about that police incident you mentioned just now but regardless of it, are you sure?"

"Yes Gail and I have always enjoyed working with you too. You've always been great and treated me so well. No, it's more the matter of the memories and ghosts of Thomas that haunt me. It was us who found him and I never want to be in a position like that again and I really doubt if I could face that upstairs room again either."

Gail felt utterly dejected at that point. Sighing, she voiced her own perspectives on the matter.

"Maiya I know you're right and actually to be honest I have felt like chucking it in within the past day or so myself. Oh well, thank goodness I hired a new assistant, an operations manager so he'll be able to help fill in where we need it most. Listen if you ever need a reference you know I'll give you a great one!"

"Thanks for understanding Gail. I really had dreaded this

phone call but now that I've spoken with you, I'm glad I did. Best of luck and I know things will work out. You're a great manager and person!"

Looking over at Aaron, she smiled. "Well Gail took it better than I thought. She's upset but she doesn't blame me at least."

"That's wonderful babe! Okay so now we can concentrate on our ideas and see what happens," Aaron said as he went in search of some paper and pens.

***

Staff Sergeant John continued reading the new report from the night before and was shocked.

According to Officer MacPherson who logged the information, Detective Paul Andrecki of the RCMP, Toronto North Detachment (New Market) had been working undercover infiltrating a secret society, which operated out of the old section of the *Monk's Abbey Golf and Country Club.* They had illegally entered and set up their headquarters for their cult on the golf and country club's premises in the area, which used to be the old monastery.

In addition to his role as a new member of the cult, he had needed to impersonate a priest at *St. Simeon's Church* as part of his profile. The tip had come from a civilian. From there it was processed in criminal intelligence then sent over to Detective Andrecki's unit in organized crime.

Officer MacPherson had logged that the room where the attempted murders were about to take place and where the 'grand master' was shot by Detective Andrecki, was referred to as the great labyrinth. The labyrinth had a name, 'Labyrinth Green".

Looking up for a moment from his computer screen, Officer John recalled where he'd seen that term before. *"Lytton's Funeral Home, Labyrinth Green, a Division of Respectful Pastures Memorial Group,"* Staff Sergeant John, spoke aloud.

Continuing reading, Staff Sergeant John noticed that the victim of the shooting incident, who was referred to as the 'grand master', was identified as Mr. Angus Radcliffe, VP of *Lytton's Funeral Home, Labyrinth Green, a Division of Respectful Pastures Memorial Group.*

Making some notes, he got on the phone to contact Detective Paul Andrecki.

Leaving him a message, he also sent him a faxed report.

Staff Sergeant John was returning to his office when his phone rang.

***

"Detective Andrecki returning your call. Thank you for the faxed report, it's very helpful."

"My pleasure. I felt we needed to talk and compare notes. I believe I have some information which could impact your case and it would tie up one of mine," Officer John stated as he held onto his faxed report.

"We've not been able to question the victim, Mr. Radcliffe because he hasn't awaked from his surgery yet. He's in semi-critical condition and in intensive care. He's not responding to the surgery or medication well. Because he's an older man, this could be hampering his healing and recovery.

"We're hopeful that he will recover and then we can get to the bottom of this strange society he's embroiled in as well as find out the length and breadth of it. Unfortunately none of the other members know anything or at least they aren't admitting to knowing anything helpful," Detective Andrecki explained as he sat back in his chair.

"I have a question about the part of you having to impersonate a priest. Why was that?" Officer John asked carefully.

Closing his eyes for a moment, Detective Andrecki considered how best to answer his question. "May I defer that question for now? I'm actually waiting to speak with a witness so once that happens then perhaps I can answer your question.

"Our unit will get onto this new information with regards to your witness, Mrs. Hench observing the caskets being moved to and from the funeral home during the night. To everyone's knowledge this was an unauthorised shift?"

"That's right. None of the funeral home staff can confirm that it is authorised or usual practice. Strangely, though I expected to find other hits across the city, province or country. Nothing so far," Staff Sergeant John reported.

Detective Andrecki rubbed his tired eyes. "Yes that is strange. We'll latch onto this and see what happens as well. If we turn up anything useful, we'll be in touch. Thanks again for the intel."

**

Staff Sergeant John opened the report about the Thomas Fieldstone murder.

"My instincts tell me the case regarding the nocturnal coffin exchange, his murder and the strange reference to Mr. Angus Radcliffe, VP of *Lytton's Funeral Home and Labyrinth Green, a Division of Respectful Pastures Memorial Group,* are all intertwined but how can I prove it and what was their common thread? Oh yes, and the strange society where Mr. Radcliffe was the 'grand master' better be added that to the puzzle."

Rubbing his eyes, he set down the report for a moment then sat back in his chair and closed his eyes. He needed to think.

Opening his eyes, he started the ball rolling to obtain a warrant for the personnel files and other relevant business files from the head office of the funeral home chain. He now had probable cause because the VP of the company, Mr. Angus Radcliffe was a suspect in the recent crime at *Monk's Abbey Golf and Country Club.*

Next, Officer John phoned Gail Gordon back. He needed to pick her brain.

"Hello Ms. Gordon, its Officer John calling back."

"Yes Staff Sergeant, what can I do for you?" Gail asked as she held onto some files that were on her desk.

"I know today will be hectic as your first day back but I wondered if I might drop by and just have another look around and ask you some questions about operational details?"

Sighing lightly she smiled. "Why the heck not? Besides, you can meet my new operations manager, Everett Logan. Come by anytime Staff Sergeant."

CHAPTER TWENTY

Entering through the front doors of *Lytton's Funeral Home*, Staff Sergeant John waited as he heard footsteps approaching.

Seeing a police officer standing inside the doorway, the older man was surprised. "Hello, I'm Rex. Are you here to see Ms. Gordon?"

"Yes Rex, I'm Staff Sergeant John."

"Please have a seat in this room. I'll let her know you're here," Rex promised as he headed to the staircase.

"Thank you Rex," Officer John said as he found a chair and sat down.

A few moments later, Gail Gordon appeared at the doorway. "Hello Staff Sergeant John. Please come with me into this private office."

"Actually I would like to see your showroom if I could."

"Oh, I see, alright, why not?" Gail said as she led him up a staircase and to the right.

A large well-lit room with a thick rug on the floor held several models of caskets.

"Any particular casket you'd like to see?" Gail asked as she stood about a foot away from him.

"No, I really needed to get a handle on the layout and the volume of caskets you order. How often and which styles are most ordered?"

"Well without going into specifics, which I can get for you but they'll take a few moments to locate in our files, we order these two models over here the most. They are very popular and if someone needs one and we can't get the model they want, we'll take it from our showroom in an emergency.

"Now the frequency of ordering these caskets varies. We also hold a couple of extra models downstairs and also in the room just off the prep room. Our supplier is really good, they can deliver usually within a day or so, sometimes sooner if it is a rush."

"Could you give me the name of your supplier?" Staff Sergeant John asked as he glanced around at the various caskets.

"Oh we have several because some don't carry the same casket so naturally we get them from a couple of different suppliers. We've been doing business with them for years so I don't think there is anything there. I know where you're going with this Staff Sergeant but as I said our suppliers have been with us for years," Gail explained as she studied the officer.

"Okay, I see. Please show me the areas where all of the caskets are stored."

"Please follow me," Gail said as she led him over to the upper room first.

Opening a door that opened onto the prep room, she showed him some large racks with several coffins lined up on the racks like shelves. "Just beyond is the prep room but we won't be going in there."

Nodding and smiling, Officer John agreed. "Okay that's fine with me."

"Not that you aren't used to seeing people in all states of trauma and death but really I doubt if you'd like a tour of the prep room," Gail stated as she led them down towards the main level.

Seeing Everett Logan, she introduced them to each other.

"Nice to meet you sir," Everett said as he took in the general appearance of the policeman.

"My pleasure as well. So, first day on the job?" Staff Sergeant John asked, while standing opposite Gail and Everett.

"Yes it is, but as Gail likely mentioned I used to be a funeral director so none of this is new to me. Still, it's kind of nice to be back in the saddle so to speak."

"Everett, if you'll excuse us I was just showing Staff Sergeant John around."

"Sure, please let me know if you need my help for anything," Everett said as he began to walk away.

Downstairs, Gail opened a heavy door into a larger room that had several caskets lining the floor. "These babies take up a lot of floor space but that's part of the process isn't it?"

Looking around, Officer John got his bearings. "So from here, could you easily get to the back parking lot?"

"Yes, there is a loading ramp and a door. We have to have it to move the coffins around right?"

"Please show me that area," Officer John asked, as he began to walk out towards the hallway.

"Sure thing, now right here is the door. Do you see it? Yes I know, it's not very easily identified but this place was built a long time ago so that's how they would do it. A horse drawn wagon would bring the coffins up to the door and then this strange old door would be unlocked and they'd slide the casket down the ramp. Now back then, they didn't have the caskets like we have today. They were much smaller and lighter."

Noticing an old trap door in the floor, Officer John pointed to it. "Where does that lead and what is it for?"

Gail crouched down and said, "that old door hasn't been used in years. I have no idea what it's for."

As she was getting up, Gail noticed something that prompted her to crouch down again. "Officer, could you shine your flashlight on this door?"

Crouching down next to Gail, Officer John shone his flashlight onto the old trap door. Just barely discernable, they saw evidence that the old trap door had recently been used. Motioning for Gail to move back she complied.

Carefully, Staff Sergeant John played his light around the edges and then the main handle and noticed that it did appear to have been recently opened.

"Ms. Gordon, do you give me permission to open this cavity?"

"Absolutely Officer John, please continue," Gail stated, as she stood further back to give him room to work.

"Could you ask Mr. Logan to bring me a shovel and anything else that could pry this heavy old door open? I need to use a wedge perhaps. Actually, I should call for back-up but this might be just an old empty cellar."

Standing up, Officer John considered the situation.

"Technically, this is a crime scene even though the team has left so that is probable cause for me requesting back up in the event this cache holds some evidence."

Radioing for backup, he waited standing next to Gail.

"Let's go up and meet them at the door otherwise they won't know where to find us."

"Good point, sure, take this staircase, it's shorter and it leads to the street."

"This place is a maze or a labyrinth isn't it?" Staff Sergeant John remarked as he climbed the stairs.

"Yes this old building does rather twist and turn. However, I think a maze is nothing but false walls and that sort of thing.

"A labyrinth I believe has one opening and one central place which is usually the heart of the structure. The rest of the design winds around and around and twists and turns but it still leads to either the opening or the central point or heart but yes, this place could be both I suppose."

Arriving outside, Staff Sergeant John watched for the police cruiser.

Gail Gordon stood next to him and did the same. Every so often, she would glance back at him and study his face.

Catching her doing this he smiled.

"Sorry, I'm a people person. I like to study people. I guess that's an occupational hazard although the people I meet aren't alive to care what I see of them," Gail said with a smile. "Tell me, what is your heritage?"

"No apologies. I'm also a people person and I must say you are a unique lady. I enjoy working with you Ms. Gordon. As to my heritage, I'm a Native Canadian; *Ojibwe* or as some people say *Ojibway*."

"That's awesome! You're very kind Officer John and I enjoy working with you too."

"How about your heritage?" Officer John asked as he studied Ms. Gordon.

"I was born in Canada but my heritage is originally from Curacao, in the Netherlands Antilles."

Smiling at Gail Gordon, Officer John was intrigued. "Do you speak Dutch fluently?"

"I do actually and I enjoy being bi-lingual. How about you, what language do the *Ojibwe* people speak?" Gail Gordon asked with great interest.

Staff Sergeant John enjoyed speaking about his heritage. He was always delighted to find someone who took an interest in people's cultures. "The *Ojibwe* language is known as *Anishinaabemowin* or *Ojibwemowin.* Our language belongs to the

Algonquian linguistic group and is descended from Proto-Algonquian."

Smiling widely at Officer John, Gail Gordon nodded. "That's totally awesome! I love it!"

The back-up police officers arrived and immediately Staff Sergeant John began to fill them in.

Gail unlocked the door they came out from and led the way down to the strange old door in the floor.

"You see this door looks as heavy as all hell and I also don't know what we'll find here. As you guys know this is still technically a crime scene even though the dust has settled," Staff Sergeant John explained as he looked from constable to constable.

"Right and so we have probable cause as well as permission from Ms. Gordon who is the acting managing funeral director. Okay, let me go and get some equipment," the younger constable said as he retraced his steps.

"Leave the door open with something or we'll have to unlock it for you," called Gail Gordon as she watched the younger policeman head up the stairs.

"Right, got you!" called back the younger police officer.

The two police officers and Ms. Gordon stared at the strange old door in the floor. Each were wondering what the trap door contained if anything.

Carrying some shovels and some heavy rope and some clips, the younger officer returned to the strange trap door.

Distributing the shovels, the three officers began to pry around the door crack to loosen it a little. The wood was old but it was stubborn. Bit by bit they began to loosen the edges until they were able to place another shovel under the opening and use it as a wedge to pry it up.

Wafting up from below, they could all smell evidence of some remains. The three police officers exchanged glances. Gail Gordon had placed a tissue over her nose.

Painstakingly repeating the maneuvers until finally the trap door was being raised, they increased the wedge angle so that it would support the increased load bearing functionality.

Staff Sergeant John shone his flashlight down into the abyss and sucked in his breath slightly. "Ah shit! We've got some remains down in there. Call the coroner and the crime team."

Gail Gordon leaned against the wall as she turned away from the putrid sight and smells. Holding her breath at intervals, she could barely stand the smell.

Funeral directors didn't often get cases where the deceased had begun to decompose but she also had her protective gear on when working in the prep room.

Turning back toward the police officers, she just watched them.

Presently, members of a crime scene team arrived and stood flashing lights into the cavity.

"Oh my… this is nasty," one of the crime scene staff remarked, as they wrinkled their nose. Brushing hair away from her face, she placed a cap on her head.

Sighing lightly, one of the other crime scene members shrugged. "Let's get it at and prepare things for the coroner."

Staff Sergeant John approached Gail Gordon. "I'm really sorry you had to witness this."

"I'm used to most things but funeral directors usually don't get cases like this. We also have our protective gear so that helps. We'll get these individuals later perhaps after they've been to the morgue and the coroner or pathologist has worked on them and cleaned them up somewhat but seeing and smelling them in the raw is pretty nasty," Gail admitted as she turned away again.

"Yeah the smell is the worst in my opinion," Staff Sergeant John said, as he noticed the coroner had arrived.

Dr. Gloria Fishman came down the stairs and after nodding at everyone, she began to do her work as the crime team members assisted her with trying to examine the deceased. Dr. Fishman had already protected herself with the necessary disposable clothing, coveralls, head cover, mask and gloves. Strong lights had been set up to shine as much light into the cavity as possible with protective tarps lining the floor.

In a muffled voice, Dr. Fishman remarked, as she shook her head. "Wow, this is nasty stuff! Okay let's try to bring this individual up and place them on this tarp. Oh shit, they're breaking up! Please let's try to keep them together as much as possible! I know it's challenging working under these circumstances."

The police officers and Gail Gordon watched as the crime team and Dr. Fishman brought up the remains. Little by little, they managed to clear the cavity of remains while bagging and labelling everything.

"That's an impossible looking feat trying to get every scrap of evidence up from that cavity. It's not very large either which makes it worse," Gail Gordon remarked to Officer John.

"Yeah I don't relish their work but they're the best so we will get everything there is to find from that cavity," Officer John said as he watched them collecting evidence.

"Well I should get back upstairs and see what's going on up there. There's nothing else I can do down here," Gail said tiredly.

"I will want to speak with you when we know more so that we can try to piece this all together. Now we know what the nocturnal coffin exchange was about," Staff Sergeant John remarked as he followed Gail upstairs.

Shaking her aching head, she had no comments.

Turning back towards the stairs, Staff Sergeant John returned into the basement near the cavity of horror.

Gail Gordon sat with her feet up and her shoes off. Her head was really aching and she needed to close her eyes for a moment.

Softly knocking on the door, Everett Logan came in. "Sorry Gail. I just wanted to see how you were doing."

Sighing loudly she shrugged. "I don't know how the hell I'm doing that's how I'm doing. Some first day of work for you eh?"

"Hey I remember some of this stuff but not quite like this mind you. Can I get you a tea or some coffee?"

"If there's any booze in the tea or coffee I'd prefer it but no, thank you I have some water here. Remind me why I became a funeral director?" Gail asked as she closed her eyes again.

Edging towards her, Everett began to massage her shoulders. "Geez you're tense. Let me loosen you up a little."

Remembering how she used to feel when he touched her, Gail sat up then spoke. "No Everett thanks anyway. Not now and not this way."

Moving away from her, he nodded. "Okay sure. Well if you want to talk just come and get me."

Gail watched him go, then shut her door. Returning to her chair she closed her eyes again as she tried to get rid of her pounding headache.

Images of Thomas Fieldstone came into her mind. Opening her eyes quickly, she turned on her computer. Searching through Thomas' recent files opened by date, she found one that had been opened the day of his murder.

It was password protected but Gail thought she knew his codes. Trying first one code then another she finally hit on the right combination. The password that she used was 'Maiya'.

***

Opening the file dated the day of his death, she read correspondence that was an email letter to Mr. Angus Radcliffe.

'Dear Mr. Angus Radcliffe,

'It has come to my attention that witnesses have observed some strange off-loading of caskets during the night after business hours. This was communicated to me some weeks ago and now again more recently. I have spoken to the persons who I think are involved but although they promised me I was mistaken, these practices still continue.

'I have also been informed that large amounts of money have been transferred from the funeral home business account to a numbered account which exists at the head office. My book-keeper assures me that this money transfer is significant and it happens often enough for it to be of concern. The numbered account is not the usual account that we forward funds to either.

'I want a full accounting of this and I want to be provided with the details of this for our audit purposes. I have authorised my staff to take whatever action necessary but you have to authorise it from head office. Your cooperation is greatly appreciated.

'If I do not hear from you with regards to these issues I will have no other recourse but to refer this to our legal counsel. I will not be held liable for the repercussions of such action.

'I look forward to your expedited reply.

'Sincerely,

'Thomas Fieldstone'

***

Gail sat back for a moment and closed her eyes. So, this could have been the reason Thomas was killed. Quickly she made two copies and transferred the file into one of her own that required a password.

Who had Thomas spoken to? This was the first she had heard of any of this. Who else could he have spoken to other than his book-keeper?

Warren Sinclair's face popped into her mind. *It had to be Warren! There was no one else!*

Gail recalled Officer John say that Warren was being held for questioning at the precinct but was he still there now?!

***

Struggling to put her shoes back on, she just left them and flew down towards the stairway in her stocking feet. Calling out she yelled, "Officer John! Would you please come up here for a moment?"

Hearing his name, he hastened up the stairs to find Gail Gordon waiting in her stocking feet.

"Please come into my office. I have to show you something!"

Immediately noticing the urgency in her voice, he came with her.

Closing the door behind her and locking it, she held the printed letter written by Thomas Fieldstone on the day of his death.

Immediately reading the letter then looking up at her, he waited.

***

"Officer John, where is Warren Sinclair? Is he still at the precinct? It has to be him who killed Thomas, there *is* no one else!"

Phoning into the precinct, he learned that Warren Sinclair had just been released. Relaying this information to Gail, he waited.

"Ms. Gordon what makes you believe it was Warren Sinclair

who killed Thomas Fieldstone?"

Taking a deep breath, she began providing her theories. "Officer John now I know that you might not appreciate this but I can tell you this is the truth. You see this file was password encrypted with the word 'Maiya'. That's Mrs. Maiya Emerson. Now she told me she quit today but that is because of several factors.

"Anyway, head office if you recall wanted to terminate or fire Ms. Emerson without cause. When I spoke and met with Mr. Angus Radcliffe he wouldn't give any reasons for their order to terminate her, he simply stated that he would fire her and that was that.

"I know that Thomas had shared this with Warren because I hadn't come into the office yet and he wrote his notation on the top of the termination notice. I know you noticed this written there. Now in our chain of command, if I'm not in the office then Warren is next in line with Thomas at the top of course. Therefore, it was proper procedure that he shared this termination notice with Warren Sinclair.

Taking a deep breath, Gail continued providing her facts. "You see, Thomas was in love with Maiya and so was Warren Sinclair. She confided in me about this several times. Thomas had been a gentleman about it but not Warren. Maiya told me that she was the rock between them and she was.

"Thomas loved her and lusted after her but he respected her so he kept all of this to a minimum and he never acted out his intentions. Maiya could tell how he felt about her but she let it go because he never became inappropriate.

"Now Warren on the other hand, the young cocky bugger that he is lusted after her and he forced himself on her a few times. He was strong and young and very hot and horny if you get my drift, and he decided that Maiya was some cougar prize for him. Those were his words. Anyway, Maiya brought this up with Thomas and he was pissed so I know he had to have confronted Warren about this.

"Now here comes the fly in the ointment. Warren is old man Angus Radcliffe's nephew so you can see how that went. Officer John, I know he did it and I can prove it indirectly through correspondence and the timelines of that night as well as Maiya Emerson would back this up.

"She might even know a lot more about this but doesn't remember due to the shock of it," Gail Gordon stated as she sat waiting for his comments.

"Ms. Gordon I wish we could arrest him on these points but we can't without real proof. We have to show probable cause for an arrest warrant and we don't have it. We are getting it by the sounds of it and I like where this is going because it shows motive but it isn't enough for a warrant.

"Now if you can get me some real evidence like this letter only more compelling, we can get going on this and get him arrested," Staff Sergeant John explained as he studied Ms. Gordon.

Sighing she nodded. "I know, I know. I was afraid you'd say

this. Look officer I will do what I can to get you that evidence because I know Warren Sinclair did it."

"Ms. Gordon, please keep this to yourself. You have told me and that's it. Don't mention this to anyone else not even your husband and not to Ms. Emerson. We'll ask her and see what she can tell us. I say this to protect you."

Smiling at him, she agreed. "Of course and thank you officer. Okay, please let me see what else I can find and I'll be in touch with you."

"Handing her his private number he smiled. "I don't usually give this to people but it is my private cell number. This number reaches me anytime of the day or night. You know Ms. Gordon; we might uncover some evidence from downstairs that will implicate Warren Sinclair after all."

"Please call me Gail. I know this is a crime scene but I need to access Thomas's files so may I still come here?"

"Sure Gail but only you. We'll be working here for some time still but you can come and go. I will clear it with everyone so they'll know and they won't give you a hard time.

"Gail could you print off everything that Mrs. Emerson told you and her formal complaints about Warren Sinclair? This would really help. Could we also access Warren's files?"

"Sure, here, let me do it for you now and see if we find anything. He isn't supposed to have any encrypted files, that courtesy was only extended to Thomas and I," Gail explained as she brought up the directory to access the staff files.

Searching through the directory, she found Warren's files. Immediately upon trying to open them, she was met with a password encryption box.

"Damn him! He isn't allowed to have encrypted files on our company computer directory! See now that is something right there. You see what I mean about him?

"Okay, let me think what could he use for a password?" Gail wondered while Officer John sat next to her.

"How about Maiya?" Staff Sergeant John offered as a password.

Gail Gordon tried it and it wasn't the right password. "Oh shit I thought you were onto something. Oh what could it be?"

Officer John had a thought come to him as he recalled a word that was used in Constable MacPherson's report from the raid the night before. "Try the word 'priestess'."

"Ooh, okay I will," Gail said as she typed the word in lower case.

Immediately it opened and they gasped as they saw file after file with Maiya's name on it and then some photo files as well.

Exchanging glances with Staff Sergeant John, she clicked on the PDF photo files.

The first photo file opened and it showed a photo of Maiya Emerson in a slightly compromising position as she was coming along the corridor and she was straightening her dress that was up at the back.

Another file opened and it showed a close up of Maiya's

breasts in her clothes.

Shaking their heads, they kept clicking on more files.

The last photo was obviously reworked with a photo enhancing program. It opened to show Maiya in the nude but one could see it was not really her body but someone else's that had been pasted and re-worked into the original picture of her.

Sighing loudly Gail and Staff Sergeant John were disgusted with what they had seen.

Noticing another file that was marked 'trophy', they opened it and found photos of him in some strange hooded outfit with a dubbed in photo of Maiya in the nude. He seemed to be chasing her in the photo and in his hand, he was carrying something.

"Oh my goodness these are so sick I can't believe it!" Gail Gordon cried out as she looked at the policeman next to her.

"These are definitely evidence of extreme sexual fantasies which border on images which depict crimes. The last photo shows a dubbed in image of Maiya being chased but she doesn't want to be in that situation with him.

"That is probable intent of a psychological desire to commit a crime if even in a fantasy. His mind wants to play out these images and he does which is very disturbing. If he moved from fantasy to reality, then we'll have a lot more but we absolutely don't want Maiya to be put at any further risk."

Immediately he contacted his precinct and arranged for protection for Mrs. Emerson. "We've got enough here to bring him in for further questioning. We can't get a warrant yet but we can try to contact him and get him into the station. Gail keep looking for more evidence and we'll get you that warrant."

"Obviously he fancies himself some cult priest and she is his priestess. My goodness I just can't believe any of this. Okay, let me keep looking," Gail promised as she kept opening file after file.

***

Staff Sergeant John returned downstairs to check on the progress of the crime scene team and the coroner.

***

Father Francesco Kubelik woke up suddenly from a disturbing dream.

He immediately was glad it was only a dream. Realising he was safely inside his friend's apartment, he lay back down on his bed. While he mulled over the parts of his dream he discovered it was a warning.

Grabbing his cell phone, he dialled the phone number to Aaron and Maiya's home. Getting their voicemail, he left a hasty message then got ready to head over to their home as quickly as he could.

Turning the corner to their street, he immediately saw police cars swarming their home and lights flashing on the cars. Pulling to a stop, Father Kubelik got out and rushed towards the commotion.

One of the police officers stopped him. "This is a crime scene. You can't come any closer. Who are you? Do you live here on this street?"

"I'm good friends with Mr. and Mrs. Emerson. I'm Father

Francesco Kubelik. I'm an Anglican priest. Please, what's happened!"

Hearing and seeing his good friend, Aaron Emerson strode over. "Father Kubelik! Please officer, let him pass, we need him!"

Hesitating for a moment, the officer finally agreed. "Okay but stay where I can see you and let me see some identification. Let me get your wallet."

After the officer read Father Kubelik's identification and pat him down, he allowed him to pass and over to the side still in his line of vision."

"Aaron, for the love of Pete what's been happening here and who is that under that cover!"

Moving closer to Father Kubelik, he lowered his voice. "Thank God it isn't Maiya but it could have been. This wacko was out to get her. It's that missing guy from the funeral home, Warren Sinclair."

Father Kubelik moved away for a moment and said to the officers nearby. "I'm a priest as that officer saw my identification. They have also searched me and I'm clean. May I come and administer to the deceased?"

Glancing over to the officer who cleared Father Kubelik, they agreed. "Okay but no touching him. Just do your prayers or whatever you do and no touching okay?"

"Sure, I understand and we never touch the dead anyway. That would be quite wrong. Please, if you can remove the cover for a moment I want to see their face," Father Kubelik said as he crouched down by the deceased.

Immediately seeing the outfit the deceased was wearing gave Father Kubelik a start. 'My goodness he's wearing a Knights Templar costume! Okay, please leave the cover open so I can pray for his soul."

Just as Father Kubelik was going to start his prayers, he detected some movement on Warren Sinclair's face.

Shouting for the police officers he said, "I think he's still alive!"

Looking down at Warren's face, he saw him slowly open his eyes.

Warren's eyes struggled to focus as he eventually realised who was crouching next to him. Behind Father Kubelik were two police officers.

"It's you…Father; bless me for I have sinned…I…"

"Warren, what have you done my son? Speak while you still can and be purged and cleansed. Go to God now while you can and receive his forgiveness and absolution this instant," Father Kubelik said as he made the sign of the cross above Warren's head and upper body.

Father Kubelik kept repeating the words *Sanctus Benedictus, Kyrie Eleison, Christe Eleison* under his breath…

Gasping as he reached out for Father Kubelik's hand, he held it weakly then spoke. "Father forgive me, for I have sinned so much…I only wanted to…but I did what I could and set her free…she could be mine now…Father I have sinned so much…give me peace…please give me peace…"

"*Pax et Bonum* my son, be at peace and goodness now and always. I absolve you in the Name of God the Father, the Son and the Holy Spirit," Father Kubelik said he made the sign of the cross once again and tensely watched Warren Sinclair open his eyes widely then gasp as he took his last breath.

Turning to one of the police officers, Father Kubelik watched while they took Warren Sinclair's pulse and found he was indeed dead.

Father Kubelik knew there was little else he could do as Warren was now deceased but he was grateful that he had been able to administer extreme unction to Warren before he died.

Praying for his mortal soul, Father Kubelik got up as he completed his prayers, brushing away tears from his eyes.

***

Returning to Aaron's side, he spoke. "Where is Maiya?"

"She's with a policewoman right now. They have her inside the house. She's extremely distraught. The EMS staff have already given her some medication and a doctor is on their way."

"I am so very sorry Aaron I just have no words to express my deepest condolences on yours and Maiya's suffering. We just left you a few hours ago! I just can't believe it! I should be in there tending to her," Father Kubelik said as he waited for Aaron's response.

"Come on then, you're coming in with me. I'll clear it with them," Aaron said as he went and spoke with the officers. Readily agreeing, they allowed Father Kubelik in the see Maiya.

Seeing the priest, she held out her arms to him and began to cry. "Oh Father Kubelik I am so glad you've come! Please come to me now!"

Rushing to her side, he hugged her tightly as he tried to console her. "There, there my dear, we are going to help you all we can. Please tell me anything you want."

While the female police officer watched, Maiya sat next to Aaron on one side and Father Kubelik on the other. "I can hardly speak of this now but I must. I can't hide from the horror of it or it will haunt me forever.

"Aaron was in the shower and I was downstairs preparing our dinner and all at once, Warren Sinclair slipped inside of our home and came up from behind me and held a huge knife to my throat. He was wearing some strange outfit with a large red cross on it, which made me wonder as he was inflicting pure evil on me and nothing worthy of such an outfit with a cross on the front of it.

"Anyway, Warren told me he had killed Thomas because he had stood in his way and he needed him to step aside but he wouldn't. Warren then said he was there to kill Aaron because he was the real block that stood in his way. He'd tried to kill Aaron before but those priests got in the way. He said this time nothing would go wrong and then he'd have me." Maiya paused for a moment then continued.

"Just as Warren was about to either cut me or go upstairs and try to kill Aaron, the police arrived here and started knocking on the door loudly. It unnerved him so much that he fell on his own knife and it killed him right in the chest. Oh Father Kubelik I saw it all!"

Hugging her tightly he smiled at Aaron. "Oh my dear Maiya you have suffered horribly and far more than anyone's share these past weeks. We're going to see that you go someplace where you can recover and heal. We have peaceful and beautiful retreats that you and Aaron would love."

Gently letting her go, she hung onto Aaron for safety and security.

The physician arrived and recommended she go to the hospital for overnight observation. Aaron went with her in the EMS ambulance.

Watching them go, Father Kubelik went over to this car. He prayed a prayer of thanksgiving to God for waking him up and getting him over to his dear friends in their time of need as well as for being able to offer extreme unction to a dying and deeply troubled soul.

CHAPTER TWENTY-ONE

Maiya Emerson lounged in a wicker patio chair overlooking a crystal lake. Aaron sat on the other side of her. Presently a series of figures approached the couple. A wide smile broke out over Aaron and Maiya's face.

Springing up from her chair, she ran into the arms of all three of her favourite priests. "Oh it can't really be you?! You are all a sight for sore eyes! I've been hoping I'd see you soon but each day; nothing. Come and sit with us my friends!"

Noticing her other friends she jumped up again and ran to Don and Cynthia Fenway, then Gail Gordon, Staff Sergeant John, Detective Paul Andrecki and finally Everett Logan.

Everyone was seated around Maiya and Aaron after the group went and brought more chairs.

"I've missed you more than anyone can imagine! But oh it is *so* wonderful to see you again!" Maiya exclaimed as she beamed at her sea of friends gathered around her.

From beyond the small hill, approached a team of waiters and catering staff as they brought food and drinks and set them up around Maiya and Aaron.

"Wow you're awesome!" remarked Aaron with joy as he watched the efficiency of the team set up for their afternoon's festivities.

Maiya just sat back and beamed with radiance and joy as she watched her friends help set up for the party. Tears of happiness came to her eyes as she realised how blessed she was to have such friends.

Then from beyond the small hill, came a large birthday cake. Maiya saw it and her eyes widened with joyous surprise. "Oh *Mon Dieu*! This is for me! It *is* my birthday isn't it? I had almost forgotten!"

Singing and clapping ensued as the three priests brought her cake closer to her.

Father Kubelik stood nearest as he called out to her. "Happy blessed birthday Maiya! We love you *so* much! Now, *please* cut your cake, I can't wait to try it!"

All three priests kissed her on her cheeks and hugged her as she prepared to make a wish then cut her cake. Applause was loud and continuous as Maiya cut her cake and handed the pieces around.

"We are doing this a little backwards, first we eat the cake, then we eat the main course and hors d' oeuvres! Oh who cares, we have fun, yes?" Maiya called out to her friends.

During the party, Officer John and Detective Andrecki approached Aaron.

"Some time we'll tell you what we found and how things were resolved but now is not the time or the place," Officer John said, as he glanced at the festivities around him. "Thank you very much for inviting me up here for your wife's birthday surprise. I wouldn't have missed it for anything!"

Detective Andrecki agreed. "This is a wonderful location and party! I'm so glad I was invited too! But yeah some time, someday we'll fill you in. But then again maybe some things are left unsaid or unfinished."

Father Kubelik joined the trio and said, "I will say this much; that advice applies equally well to the priesthood." Bringing his attention to Maiya, Father Kubelik looked back at Aaron. "She's progressing extremely well and she remembers very little from that dark and stormy time. I think it is better this way don't you?"

All four men agreed, as they turned to watch Maiya enjoying herself like a carefree youth.

"Your idea to join forces with the three priests and Detective Andrecki was a good one. I love the name of your new agency; *Redemption Investigations*," Officer John remarked as he gave each man a big smile. "Very enterprising of you all. How did you think of it?"

Aaron looked to his two colleagues and then spoke. "It was simplicity itself. After everything that had happened we all knew that we had these special and hidden talents that needed to be cultivated and brought out. Therefore, I floated the idea by my friends, to coin a phrase from Maiya and we hashed some thoughts

THE LABYRINTH OF THE CAPRICIOUS PRIEST

around and the next thing we knew *Redemption Investigations* was born. Officer John, we'd love it if you would join us too! There's more than enough work for us all."

Smiling widely at his friends he shrugged. "Let me think on it okay? I'm happy with the Toronto Police and I've got my seniority and you know what I mean but hey, I really do appreciate the invite. You just never know, I have been known to change my mind so you might find me at your door one day, hat in hand looking to join you all!"

Everyone laughed as they agreed and hoped Officer John would join them one day soon.

As the party was winding down, Aaron got up to walk along the small hill just below their cottage.

Father Kubelik came and joined him as they both looked back at Maiya having the time of her life playing queen bee to all her friends.

"Now that we're out of earshot of my wife, please tell me what *really* happened," Aaron pleaded earnestly.

Father Kubelik turned to face his friend as he spoke. "Aaron, a lot of innocent people died at the hands of that devil Mr. Angus Radcliffe and a few too many died at the hands of Mr. Warren Sinclair. Now they're both dead themselves. I am glad though that I did have the opportunity to offer Warren extreme unction before he died. He made a confession, which was his last, but I don't think it was his first.

"Just by the way he spoke I knew he'd been to church at some

315

point in his life. So, I did what I could for him and after all, that is part of why I am a priest.

"Do you believe that they finally had to close *Lytton's Funeral Home* down? There was just too much tragedy attached to that place. Once the second set of tragedies occurred, no one wanted their service held at that home. The building has been torn down and the lot left empty. I'm not sure what they'll do with it. I think they should make a small park or something nice," Father Kubelik suggested as he walked next to Aaron.

"Anyway, that's what happened there. *Monk's Abbey Golf and Country Club* is another property, which has undergone a huge metamorphosis. The old section has been torn down so now it is only the country club, golf course and restaurant proper that remain. All of those wonderful old monk's cells were demolished and those labyrinths were destroyed.

"It's just as well you moved away and sold your house Aaron. Maiya could never have remained living in the city and being exposed to constant reminders, it would have kept her ill and we couldn't have that."

Turning back from watching Maiya, Father Kubelik continued his story. "Aaron, take great care of her always because if you weren't with her I would be. You know how I feel about certain women and your wife is one of them but don't worry, I'd never cross the line but all the same just guard her with your life."

Smiling at his friend, Aaron *knew*. He'd seen their exchanges before.

"That's okay Father Kubelik; I don't intend to ever let her out of my sight again. But if I did, she would be going to one of the greatest priests alive."

Patting him on the back, Father Francesco Kubelik was honoured.

"Aaron my man and you can count on me to pray for your long life together but should the good Lord ever see fit to send you to heaven first, then I'll be right along to take over where you left off."

Laughing together, the two men continued walking along.

"Did I tell you that Warren Sinclair had fancied himself a modern day Knights Templar with an evil and sadistic twist? Apparently, one of his descendants was a bona fide Knights Templar so naturally this was his claim to fame.

"Warren forgot about the good points of being descended from a real Knights Templar and fell into a fantasy world which was evil and sadistic to say the least. Well unfortunately it got him killed but you know Aaron, it might be that he planned it that way."

Aaron shrugged as they walked along. "He might at that but thank God we'll never know. My wife worked closely with him on occasion and who knew this was what was brewing below his surface? Say, how about your sister, is she well?"

"Oh she's doing well and she sends her best wishes and love to Maiya. It's funny about all those labyrinths; if they hadn't figured so prominently among the churches and even the golf and country club we might never have solved the mystery of that horrid funeral home chain.

"My sister was instrumental in obtaining the plans for that old building so we eventually knew exactly where those evil ones were conducting their devilish meetings and in the former monastic area no less.

"It pains me how much of a blasphemy and sacrilege it all was but of course that's exactly why those devils did it that way. Speaking of the golf and country club, old Radcliffe had been a member just like you are so that's where that connection came from and he'd have known the history of the place just as you did.

"Boy that Mr. Radcliffe was nasty. He was truly an evil one and the epitome of evil itself. Not a shred of decency or remorse in him. He was heartless I'd say. Old Radcliffe was behind the thugs who used to watch your home and Maiya's workplace. We never did find out the name of their cult but he was definitely their 'grand master'. Those inquiries and research are ongoing. Aaron, do you know why they killed those people and threw them in the cavity at *Lytton's Funeral Home*?"

Aaron thought for a moment then shared his idea. "Don't tell me they were cult members who wouldn't tow the mark?"

Nodding his head, Father Kubelik agreed. "You guessed it. Yes, old Radcliffe would mete out the justice and if they wouldn't conform to the rules then he'd be judge, jury and executioner. They found their hooded robe fragments among their remains.

"Not only that but it is believed that some of the offloading and loading of coffins which took place at night were poor souls who were cremated and placed in some mass grave or paupers grave somewhere in the GTA area or beyond maybe. That way no one would figure out who they were or be able to find them."

"That is truly disgusting and so very sad, for those people never deserved anything like that. What about their families? My goodness Reverend! Obviously those unfortunate people were brain-washed by the old devil himself," Aaron stated sadly.

Suddenly Aaron recalled the old man Jensen and the auto garage.

Stopping, he faced Reverend Kubelik. "What about that auto garage you allegedly used to live above. That old man Jensen said he saw you or he assumed it was you coming out on a covered stretcher. What really happened that time?"

Laughing slightly, Reverend Kubelik nodded his head slowly. "Oh that. Yeah well, that was all part of my big disappearing act. I can laugh about it now but sure as hell not back then. Those guys old Jensen saw were some of my friends and the stretcher was empty but they made it look as if a body was under the covers.

"I know it was wicked to try to fool some people but Aaron I know you now understand it was imperative and my very life depended on the ruse being convincing. They borrowed an old hearse that was a stage prop for the movies. One of my friends is an actor."

Shaking his head Aaron had to smile too. "They sure were convincing so you can tell them they make excellent ghouls complete with antique hearse."

Sighing, Father Kubelik agreed. "Aaron, do you want to know the truth about 'Father Andrecki'?"

Smiling at the priest, Aaron stopped and said, "yes if you want to tell me."

"You see Aaron, 'Father Andrecki' came to me a couple of times in confession. One of the times it was about a long ago sin or something he thought was a sin. I helped him out with that. Then he told me about some of the things he'd witnessed in his undercover work and some of the rules and details of this strange cult.

"The odd thing was Father Andrecki must have still felt contrite or something like that because he either told someone else about these so called 'sins' or someone overheard us and then before I knew it I was a marked man. Real threats were made on my life so I wasted no time going into hiding.

"Through our network of clerics and laity, I had heard very early on that a certain 'new priest' would be filling in for me. Little did I know it was he.

"Father Andrecki was never a priest at *St. Simeon's* per say. He only said he was to other people but I met him as a visiting priest and penitent."

Seeing Aaron's confusion, he explained. "I know, it's really complicated. One moment he was a priest, then the next he wasn't but that was all part of his profile and he had to adapt to the situation so I had to keep rolling with it too and then finally I understood when that policewoman told me who he *really* was; the undercover RCMP officer. It all came together at that point."

Aaron turned back towards their party. "Father Kubelik thanks for not sharing this until now. I know you could have spoken of it several times but you always spared Maiya. Thank you."

"Because I love her Aaron. Oh not the way you do although if I was with her I sure as hell would love her but no, I love her as a sister and the most special lady I have ever met. I want only to protect her and I do, in my own eccentric way."

Smiling at him, Aaron was never more delighted they were friends. "Father Kubelik you really *are* the original capricious priest."

Stopping in front of Aaron, Father Kubelik laughed. "I thought 'Father Andrecki' was?"

Turning back towards the party, both men walked in silence with huge smiles on their faces.

***

Aaron recalled the providential afternoon that he had met Father Francesco Kubelik. Almost laughing audibly, he remembered his first impressions of the priest. Glancing at his friend walking beside him, Aaron knew that some people never changed and he was okay with that for in his own strange way neither did he.

Capricious priest or not, Father Francesco Kubelik was one hell of a man, priest and friend for life.

***

As the two men walked the labyrinth of life, they knew that

one day it would end and when it did, they would be back where they started; at the *Beginning*...

ABOUT THE AUTHOR

Merlaine Hemstraat is the author of *Peacocks among the Tamarind Trees* and various short stories. Since childhood, she has fostered her dream of becoming a writer. She has several new novels cited for publication in 2017-2018. Enjoying world travel, currently she spends her time in Toronto, Canada.

77307274R00200

Made in the USA
Lexington, KY
26 December 2017